SILVER SAVAGE

Warriors of Valose Saga 1

IONA STROM

LS ANDERS

Use your own judgment to determine if the content of this novel is appropriate for you.
This romance is a work of fiction. Names, characters, places, brands, media, and incidents are either the product of the author's imagination or are used fictitiously. Any resemblance to actual persons, living or dead, events, or locales is entirely coincidental.
NOTE: If you did not buy this ebook via Amazon KDP or download through the Kindle Unlimited program, then you are in possession of a pirated copy of my work. I suggest you delete it and never return to where you obtained it. Copyright infringement is a crime.

Created with Vellum

Also by Iona Strom

Nomadican Mates Series

Nomadican Mates Series Mega Box Set (books 1-7): Sci-Fi Alien Abduction Romance

---

Read Zaku and Ivy's Story!

Zaku: Sci-Fi Alien Romance

Warriors of Valose Saga

Silver Savage: Warriors of Valose Saga 1

Silver Seducer: Warriors of Valose Saga 2

Silver Savior: Warriors of Valose Saga 3

Silver Solace: Warriors of Valose Saga 4

Silver Scout: Warriors of Valose Saga 5

Silver Silence: Warriors of Valose Saga 6

Silver Spice: Warriors of Valose Saga 7

Silver Storm: Warriors of Valose Saga 8

Silver Steel: Warriors of Valose Saga 9

Silver Stealth: Warrior of Valose Saga 10

Glossary of Valosian Terms

Special Note:
You'll find the following **Valosian** words throughout this text. They are not misspellings but alien terms. Also, they are no longer italicized since they seemed to have been a distraction for some readers.
This is an ever-growing list and may not have captured every single Valosian word. I'm currently working on it, so don't hate me for not being perfect.

Adrenalyne- A hormone secreted by the adrenal glands in males only, which increases strength, endurance, and stamina for the sole purpose of protecting their spirit mate. Also, this hormone promotes healing.

Chiksin- The Valosian equivalent of a chicken.

Crikts- Large insects that look like cave crickets.

Dearth- A herbivorous creature similar in size and look to a deer.

Electro-bars- Electrified bars of light.

Elksen- A herbivorous creature similar in size and look to an elk.

Fates- A Valosian measurement equivalent to a foot.

Fibrous tubing- Similar to fiberoptic cable.

Flites- Small flying insects that eat the dung of rexose.

Floratrap- Is a carnivorous plant similar to a Venus flytrap, only much larger.

Hipose- A herbivorous creature similar on size and look as a hippopotamus.

Hundredths- A measurement equivalent to a hundred.

Hurs- A Valosian equivalent to an hour.

Insectoids- Nuttaki species of insect-like mammals.

Kiltus- Similar in fashion to a Scottish kilt worn only by males.

Lood- Valosian equivalent to water.

Loodfall- The Valosian equivalent to a shower. This term can also mean a waterfall.

Luminetric barrier- Impenetrable transparent shielding.

Mims- The Valosian equivalent to a minute.

Milose- A Valosian measurement equivalent to a mile.

Mothis- A flying insect with fuzzy wings.

Munthis- A Valosian equivalent to a month.

Nula- Term of endearment like sweetheart.

Nutrillium- A mineral mined on Valose with the potential to release stored energy.

Nutrone- A rare mineral found only at the highest peak of the Jurigon Mountains.

Patooga- A large feline-like beast with enormous canine teeth.

Penitentrium- A building used to house prisoners.

Rovers- A mode of transportation similar looking to a jet ski, only they are used on land. They are equipped with gravity disruptors in order to hover above the ground and use thrusters to propel them forward.

Rynose- A herbivorous beasts similar to a rhinoceros.

Sanitate system- Is the Valosian equivalent of a toilet.

Sec- The Valosian equivalent to a second.

Skypod- A lightweight metal structure meant to float using a gravity disruptor.

Solaries- Rocks which absorb solar energy and emit light as from chemiluminescence of phosphorus.

Solitarium- Isolated prison cell.

Splinth- A clear shell used to set broken bones.

Spirits- Valosian Gods.

Squidlin- Massive carnivorous sea creatures with multiple tentacles.

Suns-fall- The time in the evening when the twin suns disappear and daylight fades.

Suns-rise- The time when the twin suns appear above the horizon as a result of the daily rotation of the planet, Valose.

Thrumming or thrum- Is a low continuous vibratory sound internally created by Valosian males to comfort or enhance pleasure.

Tondru- A massive wolf-like beast.

Tragore- A device used to detect power sources.

Turculine- Very close in hue to turquoise.

Yerons- A measurement of time approximately 365 days.

About this Book

Jakkar

After losing all our females, I didn't think life could get any worse until I was stripped of my crown and exiled by my twin brother. With my world in turmoil, my spirit mate crashed into my life when I needed her the most. She was not of Valose but a stranger from another world.

Newly awakened, my ancillary heart beats for one reason only —to keep her safe. Now I must protect her from old enemies as well as new yet what came with her posed a unique danger that can't be fought with swords. There was nothing I wouldn't do for her. Unfortunately, what she wanted the most would tear apart my very soul.

Lily

I thought the abduction had been bad enough, but the crash-landing nearly killed me. Stranded on an alien world, all I wanted was to find a way to get myself and the other girls home. When the solution presented itself in the form of a kilt-wearing, hopeless romantic with serious muscles, sexy elf ears, and the belief that soul mates truly existed… Well, I was no longer in a huge rush to leave.

Acknowledgments

Copyedits and proofread
Rebecca Norman
Rosie Chapel
Owl Eyes Proofs & Edits
Del's Diabolical Editing

Cover Designed by Natasha Snow Designs
www.natashasnowdesigns.com

Map Of Valose

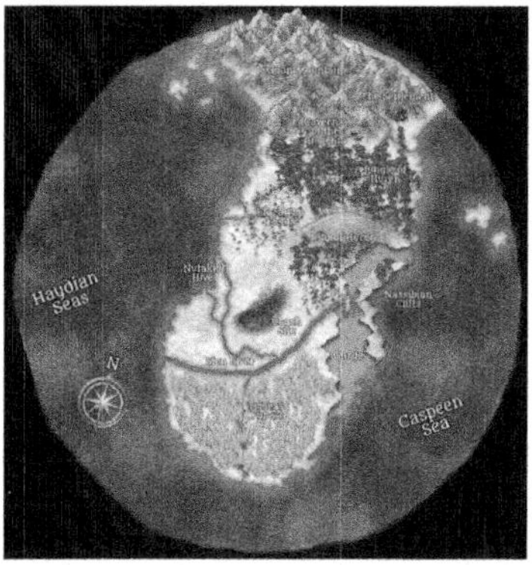

Chapter One

LILY

My body was a leaden weight as I slowly woke. Aside from the pounding behind my closed eyelids, something was off. The residual creepiness from nightmares of lanky, grayish men from last night's tortured sleep clung to me. Their spindly hands—cold and clammy—had touched me everywhere. I shivered hard from the echo of unwanted touches.

No matter how high I raised my eyebrows, my eyelids refused to budge. My jaw cracked open to call out for my friend, Amy, but no sound escaped me, my lips only mouthing her name.

My body followed the list of the floor, sliding down with a squeak against what felt like a metal plate. I finally forced one eye open.

I was lying on my side, and there was a distorted reflection of myself staring back. Sluggishly, I squeezed my eyes shut and tried again, but the view remained the same.

The room rightened itself and I slid back, my bare legs sticking to the metal floor, grabbing and pulling hard at my skin. I flopped over onto my back, and that was when the smell hit me. My nose wrinkled from the burn of ammonia. The air was saturated with it, making it difficult to drag in a full breath.

I'd never felt this tired. Exhaustion had to be why the popcorn ceiling in my apartment looked like the same polished metal as the wall I was just facing.

My head lolled to the side, and I found a row of thin, luminescent tubes set evenly apart—the diffused light pulsating in waves.

Why was I inside a strange box?

Beyond the light bars, the scene worsened—I was not alone. There were more metal boxes across a wide aisle, stacked one atop the other. There were a few vacancies, but most housed a single sleeping girl. From what I could tell, I was three cages high on my side of the room.

My eyes traveled down my body to find I was wearing the same loose, white dress with ties at the shoulders as the others. No panties that I could feel. Suddenly, I felt very exposed and curled myself into a tight ball.

Memories from my nightmares flashed back. Fear solidified into terror. Those hadn't been dreams; all that crazy shit had *really* happened. The full-body scans, the strange needle-less device that had drawn my blood, the tissue samples pinched from the inside of my cheek, all performed by creepy gray creatures with bulbous heads and beady black eyes. I ran my tongue along the inside of my mouth to find tiny craters where my flesh had been wrongfully harvested.

Down below, a dark-haired girl rolled over to face her light bars. She opened her eyes, panning around.

"Hey," I croaked. "Up here."

Her face scrunched in anger. "Shut the fuck up!" she yelled at me in a harsh whisper. "If they hear you, they'll come back and gas all of us."

My aching body stiffened. Gassed with what?

"How do you know?" I whispered back. "What does the gas do?"

"They always come when they hear one of us making noise. I don't think they like noise," she prattled on, barely above a whisper. "The gas comes out of something that looks like a handheld fog machine. I guess it's some kind of anesthetic because it instantly knocks everyone out unless you know to hold your breath until it clears. That's how I've been able to stay awake. Most girls wake up screaming, so they come right away."

"Who... Who is they?" I wasn't sure I really wanted to know.

The dark-haired girl looked at me for a long moment, then said, "Aliens."

Before this, I would have laughed at that. Aliens? Really? I wasn't one of those skeptics that believe we were all alone in the Universe, but alien abductions were figments of other people's overactive imaginations.

It appeared the figments were real, and there was nothing funny about where I was at, so I stayed quiet, taking a moment to absorb my new truth.

"We have to get out of here." I stretched out a hand and touched the thin, illuminated bars. "What the hell!" I recoiled back with a hiss.

"Keep your voice down!" The dark-haired girl propped up on an elbow, scowling up at me. "Those weird light bar things will shock you like a high voltage electric fence. There's no way out of this thing. Don't you think I've already tried?"

"There has to be a way out because I refuse to be abducted," I said, rubbing at the tingly marks left on the palm of my hand as my grogginess started to clear.

"Too late," the dark-haired girl retorted and settled back in her cage.

"I'm Lily, by the way."

"Marie."

"How long have we been here, Marie?"

She shushed me as a reminder to keep my voice down before whispering her answer. "I've been here for days, maybe a week. I don't know for sure. Anyway, it feels like forever. You've been here about half as long as me."

"Was there a redheaded girl brought in with me?" I held my breath as I waited for her response.

"No," Marie scanned the cages I couldn't see stacked up below mine. "No redheads. Only blondes and brunettes."

I didn't know whether to be relieved or upset by the news. The last thing I remembered was the two of us hopping into Amy's car for an ice cream run, yet I don't remember going inside the store or even parking the car.

I swallowed hard, knowing we never made it, and wondered what had happened to my friend.

Tears pricked my eyes. I blinked them away and pulled my legs tighter to my body, holding myself together.

"Looking for someone in particular?" Marie asked.

"What?"

"You asked about redheads." Marie turned fully to her side. "Is she a friend of yours or something?"

"Yeah. Amy. My last memory was of us together in her car."

"Maybe she's lucky enough to still be on Earth."

"Still be?" I wrinkled my nose. "Why would you say that? Where do you think we are if not Earth?"

"Honey, I have no idea where we are." Marie sliced a hand through the air. "All I know is we're moving, and we've been moving ever since I woke up the second time."

"You've been gassed twice?"

"Yeah, after the girl in the cage below yours woke up and started screaming, a skinny gray dude came in and fogged up the room," Marie spoke fast but kept her words soft. "The few of us who were beginning to wake up got knocked back out. It happened again, not too long ago when another girl started crying really loud, except that time, I held my breath until the alien with the fog machine left. It didn't take very long for the fog to dissipate, and I was the only one left awake. That's why the air smells like Mr. Clean shit himself."

"How many girls are on my side of the room?" I started counting the bodies on her side.

"Eleven, including you," she said.

"I count nine on your side," I reported.

"So, twenty girls total," Marie pondered. "There's still empty cages. I wonder if they're finished collecting girls."

"Hey! If they're still abducting from Earth, that means we're still here. Maybe this is our chance to escape the ship or whatever this thing is." I pressed my feet and hands against the metal walls, testing the strength of my cage. "If we can get out of these cages and make a bunch of noise, we could jump the fog guy and run out of here."

"Yeah," Marie looked at me excitedly. "Then we can get Scotty to beam us back down to Earth. Or better yet, maybe we can take over the ship, fly it back, land it, and save all the girls. We'd be fucking heroes."

I flipped her the bird and rolled my eyes.

"As I said, Lily, I've already tried to get out. The light bars will only shock you, and the metal is stronger than steel. So, we're stuck in here."

"The aliens got us in this box," I argued. "There has to be a way out of it."

Something beeped, and Marie cursed. "Great! They heard us. Pretend to be asleep, and don't forget to hold your breath."

A door I never noticed slid open to my horror, and in walked three of the creatures featured in my nightmares. Tall and lanky, their weird bodies were gray covered in bumpy skin topped with heads that looked like they could double as flotation devices. Embedded in their fat heads were two unblinking shark eyes, set too close together.

One carried a little black box, while the other two flanked a floating table. On it lay a girl with fiery red hair. She faced away from me, but I would recognize Amy anywhere.

They moved her to an empty cage near the floor. I watched as one of the aliens held up his palm to a small panel on the face of the cage. An orange beam shot out and scanned his palm, then the light bars disappeared. The table Amy lay on lowered to the floor. Both aliens shoved her off the table and into the cage; her body landed with a sickening thud.

Before I could think better of it, I screamed over the mistreatment of my friend. "Hey, assholes! Leave her alone."

I sat up too fast and banged my head on my metal ceiling. Falling back with a groan, I pressed my hand to my forehead. When I opened my eyes, one of the aliens was front and center on the opposite side of my light bars. Its huge face filled up the entire space.

I shrieked and scrambled back as far as my box would allow. Fear and disgust rolled over me as the alien's slashing mouth peeled wide and hissed, displaying rows of sharp teeth. Then the alien pointed the fog machine directly at me with a final glare and released a cloudy wall. I remembered what Marie said and held my breath, rolling away from the bars, covering my nose and mouth with my hands.

I could hear the alien's feet slap on the black, sparkly floor as it made a circuit around the room. Then the door slid open, and I squinted through the thick fog, hoping all the aliens had left.

Just like Marie said, the green cloud dissipated quickly, and the room cleared out.

I blasted out the air I'd been holding and sucked in fresh ammonia on a harsh cough and gagged from the stinging in my lungs. My head lightened like an inflating balloon, but I remained lucid.

I glanced down at Marie. She beamed up at me, and I returned her thumbs up. I think I just made a new friend.

I WOKE up to the sound of my name.

"Hey, Lily." Marie's whisper held a tinge of panic. "You okay?"

"Yeah, fine," I croaked. My throat was tight and raw. "How long have I been out?"

"Long enough that two more girls have joined our ranks, and I think the ship might be about to crash," Marie said matter-of-factly.

I shook my head, trying to clear it. "Why do you think the ship is crashing?"

"All the lurching the ship's been doing. Plus, we've sped up, and then there are the explosions," Marie answered, stone-cold deadpan.

"Explosions?" I tilted my head. "I don't hear anything."

"Wait for it," Marie rattled off sarcastically.

"How do you know we've sped up?"

"If you lay perfectly still, you can feel the ship's movement. It's like being on an airplane that's reached its cruising altitude, only much smoother," she explained.

"I'll have to try that later. Right now, I want to know what I missed. Did Amy ever wake up?"

"Not that I know of." Marie turned her head in Amy's direction. "I can't see any of the girls on my side of the room."

"What happened with the new girls?"

"Same ole, same ole." Marie pushed herself up from where she kept sliding down the slick, metal floor. "The gray freaks bring them in on a floating table and dump them in an empty cage."

"If the ship's about to crash, how is it you're so calm?"

Marie breathed out a long sigh. "I guess I've been scared for so long that I've grown used to it. Besides, what can I do about it but wait and see what happens next?"

"Well, I'm not ready to give up." I flopped to my back and groaned, rubbing at my temples. "Oh, wow. I can feel it. We really are moving."

"Yep. Remember to try and stay away from the light bars when the ship tilts," Marie nonchalantly whispered when the ship began to list.

"What?" I gasped.

The ship listed hard to one side, and I crumbled to the bottom of my cage. I threw out my hands to steady myself. My palms pressed tight against the walls. We banked another hard turn, and then the ship leveled off as if we were evading an enemy.

An explosion sounded out somewhere in the distance before giving us a good shaking. I swallowed my screams and held in the tremors racking my nerves.

I glanced down at Marie. Her eyes were wide, matching my terror.

My teeth rattled from the next explosion, which definitely felt a lot closer. The ship listed violently to the side before we spun around. I yelped as my back made brief contact with my light bars before I was able to gain momentum enough to scramble away.

Marie's screams joined mine as we were tossed into a spiraling descent. We were hurtling toward a crash-landing. Crashing where? I didn't know.

I fought hard to keep my body wedged into a corner to keep from touching my light bars. My fingers curled, clawing to find purchase against the slippery metal walls. The tips of my fingers burned from the friction. The bottoms of my feet squeaked across the metal floor as I scrambled as far away from the fear of electrocution.

"Hope this ends well," Marie called out.

"Yeah. Me too," I shouted back. "Thanks for friending me."

"We'll still be friends when we land," she said, though her words held little faith.

The cage beneath me unexpectedly fell away. I gasped, suddenly free-floating while still trapped within my metal confines. From what I could see, everything inside the room lacked gravity. All the cages were swimming around, gently bumping and bouncing away from each other. All the girl's inside, as weightless as the metal boxes around them, free-floated like astronauts, only trapped inside a cage.

Amy's cage floated near mine. I reached out to grab her, but the light bars shocked my hand away. "Amy!" I yelled and rubbed at my hand. "She hit the light bars on her cage, Marie, and she didn't even twitch!"

We took another hard hit. The gleaming white walls of the room appeared to be vibrating violently, yet my buoyant body registered none of it. I slapped my hands over my ears, muffling the screech of tearing metal, and hoped for the best while ice pulsed through my veins. Then, everything went eerily quiet.

"The calm before the storm," Marie mumbled.

"What do you think's happening?" I wheezed; fear tightly gripping my throat.

"Not sure," Marie answered, and I was thankful when her cage floated into view. "Before you woke up, it sounded like we were in the middle of a war. But now, I don't know. Maybe we won, or maybe we're screwed and whoever is firing on us is about to board the ship."

The gravity we lost slowly kicked in. It felt as if a hand had reached up, taken hold of me, and gently pulled me back down to the sparkling, black floor. All of the other cages and the girls within them were making the same slow descent. When we reached the floor, the cage's stacked haphazardly, littering the room in a jumbled heap.

Pained squeals accompanied the sounds of body parts touching the light bars with sizzling hisses. The cages were in complete disarray, some having landed cock-eyed against the others, some lying on their backs and to my horror I watched as one landed, and it fell facedown.

Oh my god, I hope it was an empty one.

The shriek that permeated the room set my teeth on edge. Not empty, after all. I heard Marie's sympathetic curse somewhere off in the distance. The screaming and wailing continued. I was helpless to do anything to help the girl except cringe away from the mental image of her being mercilessly zapped by the light bars—nowhere to go—just enduring the pain of slow electrocution. My throat grew tight with her agonizing wails.

The stench of burning flesh gagged me as the girl's cries fell away and then suddenly stopped as if a switch had been flipped. My ragged breaths filled the void of silence, then a chorus of weeping and mumbled confusion joined in.

Another explosion sounded even closer. Again, we were shown no mercy as whoever attacked our ship wasn't letting up. We were getting pulverized in here!

A collection of screams followed another rollover, the cages crashing into each other with resounding cracks. It was impossible to know if we were up or down and keeping track of the spinning black floor was impossible.

When the spinning finally stopped, what came next proved much worse. We were tossed in a single direction, all the cages piling up in one corner of the tilted room. The floor sat cockeyed beneath me before the backside of another cage slammed into my light bars, showering me in a spray of stinging sparks. I shut my eyes to protect them because there was no getting away from the onslaught or the compression of the rapid descent.

We fell forever. Our world was a fast tumble of terror. Tears streaked across my cheeks.

We hit hard; all the cages shifted direction in a crumbling heap. Then we bounced, flung high into the air like popcorn in an air popper before all the cages rained down with heavy thuds.

Mine landed with a crunch, and I looked at the room. Ahead, there was a jagged hole where solid wall used to be. Displayed in the rift was a mangle of strange tubes and wires.

My cage rocked back and forth as another bumped into mine. I sucked in an alarmed breath when I began to fall forward into the light bars. As I tottered backward, I threw my body toward the back wall. My slight weight was no competition for my metal confines' heft, and I began to fall forward.

"No, no, no!" I cringed.

Everything switched to slo-mo; the sparkly black floor reached up to seal my fate. Holy shit! I didn't want to die in this cage.

I scrambled for some kind of hold. The palms of my hands and the soles of my feet slipped and slid off the slick metal walls. With no handhold, I was at the mercy of my toppling cage.

The light bars shone brighter while my face grew dangerously close to my inevitable electrocution. I threw out my hands as the forward momentum of my cage thrust me into harm's way.

Anger boiled just beneath the surface of my panicked cries as my cage was about to hit the floor. First, I'd found out my fiancé had been cheating on me, then I had been abducted by aliens, and finally—the icing on my shitstorm cake—I survived a spaceship crash-landing. Yet, after all of that, I would meet my demise, being shocked to death by the very bars that held me captive.

This was such bullshit!

The cage landed hard. I bounced around like a cat on a hot side-walk, but there was no relief from the electric shocks that were now my floor. My muscles spasmed, making it hard to keep moving. Eventually, I'd tire, and then I'd be dead. I wasn't ready to give up. I fought through the tremors, the pain, the agony until the light bars began to dim; the shocks diminished. Then, with a pop and a fizzle, they disappeared altogether, taking every ounce of light with them.

My body shook uncontrollably inside the inky darkness. My ears roared with my harsh breaths as I rubbed at my trembling limbs. The light bars were gone!

Hysterical laughter rolled out of me, reverberating inside my metal box. I had cheated death. If I could lift this thing, I would be free.

I rested my forehead against the cold wall and squinted into the darkness. It was pitch-black inside my overturned prison, but I would take darkness over the punishing light from the shock bars that had burned painful lines into my skin.

Chapter Two

JAKKAR

The fiery disc rocketed across the newly risen twin suns, leaving a charred stain across the shimmering silver sky in its wake. My feet were firmly planted on the tower's platform, yet my body loosened with concern.

The disc suddenly slowed its rapid descent, breaking through the tree line in a more controlled decline. What wasn't smoldering in flames showed strange colored lights blinking around the gleaming body. It was like nothing I'd seen before.

The massive, black vessel hit the ground in a shower of dirt and debris, flushing out a flock of nesting wetlocks before bouncing once and finally coming to rest with a shuddering crunch.

"I disagree, Sia Jakkar. It looks like an asteroid to me."

I lowered the scope and watched the wetlocks soar high into the sky on leathery wings as broad as a male was tall. Their bellies flashed a brilliant white, the first and only warning to take cover or risk being plucked from the ground and fed to their hatchlings. A stunning sight to witness with so many taking to the air at once.

It was also the time I needed to control my simmering rage. I could feel the flare of color wanting to erupt over my scales.

After a moment, I could safely lay eyes on Rayyar, my personal guard, where he stood next to me on the deck of the sentry tower. My urge to throttle him was more manageable.

I knew what I saw, and that was no celestial body plummeting to the surface of Valose. Instead, the vessel had visibly slowed before crashing and even bounced off the surface before coming to rest in a smoldering, jagged heap. Asteroids always came in fast and collided with the ground, leaving a massive crater with shock waves rolling for many milose.

"Well, whatever it was, crashed 200 milose from here," I bristled. His very presence was irritating. Yet he added insult to injury by daring to argue with me. Nevertheless, I let it go and scrutinized Rayyar's reaction to my next command. "Gather a squad and enough provisions for several suns-rises. Don't forget the hauler. And be ready to meet me at the rovers in ten mims. Ensure Nullar is among them and has what he needs to scan the wreckage before we make entry. The last thing Valose needs is another alien germ to wipe out the rest of us."

"Sia, is it wise to leave the settlement with already so few warriors to guard it, only to view the remains of a crashed asteroid?"

I wasn't sure what angered me most, more questioning of my authority or Rayyar's deliberate attempt to keep me away from the crashed spacecraft. The latter only fueled my determination to discover what it was he didn't want me to see.

I took a step into his personal space, barely holding myself in check. It was nothing for me to tower over him. The only thing saving Rayyar from being pummeled to death beneath my fists was he remained a crucial link to my rancid twin brother, Sakkar. As for now, I needed him alive and believing me ignorant of his disloyalty.

Yet, I couldn't resist saying, "Do you think it wise to question your superior's order?"

Rayyar was quick to back down. His scales flushed white. "I meant no disrespect—"

"Good," I barked and stepped away. "Then carry out my orders."

I handed the scope over to Sazzar, the sentry on duty. His face was a mask of urgency. "A word, Sia?" I didn't miss his sideways glare at Rayyar.

"Why are you still here!" I chastised Rayyar. "You have your orders."

Rayyar's gaze bounced between me and Sazzar, an argument perched on his traitorous lips. If he questioned me again, I swore to the Spirits I would fling him off this platform and be damned the consequences.

I was almost disappointed when he nodded briskly and descended the rope running down the tower's center to the ground 60 fates below.

"What have you got, Sazzar?" I turned my attention to the sentry bristling at my side. "Has my brother's ship left the planet?"

"No, Sia," Sazzar answered in a rush. "But there was another fluctuation in the dome's shell."

"I wonder what problem they're having with the energy levels," I pondered aloud and peered over the top of the dense jungle at the glittering dome protecting the city of Huren.

"If there's a weakness, we could exploit it. Send in the warriors and take the city back in your name."

I clapped a hand on his broad shoulder. The corner of my lip curled up at his eagerness to fight. I, too, felt the need for retaliation. "Our time will come. But, for now, report any anomalies with the shielding directly to Nekko."

"Yes, Sia," Sazzar presented his forearm, a customary display of respect, for me to clasp. I did so, approving of his firm grasp, before turning away and starting my rapid descent down the thick rope.

I jogged through my new settlement, where many yerons ago had sat the city of Huren. The road was a broken shell of its former self, crumbling beneath my booted feet from neglect—the surrounding buildings lay in ruins and uninhabitable.

As I raced through my clan's past, I envisioned the bustling city as it once was, back before the last war of many with the Nuttaki. That tribe of primitive assholes had obtained nutrone spears and bombs from unknown origins, then laid waste to Huren and half the Valosian people, including my sire and former ruler.

Once their nutrone ran dry, the Nuttaki lost the advantage, and the Valosian warriors quickly gained the upper hand at the razor-sharp end of our swords. Ultimately, they tucked their spindly tails between their bowed legs and slunk back to their hives on the western coast.

A sparkling new Huren was rebuilt, and our scholars placed the city inside a protective dome using new technology. Proven to be impenetrable, the new shielding ended the need for sentries to guard the perimeter. For most, that was the beginning of the end of our rigorous warrior training program.

For warriors like myself, who saw the folly in relying solely on technology for protection, we continued to train and kept our skills honed and fresh for when we were once again needed.

Given the dome's current anomalies, I would venture to guess the technology my brother, Sakkar, and the city dwellers had relied so heavily upon was failing.

I turned on the next road toward what used to be the warrior training field. Now overgrown with the encroaching jungle, the open space was perfect for floating a sky full of skypods.

As I neared my temporary shelter among the clouds, I grimly noted how far it had dropped since the last suns-rise. Mine wasn't the only one. All the others had dipped as well. Soon they would touch the ground and become vulnerable to nocturnal attacks. As much as I despised relying on technology of any kind, my warriors couldn't be everywhere at once.

I prayed to the Spirits the crashed vessel yielded something useful. I was desperate for anything to help protect the males who chose to stand with me when my crown was ripped from my head, and I was exiled from the city by my twin brother.

I ascended the rope to my dwelling in the sky and pushed open the hatch in the floor. It was dark inside. My nocturnal lenses dropped over my eyes with a blink, allowing me to penetrate the darkness.

I went directly to my weapons trunk, heaved off the lid, and armed myself. Matching swords crossed my back with a leather holster that crisscrossed my breastbone. A coiled wetlock, the symbol of my family, adorned the front.

I should shed the symbol now that my brother had taken the throne for himself, but every time I went to detach it, it felt like a betrayal to my sire.

I hesitated before popping open the false bottom of my chest and retrieved the plasma gun I kept hidden inside. I checked the chamber; the remaining charge filled my small home with an eerie glow of an unknown hue.

What I held in my hand was the most destructive element on the planet of Valose. I'd only ever used it for target practice, but I'd seen it lay waste to a rexose, the largest and deadliest creature in the jungle, with a single shot.

Wistfully, I closed the chamber on the plasma gun and ran my hand over the cold metalloid. An alien's weapon brought back from one of my brother's many travels to the stars. My sire would still be alive if the warriors had been armed with these during our last battle with the Nuttaki. They had us outnumbered and outgunned, yet we fought back; even my sire had taken up arms.

If the dome around Huren failed, it would be like sending out an engraved invitation for them to attack us again. Those bastards had been trying to exterminate us for as long as I could remember.

Despite my brother's obsession with space travel, he surely had a plan to safeguard those under his protection. Right now, I needed to consider those within my own failing walls. My people were even more vulnerable to enemy attacks living inside the former city's ruins.

I knew just the male to look after them while I was away.

I tucked the plasma gun inside the pocket of my kiltus and slid down the rope to the ground. Just as I raced around the corner searching for Nekko, he appeared in front of me, having stepped out of the armory, swords crossed at his back and daggers strapped to his thighs.

"I was on my way to look for you," I said, skidding to a halt.

"Your search is over, Sia." One side of Nekko's mouth lifted in a casual smirk. Always jovial and quick-witted, he was my most loyal warrior. I trusted him more than anyone.

"I need your help."

"Anything."

"Watch over the settlement in my absence." I raised a hand to cut him off, already anticipating an argument. "That's an order and not open for debate. Keep this on you at all times in case you need it." I pulled the plasma gun from my pocket and handed it off to Nekko, who was reluctant to take it. "Let me know the moment Rayyar contacts my brother. I can't believe he hasn't already used his comm. I figured those two would already be conspiring against me to make sure Sakkar's salvage party reaches the crash site first. I also need you to send two males to Huren. Have them approach from the east, where there's less chance of being spotted. I need them to attach a scanner to the dome. Make sure Zikkar shows them how to activate the beacon so he can record any anomalies with the shielding."

"Dare I ask where you obtained this little gem?" Nekko wagged the plasma gun in the air before slipping it into his pocket.

"A successful smuggle out from under my brother's nose."

"Well, he did say we could only take what we could carry with us," Nekko smirked then sobered. "I would feel better if I were watching your back."

"As would I, but I need you here looking after the settlement. These men stood with me against my brother. I owe them a safe place to live as I do you," I said, clapping him on the shoulder. "You're my most trusted warrior. I need your help. "

Nekko's chest expanded at my words. "I am honored to be at your service. I assume Rayyar will be joining you."

"Worry not. I have him on my radar. Better to keep your enemies close."

"With your friends at your back," Nekko added with a low growl. "I don't like it. Sia Sakkar and Rayyar may already have plans to sabotage you along the way. You could be walking into a trap. I don't like it, but I will do as you ordered. May I ask the need for recording the dome?"

"More power fluctuations." I leaned in close, lowering my voice. "I believe the rumors are true. The nutrillium mines are no longer producing."

"If the dome collapses, and the Nuttaki attack—"

"Let's hope it doesn't come to that. My brother hasn't left the planet on his next voyage; maybe that's why. No nutrillium to power his vessel."

"Or him being grounded might have something to do with your sword cutting through all those wires," Nekko grunted with humor.

"Maybe," I smirked. "I know little about propulsion engines, but that compartment contained the most vulnerable-looking components."

I extended my forearm for him to clasp. The weight of solemnity settled around us.

"Use a tracker so I can check your position," Nekko said. His sideways smirk turned steely. "Ping me regularly, or I'll send out a search party."

"Who gives the orders here?" I tightened my hold on his forearm and stepped into his bulky frame. "Are you challenging me?"

Nekko bowed his head, ignorant of my jest. "No, Sia. I was only concerned for your safety."

"Relax, Nekko," a rare chuckle escaped me, "It was only a jest. I'm glad to have someone concerned for my welfare."

He visibly sagged, shaking his silvery mane at me. "You got me," Nekko wagged a finger. "For a mims there, I thought you were serious."

I stepped back, releasing his forearm. "How is the repair to the wall coming along?"

"It's almost complete." Nekko became serious. "Now that the temperature has dropped during the dark hurs, the rynose attacks are becoming more frequent. I fear those armored beasts will soon be coming in greater numbers."

"I think you're right," I considered Nekko's concerns. "The rynose's mating season is upon them. The males will be expanding their territories in search of fertile females."

My antiquated, wooden walls were just another reason to hasten our departure to the crashed spacecraft. My settlement had so few warriors, and I was forced to seek out that which I shunned.

"Now that Sakkar has closed off the nutrillium mines except for a single shaft inside Huren's dome, there's no way to check my theory." I rubbed at my aching head. "I must find an alternate power source to keep the skypods afloat and maybe something to create a protective dome around this settlement."

"If Sakkar sends out a salvage party and they reach the site before you, it will be stripped clean." Nekko's brow pinched in thought. "What of the other clans? Do you think they will risk traveling such long distances to investigate the crash site?"

"I pray to the Spirits that they dismiss it as an asteroid and stay away," I huffed. "That's all we need, another clan dispute over land boundaries."

Valose was crashing down around me, and I was powerless to stop it. I was glad for the company of the males standing alongside me, but a part of me wished they had remained inside the safety of the dome.

"...with you so I can track your movements." Nekko's words filtered through my thoughts. "The transmitter is small enough to be attached under the buckle on your kiltus out of sight of your enemy. I can't imagine Rayyar would dare venture there."

"Not unless he's looking for a merciless death."

"Please let me know before you do such a thing," Nekko snorted with laughter. "I wouldn't want to miss that long-awaited spectacle."

"Neither would I." My hands clenched into fists, yet my mood was lightened as it always did in Nekko's presence. "Enough talk. I need to be going."

I wasn't surprised when Nekko removed the tracker from his pocket and ran his thumb over the tiny device, making some sort of adjustments. I should take the time to learn more about my people's ever-growing technologies, but I lacked the patience for such tedious things.

Nekko handed me the device, and I attached it under my buckle. "Predicting my next move, Nekko?"

"Always, Sia," he grinned. "We've known each other since we were nurslings. I know you almost as well as I know myself."

There was no cockiness in his response—merely a casual remark born of familiarity between two males who had spent a lifetime of suns-rises together.

"You are the brother I wished I had." The words tumbled from my mouth before I could stop them. The urgency to safeguard my people must be having strange effects. I wasn't known for emotional declarations.

Nekko considered me for a long moment. "I think the same of you, Sia."

"Jakkar," I corrected. "Technically, I am no longer your ruler."

"Yet, you need no crown for others to follow you," Nekko stated flatly. "I would follow you anywhere, Sia Jakkar."

Just as the moment's intensity turned awkward, the warning alarm flashed from the tower. The Nuttaki were on the move, and I knew just where they were headed.

"You better get going. Looks like you've got another enemy to outrun," Nekko clapped me on the shoulder before we went our separate ways, him racing off to the tower while I ran to the main gate.

The squad Rayyar gathered awaited my arrival with steely resolve as if prepared for war. I flashed a silver palm, greeting the males ready to travel with me into the thick of an unyielding jungle.

Draggar, Vallon, and Aggar returned my gesture, flashing silver palms. However, the fourth, Rayyar, was slow to respond, a deliberate slight to my leadership. Jaw clenched, it took everything in me not to snatch his traitorous ass off his rover and beat him into the ground.

I must suppress the urge to deliver the beating Rayyar deserved for his betrayal if I was to keep tabs on my brother. It sickened me that I had to allow the enemy into my settlement to keep it safe. Yet, if Sakkar ever planned an attack, I didn't want to be completely blindsided.

My squad was mounted on their rovers with Draggar operating the hauler—a larger version of a rover with an open bed for hauling—except for one. "Where's Nullar?"

Draggar pointed. I followed the direction of the warrior's finger to see a struggling Nullar juggling a load of medical equipment as he high tailed it over.

Nullar was a scholar, not born of the warrior class, so I didn't expect him to be as efficient as the others. Nevertheless, we needed to move fast, so I rushed to help him stow his equipment into the compartments of his rover.

Whether or not Nullar realized it, he was the most important male in the squad. Once we reached the crash site, the scanners only he knew enough to operate would be used before we could begin to scavenge the vessel.

I mounted my rover, swinging a leg over the seat, and addressed my males. "As you saw the warning alarm, the Nuttaki are on the move, which means we must get to the site first. No stopping. We ride through the dark hurs until we reach the site in diamond formation with Nullar in the center. He is to be protected above all others. No one is allowed to enter the crashed vessel until he deems it safe." The males grumbled their agreement and formed up. "Rayyar, you are to ride on my left-front."

So, I can keep a sharp eye on you, I said only to myself.

Rayyar grudgingly did as I ordered.

Leaning forward, I rested my chest against the elongated seat and grabbed ahold of the handgrips. I placed my feet on the thrusters behind me and engaged the gravity disruptor. My rover floated above the ground, and I shifted my weight into a more comfortable position, preparing for a long journey until we reached the crash site.

"Let's travel," I shouted to my males.

The wooden gates opened with an embarrassing creak. The sentry manning the portal stepped aside, allowing us passage.

The squad accelerated out of the settlement and into the jungle like a nutrone burst from a blaster. We kept low to avoid being smacked off our rovers by the dense foliage of the jungle.

A clutch of chiksin paused in their grazing of wispt grass to watch as we rocketed past. Small and docile, the fowl didn't pose any threat.

I sent up a silent plea to the Spirits that we didn't come across anything that did.

Chapter Three

LILY

Now that my screams had stopped, Marie's muffled calls reached my ringing ears.

"Lily! Are you okay?" Marie called out again. "Lily? Oh my god, please answer."

"Here," I squeaked. My voice was a hoarse whisper. "I'm… I'm in here."

I couldn't catch my breath. My throat was screamed raw. There was no stopping my body from shaking, my muscles contracting in quick bursts from all the shocks I had endured.

"Lily," came Marie's anguished cry.

I took a deep breath and tried to answer her again. "I'm here! Here!" I pounded a quaking fist on the metal wall.

"Lily! Oh, thank God," Marie breathed. "I thought I'd lost you. What happened?"

Curled into a ball, I trembled all over. I just wanted to rest for a minute—to catch my breath—yet I was scared the light bars would come back on, and then I'd be fucked. I wouldn't last long against the second round of low-level electrocution as weak as I was.

"My light bars went out," I hollered out the best I could.

"What?" Marie called back. "Are you freaking kidding me? So, you can get out."

"Trapped," I said breathlessly. "Overturned box."

"Lily, you have to get out of there," Marie's voice turned frantic. "Can you lift the box?"

I sagged into the strange, spongy floor. I needed to try, but I was so exhausted.

"Don't you dare give up, Lily!" Marie shouted as if she knew where my mind went. "Lift the box and get the fuck out of there."

Marie was right. I couldn't just lay here. I had to get myself out before I ran out of air, or the bars flickered back to life. I needed to woman up and get this stupid thing off me.

With great effort, I got my legs under me. There wasn't much room, so I squatted low and ran my hands along the floor until I found the lip of my cage. I tried to wriggle my fingers under one edge, but it sat tight to the floor.

I hugged my arms around myself to conserve energy while I thought. Marie kept calling, but I stayed quiet. It would take too much effort to raise my voice loud enough for her to hear me through the metal.

Plan hashed, I duck-walked forward until my knees touched cold metal. I placed the palms of my hands to my low ceiling near the corner and pushed for all I was worth. A slice of light spilled in under the lip. Encouraged, my arms and legs strained against the heavy load. Sweat beaded on my forehead and rolled between my breasts.

I was making progress, slowly lifting the box until it rested on one edge, but I was stuck. I'd only lifted it about a foot off the floor so I couldn't get out from under it without removing my hands from the ceiling.

It was a shitty plan, and the stupid cage was heavier than I predicted. The thing must weigh over a hundred-freaking pounds.

I would be free if I could muster enough strength to tip the box the rest of the way over. I kept lifting. My arms and thighs shook from the effort, but I raised it another few inches.

I gritted my teeth and grunted against the strain. My limbs had turned into noodles, and I was scared I wouldn't be able to hold it up much longer.

Marie hadn't stopped chatting, but I was so focused on saving myself, I wasn't making sense out of a single word she was saying. Nevertheless, the encouraging sounds made me believe she was cheering me on.

I was so close; I couldn't give up now. Just a little more, and I could lunge out and maybe clear the metal box before it fell to the floor.

Gathering every ounce of strength, I focused solely on pushing against my container's extreme weight. A cry was ripped from me as I put all my effort into lifting another couple of inches. Sweat dripped in my eyes, stinging and burning.

All right. This was it—the moment to freedom or fuckdom.

I took a few deep breaths and willed my arms and legs to power lift the cage enough to where I could scramble out from under it.

Sheer determination came to my aid. My knees nearly buckled with the force pressing down on me, but I fought back and hefted the damn cage up another foot.

Fuck it! It was now or never, and this shit wasn't getting any lighter. I flung myself out of the opening I created with one last heft. The metal box came down hard, landing with a muted thud on the spongy, black floor.

I laid face down, an exhausted grin on my face, and looked around the room with a view no longer obstructed by light bars. Cages were strewn everywhere. Some toppled on their sides, others on their backs, most piled up at odd angles.

But I was free!

The pain was slow to register. When it did, I looked down my body to find my left foot still under the cage. I struggled and tried to pull it free; the weight of the metal box kept it trapped.

"Ohfuckohfuckohfuck..."

The pain was searing, and every time I moved, it only made it worse. I could barely lift the box using my entire body; how could I lift it with only my arms to pull my foot free?

Despite the pain in my ankle, I rolled onto my back and sat up. The skin around my ankle tore away as I did. Nausea steam-rolled over me. My vision wavered, and I turned my head to the side, and dry heaved.

My empty stomach was a knot in my throat. I lay back on the floor and tried to calm my ragged breaths.

Tears coursed down my temples to puddle inside my ears. The only thing certain was if the light bars reactivated, and my foot was still under there, I would be electrocuted.

I didn't get this far to die lying outside my cage with a fresh taste of freedom.

I sat up slowly, contemplating my next move. Scooting down to the cage, I wrapped my fingers under the lip and strained to lift it enough to free my foot. I felt some easement of pressure but no visible alleviation. Nevertheless, I didn't give up the momentum. I knew what I had to do.

I gave the lifting all I had, turned my head away from the carnage, and ripped my foot out from under the crushing weight.

I fell back on the floor, truly free. My left leg twitched uncontrollably. The pain in my ankle and foot was so profound that my cries were silent.

I forced myself into a sitting position and kept my eyes averted. I didn't want to look at the damage. I wondered if my foot was even still attached to my body.

Marie's voice gained my attention. I found her off to one side, her cage sporting a large dent, yet her light bars remained. Her smile was tight. A trickle of blood dripped from her temple. Her face was ashen as she looked me over.

"You're okay, Lily," Marie reassured me. "You found a way out just like you said you would."

I nodded and wiped the moisture off my face. "How bad is it?"

"Broken." Marie glanced at my ankle and winced. "Definitely broken, but I think you'll live."

Muffled cries and women's voices began to filter out from the mess of cages. I could see bodies and movement behind the light bars. The room appeared to be on a permanent slant.

"Don't touch the bars. They're electrified," Marie rushed to explain when zaps accompanied surprised outcries.

"Okay. Okay," I exhaled and came to terms with my painful injury. I had to help the others. I'll just hop around and not look at my foot. I never could stand the sight of my own blood, so I'd probably pass out if I looked at it. "Who's all here? Sound off, ladies."

"Me. Willow," came a voice from inside the pile. "I can barely see you through a crack. There's another girl in front of me, but she's not moving."

"Isobel." A brunette waved at me from the top of the pile. I feared for her safety, precariously perched so high up.

"Rose. Over here," said a small voice from around the corner. I leaned to the side and could just make out her curly, reddish-brown hair and slight form.

"Layla," whined a pretty blonde. Her metal cage sat cockeyed and wedged between many.

"Hi, everybody. I'm Marie."

"Hi," I said to everyone and swallowed hard over how few had answered. There had been twenty or so women. "I'm Lily. I suppose since I'm the only one free, that makes me your rescuer. I hope." I whispered the last.

"Well, Lily, what are you waiting for?" Layla demanded. "Get me out of here."

"I don't know how yet, so I guess that means you're stuck for now," I snapped back.

I instantly disliked her, but I shoved aside my distaste for Layla because Amy hadn't answered. Panic set in, and I pushed off the floor to stand on my good foot. I threw out my arms and wobbled before gaining my balance on the slanted floor. Left knee bent, my foot dangled painfully as I hopped toward the cluster of cages, first looking inside the ones facing me.

My hop faltered as I was met with a horrific scene. A girl with eyes wide open was lying at the bottom of one cage in a crumpled heap. Her vacant stare was a chilly testament that not all the captives made it through the crash.

I peered into the next. Obvious contusions had claimed another life. I rubbed at my aching head. Everything else took a back seat with my ankle pain, but my body was bruised with stinging stripes burned into my palms and legs. I probably looked like I'd been in a train wreck.

The next one was blessedly empty.

I crouched to peer inside the one below the empty one and found a prone form. The girl, with a cap of blonde hair, wasn't moving. I assumed she was dead until I noticed her chest's slight rise and fall.

"Hey," I call out to her. "Hello in there. Are you all right?"

No response.

"Lily," Marie called out. "I see red hair over here."

My injured foot forgotten, I started to run in Marie's direction until I crumpled to the floor in a shock of white pain.

"Ohmygod, Lily!" Marie gasped. "Are you all right?"

"Fine," I gritted out, dragging myself in her direction—my need to find Amy outweighed everything else.

I switched to a crawl until I was directly in front of Marie's cage. "Hi, friend," she smiled at me.

"Hi," I returned. My bottom lip trembled with emotion. I absently noticed a scattering of freckles across her nose and cheeks, giving her a youthful appearance, but the trail of blood running down one side of her face commanded my attention. "You're bleeding. Are you okay?"

"About as well as can be expected. I'm alive, so there's that. I think that's your friend over there," Marie pointed in a direction over my shoulder.

I turned to see a mass of red hair in an overturned cage. I stumbled, crawled, and fought my way over to her. It was Amy. That flaming red hair couldn't belong to anyone else. I held my breath and took a look inside. Drooping green eyes gazed up at me.

"Ohmygod! Amy!"

"Werr we?" Amy slurred. "Wus happn?"

Her slurred speech and the tremendous knot on her forehead screamed concussion. So thrilled to find her alive, yet at the same time, terrified over her condition. And, how to best answer her questions without completely freaking her out?

"We were... kidnapped, and then we crashed." I decided to remain vague until I could get her out and find medical help.

I fought back hysterical laughter. Medical help from where? As much as I wanted to believe we crash-landed somewhere on Earth, I had a bad feeling we hadn't.

Amy's mouth worked to form words, but no sound came out. I needed to stop the slow veil of panic beginning to drop. "I escaped, and I'm going to help you and the others get out."

Amy's fiery brows pinched together. "Otthersh?"

"Yeah," I said as brightly as I could. "We have a few new friends you'll get to meet as soon as I find the... key to turn off the light bars. Okay? Easy-peasy."

"Eash-e peassh," Amy slurred.

I drank in the sight of her. My best friend couldn't die crumpled in the bottom of an alien's cage. I wouldn't allow it.

"I will do everything I can to get you out, Amy. I promise."

"Dunt leeves, Lill." Amy looked up at me, a desperate pleading on her battered face.

"I have to," my voice wavered. I blinked hard to keep tears from falling. I had to stay strong for her. "I won't be long. Just rest, and I'll be back before you know it."

Amy's face was a mask of questions. She looked too groggy to ask any of them, for which I was kind of glad. I had no idea what to tell her except the truth. But honestly, I wasn't ready to put a voice to what happened to us.

"Try not to worry." I was sure my smile looked as fake as it felt. "I'll be right back. Love you, Amy."

"Luuvs uu," Amy's reply was free of her usual misty-eyed humility. Out of all her visible injuries, that worried me the most.

My gaze panned the room. It was a total disaster, but the sniffles and groans of the other women waiting for me to help them were even more overwhelming. I had to do something and fast. Fear shot down my spine, wondering if the aliens would come back to check on us?

Marie seemed to know more than anyone else about our situation, so I forced myself to calm and looked back at her.

"Hey," I sidled up to Marie's cage, cringing when my damaged ankle sent a jolt of pain up my calf and tried to keep my voice low. "You're still bleeding."

"Yeah." Marie swiped away a fresh trickle of blood. "Head wounds usually bleed a lot."

"Please tell me you're speaking from a medical background."

"Nope. Sorry. Not me," Marie said, swiping again. "Marie's the name, and accounting's my game. I'm the only sister of two rambunctious brothers that thought they were superheroes. They were always doing something monumentally dangerous to turn our mother's hair gray."

"I see," I laughed. "Do you know if there's a way to open the cages besides the alien hand scanner? Maybe a hidden keypad or something?"

"Not that I ever saw," Marie said thoughtfully. "How did yours open?"

"I don't know." I shook my head. "I heard a fizzle and a pop, and then they just glitched off."

"I wonder if the impact from your hard landing turned it off somehow." Marie wiped at her face.

I considered her words. "I wonder if I could find something to bash into the hand scanner if it would duplicate what happened to mine."

"It's worth a try," Marie agreed.

"Is anyone going to deactivate this glowing shit and get me out of here any time soon?" The whiny blonde, Layla, complained.

"Where's the alien with the gas machine when you need it?" Marie grumbled.

I laughed a little. How could I not when it was exactly what I was thinking? I took a fortifying breath and prepared myself to move around the room, searching for some kind of hard object to whack the hand scanners.

"Watch after Amy for me?" I asked Marie. "Keep her talking, so she doesn't fall asleep. She might have a concussion."

"Absolutely," Marie gave me a firm nod.

"Hello," Layla bellowed. "I can hear the two of you whispering. Are you planning a rescue or what?"

"Lily's hurt, bitch." I jumped when Marie shouted. "She's doing what she can. Be glad one of us is out and able to help."

"Yeah, yeah. Whatever..." Layla mumbled.

"It's tempting to leave her ass in there," Marie cursed.

I snickered and gingerly moved into the middle of the disorderly room. It was easier to crawl, so I took to my hands and knees, trading one pain for another. Every time my palms touched the floor caused a searing sting. I sucked it up and searched the wreckage for something to smash into the hand scanners.

Once I searched the entire room, I found nothing aside from overturned cages—

Wait!

My head swung around to a tear in the wall, and I scrambled over to it. Unfortunately, a cage blocked the hole.

I hopped around to the front and stifled a scream. Inside was a girl with her head split open. The shock of white that was her skull was in sharp contrast to the blood covering her face.

"I'm so sorry," I whispered and gently touched the side of her cage. It made me sick knowing she and others never made it out of their prisons.

I looked back to find expectant faces staring back. Marie gave me a thumbs up.

Shit! I had to help these women get out—even the dead ones. I refused to leave a single person, dead or alive, inside these alien prisons. My gaze shifted to the haughty blonde, Layla.

Well, maybe just one. I grinned to myself.

Gawds, she was like the love child of a stuck-up cheerleader and a snobby homecoming queen. She glared at me, but I ignored her.

I planted my stinging palms on the sides of the cage. Then, standing on one leg, I pushed for all I was worth. At first, it didn't feel as if it was going anywhere, then it moved, sliding over just enough for me to squeeze through the hole in the wall.

Excitement flared when I heard the girls behind me cheering. I peered through the hole to see the same black, sparkling floor I was standing on. It was littered with strange tubes and wires. I wasn't super thrilled about venturing out on my own, but what other choice could I make?

"Okay," I said to everyone. "I'm headed out. I'll be back as soon as I can."

"Be careful," Marie called out along with the others. Even Layla grumbled something encouraging.

I leaned forward and poked my head out to find a smooth, white-walled corridor. Like a tunnel, the ceiling and walls were seamless. Tiny lights flashed from various panels dotted along the path. Debris was strewn everywhere.

I didn't see any aliens. I hoped those fuckers all died in the crash. It would be no less than they deserved.

I went out headfirst, placing my tender palms on the floor to wiggle the rest of the way out, careful not to cut myself on the torn edges of what looked like a wall made of heavy-duty plastic.

I looked one way and then the other. One end was a log jam of large, boxy equipment all about the size of small refrigerators. Everything was white like the walls with lots of sharp corners, which explained the corridor's damage.

The opposite direction was the backdrop to a horror movie waiting to happen. It was dark as sin at the far end. Portions of the illuminated walls flickered while other parts had gone completely dark.

I shored up my courage and pushed the ache of my broken ankle and the sting of my charred palms aside. Others were depending on me to free them. And I had made a promise to my best friend I intended to keep—even if I was scared shitless.

Off I went, dragging my jacked-up foot behind me while my palms protested the feel of the squishy floor beneath them. I rummaged through the glass wire and hollow tubes littering the corridor as I trudged along. Then I came across the barest outline of a closed door with a small blinking panel on the wall next to it.

I got to my knees and considered trying to open it, but fear got the better of me. What if one of those gray freaks was inside? It wasn't worth the risk of running into my abductors. If I got myself captured, or worse, the others chances of being rescued would be lost.

I backed away and continued down the darkening corridor. I passed another closed door and then two more and kept going for what felt like forever until I reached a room with light spilling from its open doorway.

It was an open invitation of the scariest kind. My breaths came in short pants as I hugged the wall and waited. No sounds came from within. I licked my parched lips and chanced a peek inside.

It was some kind of strange lab with long tables jutting out from the walls. Equipment was strewn all over the floor. Yet, oddly, some of it looked familiar, like the alien version of microscopes that were toppled here and there, and beakers that littered the floor were similar to the laboratory equipment which I made my living.

With a hard swallow, I moved inside the room. I rightened the first microscope I came to. Sleek in design with soft curves, it was definitely high-tech. The laboratory technologist in me wanted to play with it. Instead, I lifted it, testing the weight. It was heavy enough to use as a bludgeon but light enough I thought I could carry it back.

Now that I was fully inside the room, I began to find more useful items. First, I collected a folded pile of the shapeless dresses we all wore. Then, I unfolded one and placed the microscope and the other dresses in the center, fashioning a sack out of the garment by folding the corners.

Moving on, I found a pipe with an eerie blue light on one end. I didn't know its use, but I was taking it with me. That too went in my makeshift sack.

I waded through a sea of—I guess—specimen cups? All filled with various colors of fluids. I didn't stop to examine what they might contain because I had my eye on what I hoped was a knife. I grabbed it by the handle where it rested on a table and flashed the blade's razor-sharp edge in the glow of the overhead lights.

It wasn't as much a knife as it was a giant scalpel. Swallowing hard, I shivered over the implications—sick alien bastards. If pounding on the hand scanner didn't work, maybe I could use it to cut through the metal cage walls and get the girls out that way.

I held on to my new weapon and headed for another toppled stack of dresses. These might come in handy for dressing wounds and—

I recoiled back so fast that I slammed into the far wall. I meant to scream, but fear had ripped every ounce of air from my lungs. Under the dresses was a face of the gray alien variety. The creature wasn't moving, and it appeared to be dead. Nevertheless, I wanted nothing to do with that thing. Dead or alive, it freaked me the fuck out.

I sat, panting, with my back pressed against the wall, just staring at the alien responsible for my shitty situation, my broken ankle, the deaths of innocent women, and stealing all of us away from our homes.

What I thought was dead blinked open bulbous eyes. Frozen with fear, I watched as the alien wrapped its long, segmented fingers around the machine that kept it pinned to the floor. A fumping noise erupted from its open mouth, and it uselessly pushed against the machine.

Once I realized the alien was stuck, some of my horrified shock at finding the thing gave way to images of the women trapped in those metal boxes. With that huge contusion, Amy's face was the first image to flash in my mind, then Marie and the endless trickle of blood from her head wound. Finally, the bodies of the women I had found dead.

As the images scrolled through my mind like a tragic movie, the more anger replaced fear, and the harder I clutched the handle of my new best friend.

The alien jerked, realizing it was no longer alone, and turned its head. With a gnarled hand, it reached out to me. Those bulbous eyes once narrowed on me in disgust were wide open and pleading. Its mouth cracked open as if to speak, but I interrupted.

"As if I would help you," I seethed.

The glint of my blade triggered my next move. Guided by blinding rage, I went all Norman Bates and reared back my arm, ready to stab a death blow. But, just as my giant scalpel was about to hit home, I paused. Killing this alien fast would be like showing mercy, and I had nothing for this motherfucker.

"You can stay trapped. Die a slow death, you piece of shit," I hissed, surprised to find so much hatred inside myself.

I was one of those people who showed mercy to even the scariest creatures. Just last week, I was relocating a furry-legged wolf spider back to the outdoors, even though it took everything in me not to freak out as I was running to the door with it trapped inside a paper cup.

This gray freak lying only a few feet away wasn't a spider that had accidentally wandered into my apartment. No. This thing had stolen me, my best friend, and a bunch of other girls away from our homes and locked us inside metal boxes with electrocution rods for bars.

It didn't deserve anyone's mercy!

Like nothing I'd ever heard, a growl erupted from between several rows of razor-sharp teeth. The sound peppered my skin in gooseflesh. I fought back my adrenal glands screaming at me to get away from it as fast as possible. Yet, I remained frozen on my knees next to the enemy, holding my weapon aloft.

It thrust out a long arm and grabbed the scalpel. I recoiled away and fell back on my ass, its fingers flexing and grasping at the air.

What was so obvious became clearer than a cloudless sky on a summer's day.

"Of course," I murmured aloud. "How could I be so stupid?" I scooted closer to the trapped alien. "You want my scalpel, freak? Yeah, I'll bet you do. But I've got a surprise for you."

As the alien flailed its stringy arm in an attempt to grab me, its lips flapped like it was trying to speak. I bode my time, waiting for the perfect moment. Then, as its arm stretched to its max capacity, I reared back and chopped down on its thin wrist.

Just like a tree branch under a lumberjack's ax, the crunch of the alien's bones beneath my blade ricocheted off the smooth walls of the lab.

I assumed the orange goo that gurgled out in slow, thick drips from the severed limb was the alien's blood. My gag reflex kicked into overdrive, and I leaned to the side, barfing nothing from my empty stomach.

The room fell utterly silent. I watched in horrified fascination as the alien raised its bloody stub. Its bulbous eyes grew impossibly large, bulging with shock over the loss of its hand.

With an audible inhalation, the alien released a screech that shattered my bones. So loud, I knew anything left alive on this ship heard it. I sure as fuck didn't want to be here if more aliens showed up to investigate.

I was squeamish about picking up the alien's disarticulated hand, but I needed to woman up. The girls needed out of their cages, so I dropped my proverbial lady balls and snagged a dress off the folded pile and threw it over the hand. I wrapped it up and crawled to my makeshift sack of scavenged items.

Dragging my heavy sack, I scurried to the door and peeked out into the corridor—all clear. I grinned like a loon, quickly crawling back to the prison room where I left my best friend and the rest of the women.

Fuck beating on the hand scanner. I had an actual hand! I couldn't wait to see the look on Marie's face when I whipped it out and showed it to her.

"Thank God!" Marie swore when I flopped into the room through the jagged hole. "After that hair-raising screech, I thought something horrible happened to you."

"Not to me." I winked and stumbled, falling over and onto my side.

"What in the hell made that noise, and why do you look like the cat who swallowed the canary?"

"Are you okay?" Rose asked in a small voice.

"What's that horrible smell?" Layla griped.

"Lily, what happened out there?" Marie spoke over the rest.

Showered with questions, I sat crumpled on the floor and stared at my malformed ankle. My teeth clattered together as I cringed away from the sight of my injury.

My foot looked worse than it did before I left, my toes had turned a solid blue, and the shredded skin around my ankle was turning white and hard as the tissue shriveled with death.

"Did you find anything to help get us out of here?" Willow's thin voice filtered through the mound of cages where she was trapped.

Before I could help them, I needed to help myself. So, I grabbed a handful of folded dresses and began spreading them out. "Maybe," I answered Willow.

"What was that screeching?" Marie butted in. "We didn't think it would ever stop."

In answer, I pulled out the leaking bundle. The smell knocked me back on my ass. I held my breath while unwrapping it.

Sharp inhales and a few screams followed as I held up the severed alien's hand. Wow. It really stunk. When I first hacked it off, I didn't remember it smelling, but the hand looked more black than gray, especially at the fingertips.

"Is that a fucking hand?" Marie shrank back.

"Yep."

"How did you get it?" Willow asked.

"I cut it off an alien I found trapped under some overturned machines down the hall," I told them as I wrapped the chopped-off end of the wrist in a clean dress. "I figured I could use it to release the light bars using the hand scanner to free everyone."

"Holy shit balls!" Marie bellowed. "You're my hero."

"Be my hero, too," Layla yelled out.

I shared in Marie's eye roll. Layla had stayed quiet, and I almost forgot about her. Almost.

"Leave her for last," Marie whispered loudly.

"Hello, bitches," Layla huffed. "I can hear you."

It was bad enough luck to be abducted by aliens, but to get stuck with a troll-like Layla, too? Completely unfair.

I ignored the banter around me and cut the dresses I'd found into strips, and wrapped up my ankle. Bile bubbled up my throat at the crunching of my bones as I bound them. I swayed, blurry-eyed over the pain.

I gulped back air to calm my stomach before crawling to Marie with the severed hand. Marie recoiled away from the sickening appendage. The thing looked like cyanotic snow crab legs, the fingers thin and jointed. The tips had turned a sickening black.

I waved the hand in front of her scanner and held my breath. To my disappointment, nothing happened.

"Maybe hold it closer," Marie suggested.

I nodded and touched the stinking hand to the scanner—still nothing. I straightened the fingers where they'd curled into the palm. The popping sounds gagged me. I held the hand up again.

Still nothing. Tears pressed behind my eyes, but I wouldn't cry in front of these girls. I straightened my spine and blinked hard. Breaking down would only make everything worse.

"Do you think the hand scanner only works for a specific alien? Maybe you got the wrong guy." Marie's reasoning hit me with a wave of disappointment.

"Fuckfuckfuck," I cursed through clenched teeth. "Let me try someone else's cage."

I crawled to Amy's cage. "You hanging in there, Amy?"

"S'all good," Amy slurred back.

I held up the alien's hand to Amy's scanner. And... nothing.

"Wushthat?" I felt the fear in Amy's voice.

"I'll explain later. Promise," I told her before crawling to Rose.

"I can't believe this shit," I mumbled after another unsuccessful wave across Rose's scanner.

I looked at the ghastly appendage, then all around at the cages with expectant faces staring back. My stomach grumbled, and I placed a hand over my mid-section where the hollow ache painfully clenched.

"When was the last time you ate or drank anything?" I looked at Marie for answers.

Marie's face scrunched up in thought. "Um, I don't know. I guess my last meal was back on Earth at my apartment."

"But you said we'd been here about a week," I said, shocked. "How are we not starving?"

"With no water, how are we still alive?" Isobel added from her cage.

"The aliens came in every so often and stabbed some sort of stick into our thighs through the light bars," Marie provided. "Reminded me of a cattle prod with a needless syringe attached to one end. There was some sort of weird, greenish fluid that got injected into our bodies."

"What kind of greenish fluid?" Layla grumbled.

"How in the hell should I know," Marie shrugged. "It's some alien shit that I think keeps us from being hungry or thirsty. I can't even remember the last time I had to pee."

"So, you think it feeds our bodies somehow?" Willow gulped from somewhere inside the pile of cages.

I raised up on my knees and tried to locate where her voice originated, but I couldn't see her at all. It scared me to think she was in the center of all that mess.

"That's my guess," Marie said.

"What are you planning to do?" Marie's eyes followed me as I crawled past her cage.

"Moving on to plan B. I'm gonna slam that heavy-ass microscope into the hand scanner."

"Hells yes, She-Ra!" Marie threw up her hands and crossed her fingers. "Maybe that'll do it."

I envied Marie. Not much seemed to ruffle her feathers. Yet here I was with my heart living in my throat and the weight of responsibility heavy on my shoulders. I wished I could be as composed as her.

I grabbed the weighty microscope and hefted it over to Marie's cage. We exchanged optimistic smiles, and Marie scooted back as far away from the scanner as her metal box would allow. I lifted the microscope, and at Marie's nod, I slammed the base into her scanner, then waited. When no fizzle and pop happened, I set my bludgeon down and took a second to rest my arms.

"Okay, Marie, let's try this again," I told her. All I needed to do was hit the scanner a few more times, and her light bars would fizzle out, just like mine had. "I just need to hit it again."

"Okay," Marie agreed. "Let her rip."

I drew in a deep breath and grunted as I lifted the microscope off the floor. It was a shame I was beating the crap out of some alien technology. The laboratory technologist in me would love to take a peek at some alien microorganisms.

I reared back and slammed the base of the microscope against the scanner. Sparks flew, catching me off guard. I yelped and fell back on my ass. Marie looked equally as stunned.

"Was that a good thing or bad?" Marie swallowed hard, remaining tightly pressed against the back wall.

"Don't know," I admitted. The light bars looked unchanged. "Shall I try again?"

"Might as well. It isn't as if I have a ton of choices here."

I reached down deep and gathered a burst of energy. Then, with another heave-ho, I slammed the microscope's base into the scanner. For one breathless heartbeat, Marie's light bars wavered. Wide-eyed, we waited for the inevitable pop and fizzle.

At first, nothing... Then a blinding power surge. Marie's light bars appeared to swell so much that the electrifying light became a wall, blocking Marie from my view.

Panic became a tangible thing. "Marie! Are you all right in there?"

"So far," Marie squeaked. "Don't do anything else. Let's not blow the thing up with me inside."

"Right," I panted. "You're right. I'll just have to find another way to get you out."

I scooted away from Marie's brightly lit cage, happy to see that the light bars were already beginning to dim back to normal. Fuck! That was scary. I wanted to free these women but not kill them in the process.

My eyes landed on the oversized scalpel I used to chop off the alien's hand. I grabbed it and carried it over to the side of Marie's cage to open it up like a sardine can. "Marie, scoot back as far to the other side as you can. I'm gonna try and cut you out."

"Okay." I heard her shuffling around. "I'm good. Go ahead."

"Here goes," I warned.

I settled my weight on my knees and raised my hand over my head, thrusting the scalpel into the metal wall. The pointed end of the blade ricocheted off the metal with a resounding chink instead of biting in as I'd hoped.

I shook my head in utter disbelief, skimming my fingertips over the metal where my blade hit. There wasn't a single scratch left behind. I hit the damn thing pretty hard, too.

"How'd it go?" she called out.

"Not as well as I expected."

"Well, crap."

A twinkle of something metallic glittered from the floor. I touched it to find it wasn't the weird, sparkly stones embedded in the spongy substrate. Then I examined my scalpel and cursed. The pointed tip had broken off.

"Crap is right," I commented, picking up the broken-off tip. "What is this shit made of? I'd bet it's bulletproof."

"I don't see a dent or anything on my side," Marie stated.

"There's nothing out here either."

"Are you serious?" Marie cursed. "That knife thing you've got looks really sharp."

"Oh, it is—or was. It cut through the alien's wrist like hot butter."

"If hitting the scanner doesn't work and cutting us out is a no-go, what other options do we have?" Isobel's panicked voice sounded out from the opposite side of the room.

I positioned myself in front of Marie's cage to look over at Amy, who had fallen unconscious. Panic ate at me. I zeroed in on her chest to see the rise and fall of her deep, even breaths. I felt better knowing she was still alive.

"Amy," I called. Her unresponsiveness only ramped up my agitation. I hated that I couldn't get to her.

After wracking my brain for new ideas, I addressed the room. "I'm open to suggestions. I'm not giving up, but I'm fresh out of ideas."

A harsh scrape of metal on metal set my teeth on edge and threw the room into silence. Something or someone was on its way.

My eyes swung to the jagged hole in the wall. Whatever the fuck made that noise couldn't be good. With no way to barricade the hole, we were sitting ducks.

With my blood frozen in my veins, I positioned myself beside the hole with the microscope at my feet. I held the light bar in one hand and the scalpel in the other and waited. If something wanted to come in here and fuck with my girls, they would have to get through me first.

Chapter Four

JAKKAR

Rayyar's rover had been in my sights throughout the entire journey. His hands never left the grips to even so much as scratch his ass, so I knew he hadn't tried to make contact with Sakkar.

Suspicion was a malignancy inside my gut that was taking on a life of its own. My warrior's instinct was humming that the traitor was hiding something about the crashed vessel.

The dark hurs came and went, and yet we rode on. My back ached and my thighs cramped from the brutal hurs straddling my rover. As a seasoned Valose warrior I'd been through worse.

As the following suns-rise burned a vivid blue over the dark horizon, the crashed vessel loomed large ahead of us. It was enormous and much larger than I anticipated. I could just make out the opposite end, far off in the distance. It lay dormant, yet forbidding, like a great, crumbled beast waiting, ready to strike.

Our squad slowed and took cover beneath the enormous leaves of a yulin tree to prepare a camp. I signaled for Nullar and Aggar to follow me to get a closer look at the wreckage.

We stayed hidden against the backdrop of the jungle. Our scales assumed our surroundings blues, silvers, and whites, camouflaging us from predators wanting to make a meal out of us.

Aggar searched as wide an area around the crash site as his scanner would allow while I peered through a scope, looking for the best way inside the mangled heap.

"I'm detecting three Valosian males on the far side of our location. Also, a horde of Nuttaki approaching from the west," Aggar quietly reported.

"No dangerous microorganisms present, Sia," Nullar spoke softly and looked from one device to another. "The atmosphere inside the structure lacks sufficient oxygen. I would recommend wearing rebreathers once we go inside."

"The Valosians have to be Sakkar's salvage squad. They are of no concern. The ship is large enough we can avoid them," I reasoned. "However, the Nuttaki could prove problematic. How many rebreathers do we have?"

"Only three, Sia."

I grunted an acknowledgment. "I would have preferred to take a larger squad inside, but we'll have to make do with just the three of us."

Aggar swung around and nearly dropped his scanner. "Sia, you can't mean to join us."

"That's exactly what I mean to do." I turned to him fully. "Rayyar will be told he's in charge of the camp. I don't trust him to scavenge the craft. Draggar will keep him in line while we explore the crashed vessel. That leaves the next best swordsman, me, to protect the two of you during this salvage operation."

We cautiously moved back into the foliage, the thick of the jungle swallowing us whole.

"But you are the Sia of Clan Huren," Aggar argued as we trekked back to the campsite. "Your life is more important than any of ours. We are to protect you, not put you in harm's way."

I stopped dead in my tracks. "Listen to me, the two of you. Once Sakkar stripped me of my crown, I ceased being the Sia of Clan Huren. I only assumed leadership of the settlement to protect those that followed me out of the gate. I'm responsible for all those lives. Your lives."

The males followed me as we pushed through the heavy foliage and back to camp.

"As far as importance, Nullar's role as our only medic far outweighs me as a warrior. I can be replaced much easier than he can," I raged on.

"I disagree, Sia." It was Nullar's turn to speak up. "Without your expert tactics and survival skills, we would all be doomed living outside the protective dome of Huren."

"If anything ever happens to me," I looked directly at Aggar. "You must trust Nekko to take my place. Do you understand?"

"Yes, Sia." Aggar nodded gravely.

"Enough talk." I shared a look between the two of them. "We have a mission to fulfill. The settlement is depending on us to bring back what we need to survive, so let's focus on the task at hand and strip that steaming pile of alien rubble of everything it's got."

My words seemed to breathe new energy into my males. Aggar bounced on his toes, ready for a fight, and Nullar swelled with what I could only describe as pride.

We all knew we were running out of every power source we had. We would soon be thrown back into a primitive age and forced to eke out an existence like our ancestors. Like Clan Jurigon, the mountain peoples of Valose were rumored to live like the cave dwellers back in the age before nutrillium.

A primitive people, who lived off the land, wore animal skins, and made caves their homes. They were ruffians, and they would kill anyone who ventured into their territory, no questions asked.

Together, the three of us hustled back to the waiting squad. Draggar swung around to meet the slight rustling of the foliage as we rejoined the group. The male was primed with pent-up energy, ready to pounce on the slightest sound.

"Nullar suggested we go in with rebreathers. There aren't enough for all of us. I, Nullar, and Aggar will enter on the south side," I explained over grumbled complaints from the others. "I need the rest of you to lie low and monitor the Nuttaki horde headed this way."

Any objections to my plan died upon the mention of a possible confrontation with the Nuttaki. Valosian warriors craved the splash of Nuttaki blood on the end of their swords.

"Aggar will leave a scanner so you can monitor the horde's whereabouts and report to us on the inside of the ship. *Do not* engage them," I said sternly. Every male shifted on agitated feet. "They are too great in number. I suspect they are as curious about the crashed ship as we are and will venture inside. Relocate if they trek this way. Are my orders in any way unclear?"

"No, Sia," was spoken from every male.

"Sakkar's squad is here for the ship," I added. "There are only three, but we need to know where they are at all times, along with the Nuttaki horde. We are here to salvage what we can, not engage in combat, so remain out of sight."

The males rolled their heavy shoulders and flexed their sword arms. The most challenging order for a true Valosian warrior was being told to stand down. Fighting was in our blood, slaying the enemy as essential as breathing.

"Rayyar, you are in charge of the camp in my absence. Nullar and Aggar, gather what you need while I have a brief word with Draggar," I commanded. "There's a lot of wreckage to cover. I want to be in and out before the horde is upon us."

After a quick word with Draggar to keep a close eye on Rayyar, I set a brutal pace through the jungle toward the crashed spacecraft. With luck from the Spirits, we would find a treasure we so desperately needed.

We'd made good time reaching the south side of the ship. The tear in the hull was what I suspected it to be, large enough for a male to easily climb through. We paused only long enough to don rebreathers.

Aggar was the first to go inside, then Nullar. I brought up the rear, checking behind us to ensure we weren't followed. The air inside the ship was swimming with sooty debris, and I was glad for the mask covering my face. The rebreather was meant to protect against airborne pathogens, but it worked just as well to clean up the dirty air.

It was incredibly dark inside, but I adjusted quickly as my dark penetrating lenses dropped over my eyes with a quick blink. My swords unsheathed with the sing of metal, and I guarded my males as we pushed our way through a room strewn with bizarre objects, none of which I recognized.

Everything was so strange. My curiosity thrummed to be appeased, but I didn't dare take my attention away from my duty. Seeing all of this, I could almost understand Sakkar's fascination with what lay beyond the stars.

We reached a door stuck halfway open. Aggar shouldered it with a resounding boom. As one, we fell to our haunches and froze. But, aside from the weird bleeps and soft whirring of something overhead, the ship remained still and quiet.

Into a tunnel-like corridor, we filed out one at a time. Aggar stopped to scan glossy tubes spilling from a tear in the other-wise smooth wall. The device he held beeped, and Aggar grinned.

"It's fibrous tubing." Aggar kept his voice low despite his excitement. "The same as what Huren uses to carry energy from one cellpod to another and makes the dome whole and impene-trable. We can use this to make shielding for the settlement."

"How much of it do you need?" I ask, unshouldering my pack.

"As much as we can carry," Aggar said, carefully pulling the tangle of tubing from the wall.

He coiled it into a large ring, and we stuffed it inside my pack. The weight was a surprise, and I had to heft the pack onto my shoulder. I quickly adjusted to distribute the weight more evenly, so I wasn't burdened if I had to fight.

We continued down the corridor, checking closed doors that remained locked no matter what Aggar did to try and open them.

I nearly stumbled over Nullar when he suddenly stopped and crouched down to get a closer scan of the sparkling chunks embedded in the squishy floor. "Incredible! They're organic."

"What is?"

"The glittering crystals in the floor," Nullar spoke in awe of his finding. "The air here is oxygen-deficient, but these crystals create a breathable atmosphere."

"Are they something we can use?" Aggar unsheathed a dagger, ready to start digging them up.

"No," Nullar said, standing. "Just something unusual that I found interesting."

A prolonged screech from far away curdled my blood—no creatures on Valose sounded like that.

Eyes wide, our scales shifted from our usual resting silver to the stark white of the walls, an involuntary camouflage response ingrained in our genetic makeup to protect us from the array of predators salivating to make us their next meal. We waited, frozen in place, until the screeching faded away.

Aggar pulled the comm from his pocket, ready to ping the squad outside, when Draggar reported, "The Nuttaki horde is closing east of your location."

"Received," Aggar answered. "What of Sakkar's males?"

"Screwing around on the north end of the crash. They haven't even made entry."

The last one worried me the most. "What are they waiting for?"

"Received," Aggar answered. "Do you detect anything else moving around us?"

"Stand by." There was a pause, then Draggar returned. "Not that I can detect. My scanner is having trouble penetrating the hull of the spacecraft. Why?"

"Just an odd sound we can't identify."

"Do you need assistance?" I heard rustling and pictured Draggar gearing up to join us.

Aggar looked at me. "Tell him to stay put," I answered with a shake of my head.

"No. Stay where you are," Aggar relayed. "Keep us posted on any additional movements."

"Received," Draggar ended the comm.

"What have Sakkar's men found so interesting that they haven't made entry?" Aggar turned and asked the same question banging around inside my head.

"Maybe they can't find a way inside," Nullar reasoned.

"Maybe," I added. "Let's stay focused. Only look for what we can use, Nullar. We don't have time for exploration."

Aggar fiddled with a blinking pane next to the impression of a door. I wasn't surprised when nothing happened, so we continued.

Nullar kept up his scan of the ship with nothing else to report until we reached an impasse in the form of an open door leading to a vertical shaft. I cautiously leaned inside, looking up and down the long tube.

"The lift is wedged in the bottom of the shaft," I described to the others what I saw. "It's not so far we can't jump down. I'll go first and see if there's another door on a lower level."

"Sia, I should be the one to go. We don't have any idea what made that sound. I seriously doubt we are alone aboard this vessel," Aggar said, stepping forward. "The settlement needs a leader."

"We've already discussed this. I can be replaced. Without you, I have no technical expertise. I have no idea what any of this does," I gestured around. "To me, all of this looks like a pile of rubbish."

Nullar's scanner let out a ping. He made an adjustment, and the device repeated the sound. "I'm picking up lifeform readings on the level below us. Neither Valose nor Nuttaki."

Aggar peered over his shoulder at the face of the device. "What are they?"

"I don't know." Nullar shook his head. "There are ten beings in all, yet one is not like the others. A different species, it seems."

"As large as this vessel is, I'm surprised we haven't already found some… thing." Aggar moved away and peered down into the lift's shaft. "Well, we can go back the way we came and try to find another corridor to explore or chance an alien encounter in hopes of finding the power sources we need."

"Most of the creatures are together inside a room far down the corridor below us," Nullar pointed out. "Two are scattered about. Looks like they're in different rooms across from one another."

I'd never seen an alien before. Though my mind conjured only the worst thing imaginable, I wanted to see one very much. To meet the creature that created this vessel and knew how to fly it through space.

"It is settled," I said, positioning myself on the edge of the shaft's doorway. "We go down. Wait here until I give the all-clear."

I didn't wait for Aggar's argument before stepping off the edge. Instead, I dropped as soundlessly as possible to the lift stuck inside the shaft. A sliver of light cut a wedge through the darkness, letting me know I found a door to the lower level.

I could just fit my hand inside the crack. I shoved aside the door with a piercing scrape with a grunt, disappearing the slab inside a pocket in the wall. Metal grinding against metal disrupted the quiet. The noise ricocheted off the walls and down the corridor. I stepped back into the shadows of the tight space and waited.

Whatever the beings were on this level now knew they were no longer alone. I looked up to find the alarmed faces of my males peering down at me.

Aggar had a white-knuckled grip on his sword, eyes bright and alert, waiting for the slightest sound or movement. I knew if anything came through the door I had just opened he would be all over it before I could blink.

I waited for another heartbeat, then two, before deciding it was time to move forward. I motioned up to Aggar I was going through the door. His face fell into a harsh frown of disapproval.

No sooner than I stepped through did I hear Aggar's boots land behind me in a soft thud. Unfortunately, Nullar was not as deft, landing with a loud bang. We dropped low and remained unmoving, waiting, and listening for a reaction from the beings on this level.

I looked to Nullar, who was peering down into the face of his scanner. "None are moving," he mouthed to me.

I nodded my understanding and gestured to Aggar we should proceed down the corridor. I pushed ahead of a grumbling Aggar. Faint complaints of hardheaded Sia's placing themselves in unnecessary danger went ignored as I focused on navigating the dark corridor. A few fates ahead, the walls sporadically illuminated from within like the solaries rocks we use during the dark hurs. As we advanced, portions of the walls began to flicker on.

I paused and looked over my shoulder at Nullar, monitoring the lifeforms. He motioned to an open door farther down that there was one inside.

Cautiously, we proceeded, picking our way through the tangle of tubing littering the floor. When we reached the open door, we hugged the wall. With swords drawn, I listened intently for any sounds coming from within.

I held my breath and peered around the jamb, ready to lay eyes on my first alien. The room beyond presented nothing other than more alien objects in complete disarray until a slight movement on the floor caught my eye.

I signaled to Aggar that I was going in. The warrior rushed to my side but not before I took a cautious step into the room. I picked my way through the mess, sweeping my swords from side to side until I spotted a creature trapped under a large, boxy machine.

It lay in a puddle of what I can only guess was its blood, a shocking color, the likes of which I'd never seen. Its splotchy skin was the pallor of death, a grotesque contrast against the bright hue of what pooled beneath its thin body.

I had wanted to see an alien; now, I wished I hadn't.

Large and round, the head turned to land two beady eyes on me. Thin lips stretched wide, displaying rows of jagged teeth. I got the distinct impression it wanted to harm me.

I fell into a fighting stance despite it being trapped and returned its snarl.

"By all the Spirits, what is that thing?" Aggar murmured close behind me.

"I don't think I want to know." The thing reached out a stumped, spindly arm, and I took a reflexive step back. "I wonder how many more there are."

"The hand has been severed." Nullar's voice was filled with awe as he stepped closer to scan our first alien encounter. "It doesn't appear to have been from the crash. The cut is too clean."

"What about the others?" I nudged Nullar away from the creature when he got too close. "You said they were a different species. Have any of the others moved from their rooms?"

"No, Sia. The others remain where they are," Nullar said, then switched the device, scanning the alien. "Its blood is a bizarre hue. Do you think it speaks our language?"

"I can understand you just fine, Valosian," the alien breathed hard, fighting to speak.

I didn't glance around at the other males, but I was sure their mouths were unhinged the same as my own. Hearing my native tongue spoken from the slashing mouth of the bizarre alien was unsettling.

It knew of us, yet we knew nothing of it. At least, I didn't. My brother, Sakkar, on the other hand, knew plenty.

"What are you?" Nullar wore a look of fascination.

I would just as soon cut the thing down than hear it speak again. But my warrior's intuition screamed that this was my enemy.

"Trapped," the alien retorted. "My species is Gretolic." Its dull eyes began to gleam an unholy light from within its skull. "Now lift the tridor machine off of me."

Something inside my head twitched. My swords began to lower, the alien's words swirled around inside my mind trying to latch on—trying to stick. The more I resisted, the more I wanted to comply.

Movement out of my periphery snapped me out of my momentary lapse in judgment when Nullar set aside his scanner to obey the alien's request.

"A trick of the mind, Nullar," I scolded, breaking the alien's spell. "Do not listen to it."

Aggar gave his head a firm shake.

"If I were at full capacity, the three of you would easily be my slaves," the Gretolic sneered and coughed as we backed away.

I recalled my brother's story after one of his travels to the stars. He claimed he had discovered beings that could control others with their minds. I laughed at him, thinking it was a joke. Mind control over another? Fantastical.

Now, I knew I wrongfully doubted him. Despite the alien's thin body and gangly limbs, to be able to wield influence over another with a few simple words was a formidable foe. Sword against syllables? They were in no way compatible weapons.

"What do we do with it?" Aggar looked around the disheveled room. "Maybe we can bind it with something."

"I don't think it's going anywhere. If it could free itself, it would have already done so," I replied. "We need to get away from it before it can do us any real harm. Grab your scanner, Nullar."

I sensed Nullar's reluctance to leave. His scientific mind wanted to stay and explore this species, while my warrior mind wanted to protect the males at my side, even if it meant finishing off what another started to keep my males safe, then to the Spirits with this alien.

Out in the hallway, the grip of the alien's mind control loosened until the fog of its influence completely faded away.

"We need to shut this door." I kept my voice low and looked to Aggar.

"Agreed." Aggar went to work on the door's panel.

The device he held up flashed and beeped. I had doubts that the device would work as I hadn't seen it do anything yet. However, I didn't fault Aggar. The technology on this ship far exceeded ours.

A click followed by a long beep before the door slid closed on a whisper.

Aggar spun around on his heel, wearing a huge, satisfied grin. "Shut, Sia."

"I see." I nodded to the male. "I had no doubt."

"You're a bad liar, Sia," Aggar stifled a laugh. "Wait until I tell Zikkar most of his equipment has proven useless."

"He won't believe you. Then I'll have to place him in restraints to keep him from coming out here on his own," I whispered back. "He'll insist on testing his equipment for himself. You know how defensive he is about his technology."

"I do."

Nullar moved to the door across the hallway, pointing it out. "One of the other species is inside here."

"What of the group?"

"Down there." Nullar pointed ahead. "Looks like there's a hole torn in the wall."

Sure enough, light from the room showed itself, spilling out through a jagged tear in the wall.

"We leave the one for now," I spoke low and gestured toward the hole.

Using the spongy floor to hide our progress, we kept close to the side. Once there, we pressed our backs against the wall, finding it strangely warm. I placed a finger across my lips and motioned for Aggar to take the position at my back. He scowled but did as he was told.

I peered around the jagged edge and recoiled. I didn't know what I expected to find, but a cargo hold full of metal boxes heaped one atop the other, wasn't it.

I leaned in for a second look. Just as I thought. Cages. They were a metalloid with electro-bars to keep whatever was inside from escaping. What kind of animal was the Gretolic transporting?

Movement within one of the cages caught my eye. I couldn't make out the cargo from this distance, but from what I could tell, the animal was fairly large, covered with a bizarre colored skin, hairless except for a thatch of fur of a light hue, and sheathed in a white covering.

I turned to my males. "It's a cargo hold full of caged animals," I kept my voice low. "I don't believe they're a threat. But let's be cautious anyway. Nullar, does your scanner give details on this species?"

"Only the standard vitals. Heartbeat, body temperature, rate of respiration," Nullar explained while tapping the screen. "Respirations are high. Heartbeats are fast. This could all be normal for whatever's in there. My guess is the creatures are in distress."

"All the more reason to be cautious," Aggar said and tried to push his way ahead of me. "Which means I should go first."

"No," I shoved him back. "I am to protect you. Your goal is to find the power sources we need."

"You are our Sia," Aggar argued through gritted teeth. "Not our guard."

"When will all of you get it through your thick heads that I am no longer your ruler?" I hissed. "I was divested of my crown. It is my duty to protect those that stood with me against my brother."

How could I explain to these males to make them understand my obligation to keep them safe? It's my fault I lost my crown to my brother. No one else. It was an unexpected honor, the handful of males who united with me to share in my exile and followed me out the city's gate. The least I could do for their loyalty was keep them safe.

"Crown or not, Sia Jakkar, you are the true ruler of Huren," Aggar balked. "Your brother, Sakkar, will never be viewed as the rightful Sia. He lives a decadent and selfish life. He does not truly care for the people of Valose as you do."

I expelled a defeated breath. Aggar was right. My brother was exactly as he described. Only mims separated our births. After my sire, I was the eldest twin and next in line to wear the crown. However, Sakkar had other ideas and used his influence over the Royal Council to unseat me, taking the crown for himself.

"This is not the place for a discussion." I threw up a hand to end Aggar's next words. "I'm going first. Watch my back."

Aggar grumbled out a few choice curses as I turned and stepped through the jagged hole. Swords out and at the ready, I was met with a jumble of cages, one with a creature inside that was obviously dead. I was struck by how similar in build it was to a Valosian person.

I studied the cage. It was equipped with a hand scanner to release the electro-bars. Probably calibrated to the freaky Gretolic, but I placed my hand over the scanner anyway, not surprised when nothing happened.

"Dunt u tooch hur!"

I jerked back, caught off guard when confronted by one of the uncaged animals.

I stood to my full height, falling into a defensive stance. The creature did the same. Now that I had an unobstructed view, it wasn't a creature at all. And not an animal, either. Definitely alien, though.

And, most definitely, female.

I could feel my pupils widen as I took her in. She was an extraordinary being with a long, dark mane that framed a lovely face set in a fierce mask. Short in stature, her feminine curves were obscured by the white, shapeless garment she wore, yet not so hidden that I couldn't decipher the swell of her breasts or the curve of her hips.

It was shocking how her features were so much like my own, yet so very different. The most striking thing about her was her coloring. Her flesh was an odd pale shade, her eyes almost the color of a turbulent sea. What grew out of her scalp was darker than any storm cloud. Even darker than a hole in a bottomless pit. I'd never seen such a riot of colors, the likes of which had no names.

She was fearless as she stood against me. Favoring one foot, she shifted her weight and nearly toppled over. But, despite her injury, she held her ground, holding weapons in both hands.

It would be easy to cut her down, but I wouldn't. It wasn't in my nature to kill that which was smaller than me. Valose warriors were the protectors of our race, sworn to protect those who could not defend themselves.

Despite her petite size, inside her chest beat the heart of a warrior. She stood alone, ready to defend the others still trapped in their metal prisons.

Warmth spread inside my chest. For the first time, I felt a tug on my spirit. This could not be happening. In the whole of my lifetime, I never felt the calling of my spirit to join with another. Why now? And, why with a female not of my world?

"I won't hurt you," I said, slowly lowering my swords. I eased down to rest on my haunches and placed my swords on the ground. I bowed my head in a show of amity. "You're injured. Let me help you."

Her ankle was grossly misshapen. It was a wonder she could put any weight on it at all. Unsteady, she teetered before rebalancing on her good leg.

I pointed to her injury. "My medic can fix your ankle if you'll let me help you."

She didn't answer, only remained wary of me. Watchful. If she couldn't understand my language, I would figure out another way to communicate with her until a translator could be found.

I left my swords at my feet, removed my pack, and slowly rose with palms up. She hopped back a step but raised her weapons higher. It was a show of defiance with a hint of fear. I didn't want to scare her more than she already was, so my steps toward her were slow and easy.

"Staaway fruum me," she hurled unfamiliar words at me, but I kept coming. "Leeev uus alown."

Her eyes flared with panic. She lurched to one side and then the other, dropping the stick with the blue light. Wobbling on one foot, she screamed at me and sliced the air with the odd dagger she held. Two more steps, and her balance faltered. Just before she toppled over, I rushed forward, knocked the blade from her hand, and swept her into my arms.

She struggled against me; the female was a fighter. I held her tight, so she couldn't pull away and do more damage to her ankle. After a fierce bout of thrashing and writhing, she tired. Her body became pliant and warm against mine.

"Leet mee gow!" she wiggled against my hold in vain.

Shouts from all around echoed through the cargo hold. The others, still caged, went wild in defense of the one in my arms. I ignored all of them. The female I held commanded all my attention. Her spirit called to mine, touching my soul with wispy tendrils that tugged, wanting me to join with hers.

She was mine.

How could this be possible? She was a being from beyond the stars, yet we were destined to become one. To be mated for life and upon death, join each other in the spirit world for all eternity.

For the first time in a long while, I felt something other than anger and disquiet. I felt happy, contented just to hold her. My soul began to thrum, something only spirit mates did. It was a song of the souls, a rhythmic vibration of enticement to let the female know the male was ready to begin the bond.

My female ceased her struggles and stared into my eyes. I felt the corners of my lips lift into a smile. Her breath hitched, and she placed a delicate palm to the center of my chest. Awash in a rush of heat, my scales swirled with flashes of blues and silvers, but I wasn't prepared for what happened next.

I felt my ancillary heart beat for the first time. I had been awakened.

Chapter Five

LILY

Holy shit!

This guy was huge—nearly seven feet tall—bare-chested and wearing only calf-high boots with a modified kilt slung obscenely low around his hips. It was impossible not to stare.

His muscles had muscles. I had never seen a guy this jacked, yet he held me like precious cargo and looked at me with shining silver eyes as if I'd hung the moon. I was so tempted to relax and let him be my savior, but he had other features that gave me pause.

Aside from the fierce intensity rolling off him in waves, his skin had changed from a shimmering silver into a white that matched the walls. Except for his kilt's flecked blue, white, and silver material, he went nearly invisible.

And his ears! They were pronounced and pointed like an elf. But he wasn't the slim stature of the elves from The Lord of the Rings. He was more like Legolas on steroids with the scruff of a five o'clock shadow.

With all that going on, the most unnerving thing was to be his sole focus. I had never been eyeballed so thoroughly. And I had no idea what he wanted because I couldn't understand a single word he uttered.

Now that he was calm, his skin had changed back to the silvery blue it was before. He was multi-faceted as if covered in a thin layer of glitter, except for his hair, which was white and hung long and thick, flowing like liquid metal down his broad back.

Covering the lower half of his face was a clear cup with a small cartridge attached. It reminded me of an oxygen mask.

He smelled fantastic, too, as if he'd been hanging out inside an incense shop. I took great pulls of the aromatic air that swirled around him. However, his wonderful scent wasn't what harnessed my complete attention. The guy was vibrating a soothing melody from within.

I placed my hand to the center of his bare chest to feel the low-level vibrations. I should be freaking out in the arms of an alien, but whatever this guy was doing was calming. I wanted nothing more than to snuggle into his warmth and give in to the strange tug tingling my insides.

He turned with me in his arms, and I caught sight of two more just like him. Well, not exactly like him. He was way larger and much more handsome.

Oh my god, I must be delusional. I just thought of an alien elf guy as handsome. I should think him strange or bizarre, not be attracted to his rock-hard body or square-cut jaw and full lips. Nope. The swirl of his silver irises should have made me shake in my shoes, not tremble from his magnetism.

"Nullar, mi de jurt," my alien elf said and nodded to my broken ankle.

It immediately began to throb. I'd forgotten all about the pain, so caught up with my silvery muscle man.

The smaller of the two aliens approached, and fear streaked through me. I tensed up and wrapped my arms around my alien elf's neck, seeking protection.

He spoke soothing words and lowered us to the floor, but I couldn't squash my fear. I had no idea what the smaller one planned to do. I shouldn't trust any of them, so why did I feel trust for the alien still holding me so tenderly?

"Hey, assholes!" Marie's voice rang loud and clear, pushing away the hazy spell I had fallen under. "Leave her alone."

My alien elf's pointed ears twitched and swiveled in the direction of Marie's shout just like an animal would when it heard a noise. It was the most peculiar thing I had ever seen, and I struggled against his hold in earnest.

My alien—No! —Not mine. He wasn't mine. Attraction aside, this fucker could be about to carve me up and eat me. All of us girls were locked in cages like livestock. For all we knew, we could be a delicacy on this planet. Those creepy gray guys could be like food delivery, and we were the main course.

My alien kept up the vibrating melody and gentle words while I fought against his hold. My fears evaporated as soon as his big, luminescent gaze locked onto mine. I grabbed onto the lifeline of safety within those silvery depths. I couldn't explain why I trusted him, but I did.

He handled my injured ankle with care, holding it still for the smaller guy to examine. I tensed up when he hovered a flat device over my injury. It didn't hurt, but it didn't feel like it was doing much of anything either.

There was no explanation for why I gave the smaller elf liberty to touch me, but he had a professional demeanor and something that looked a helluva lot like a medical bag. Maybe if he proved competent in treating my ankle, he could help Amy and the others.

I kept a watchful eye on the third guy that began to meander around the room. He was slightly smaller in build than my elf but still heavily muscled. He had a pair of wicked-looking swords crossed at his back, similar to the ones my elf laid at his feet in a show of peace.

They all had that same long, fluid hair, worn in a fashion to display their pointy ears.

The third elf stopped and dropped into a crouch in front of Marie's cage. "Sye, thut chu elotro wete," he said, standing and stepping away when she hissed at him like a wildcat.

I wished I knew what they were saying. "Marie, calm down. I think they're here to help us."

"When you get done making googly eyes, ask Legolas if he knows how to get us the fuck out of here," she said, banging a fist against her metal wall.

I didn't blame her for being upset. This entire situation was nerve-wracking. Why I wasn't scared to death was something I would mull over later.

"Hi, big silver elf dude. I'm Lily," I looked up into his face and spoke. "Can you understand me at all? We need to free the other girls."

His eyes followed my hand as I motioned to the cages.

"They need medical attention." I pointed to my ankle being painted with a white ointment. "We need to get the girls out of the metal boxes."

My elf tilted his head, considering me before looking back at the third elf. "Nu ta gez, Aggar, vune tak."

"Ta elotro wete, Sye, fu nute la tok," the third elf replied, holding a strange device.

The two carried on an entire conversation while the medical elf worked on my ankle. I was fitted with a clear boot that he somehow inflated to make a cast. Whatever the white ointment was had to be a topical pain reliever because I no longer felt any pain.

The chirping of the device held by the third elf swung my head around. He held it up to Marie's hand scanner. After a few seconds and nothing happened, he made some adjustments and tried again. And... nada.

"That's fantastic," Marie huffed. "Not even the alien elf can get this shit open."

"Na tuk te frush," the third alien wagged a finger at her.

"Yeah, yeah, big silver dude, save the stink eye for someone who gives a fuck." Marie slumped back against her metal wall. "Now what, Lily?"

"Give them a chance. Bitching at them isn't helping."

"Easy for you to say." Marie cut her hand through the air. "You're out there, and we're all still stuck in here. I've been trapped in here for days and awake almost the whole time." The last spoken with a quiver Marie tried hard to hide.

The other girls who had been quieter than church mice started to chime in. The room soon erupted into a chatter of fearful emotions.

"We have to find some way to communicate with them," I said, tapping my elf on the chest to gain his attention before touching my mouth and then my ear. "Talk. We need to be able to understand each other."

"Mek te luk," he nodded, and I took that as a good sign he understood me.

The third elf pulled a different device from his backpack and waved it in front of Rose's light bars. When that didn't work, I looked around the room. My eyes landed on the shriveling alien hand, and I wiggled to get free of my elf's loose hold.

I was surprised when he let me go, and I hopped over to the severed appendage, pointing down to where I left it on the floor. "This is the hand from one of the aliens that took us. This one didn't work, but maybe another one will."

Not that I wanted ever to see one of those gray freaks again, but I really wanted the girls to be free, so the medical elf could help them, especially Amy, who had remained quiet.

My elf's eyes went wide when he saw what I was pointing at. The third alien approached and crouched down—his nose wrinkling from the putrid stench.

The elves chatted and seemed to come to some kind of conclusion. Finally, something was decided, and the third elf went out the hole in the wall and into the corridor.

The medical elf gestured for me to sit on the floor, but I had other ideas. Now that I saw firsthand that the medical elf was legit, and they weren't planning to snack on us, getting Amy checked out was more important than the remainder of my minor injuries.

I motioned for him to follow. My elf came along too as if to guard me.

"Can you help her from out here?" I pointed to an unconscious Amy.

The medical elf peered in at her through the light bars. His eyes were wide and unreadable. Then, after a moment, he fished through his medical bag, pulled out a tubular device, and aimed it toward Amy. It did some sort of light show that the medical elf could read.

"Vu lek te nook," he explained to me.

I shrugged my shoulders, hoping what he was telling me was good. "Yeah, I got nothing."

Sounds of a struggle filtered in from the corridor. I looked to the jagged hole and shrieked.

Chapter Six

JAKKAR

Instinctively, my ears flattened against my head to protect my sensitive auditory system. I knew I must calm my female fast. Her screams were blaring. With all the noise she was making, more of those Gretolics would surely be alerted to our presence.

Even though the alien Aggar dragged inside was unconscious, I was humbled when my female lunged at me for protection. Already, she felt the bond. At first, I was concerned with the differences in our species, she wouldn't respond the same as a Valosian female.

I held her close and thrummed to soothe her. It worked to cease her screams, yet her breathing became harsher the closer Aggar dragged the alien.

"It's all right, my heart. The creature is unconscious. It can no longer harm you with its mind," I crooned, desperate for her to understand. "Aggar, any progress on a translator?"

"Try this." Aggar paused mid-drag and tossed me two small devices. "It's the alien's translator. That's how it knew our language."

I studied the strange devices. "How does it work?"

"Place it behind your ear and hers." Aggar touched behind his earlobe and nodded to my female. "Then get her to talk so the translator can determine what language she's speaking, and vice versa."

I scrutinized the devices before holding them out to Nullar. "Would you sanitize these?" Nullar nodded and flashed the devices with a sanitary beam.

"I opened the door to the room Nullar said had a single female inside," Aggar said, gesturing around the room. "The lone female was hiding. I caught her, but she slipped away."

"Did you see which direction she went?"

"No, Sia." Aggar dropped his chin in regret.

"That's unfortunate. We may not have time to search for her."

"They're clean," Nullar said once he sanitized the translators. "Will you explain to your female that I need to finish with her wounds? Also, the one with the bright mane is in desperate need of a cerebral release. I can't do that until she's out of the cage."

"I hope to tell her." I skeptically placed the translator behind my ear and addressed my female. "Speak words to me so this device can ascertain your language."

She peered up at me with large, luminous eyes and pointed. "Thatstha thing that abductedus."

Her words were a garbled mess, yet some of what she said translated into Valosian, but the rest was a mishmash of nonsense.

I placed the other device behind her ear before she could object. She yelped and jumped when the thing sucked onto her flesh. She touched the device and looked at me with questioning eyes.

"Keep her talking," Aggar instructed. "The more words that are fed into the device, the faster you'll be able to communicate with her."

"Aggar, release the bright maned one first." Nullar waved him over.

"Aggar will free your companion so Nullar can treat her injuries."

My female froze at my words. "I undurstuud some of wut you sed!"

"Keep talking and move this way," I explained, circling her shoulders and ushering her away from the bright maned female's cage.

"But my freend!" she squeaked, dragging her feet.

"Nullar will help her, but Aggar has to release her first."

Her brows knitted together, and she nodded, allowing me to move her a few fates away, giving Aggar room to work.

Aggar held the unconscious alien's hand up to the cage's scanner. An orange beam shot out to the astonishment of all and scanned the alien's spindly appendage. As soon as the electrobars were released, my female jerked out of my hold and scrambled to the bright maned female's side.

Nullar tried to reason with her as she crawled inside with the other female. "A-mee! Uhmigod, A-mee wake up."

I touched her leg, startling her. "My female, please allow Nullar to treat her injuries."

My female gaped at me. "How do I understand everything you just said?"

"The creature's translators." I touched the device behind my ear and then hers.

"How can you understand me?"

"The device translates your words for me and mine to yours." I motioned for her to come out. "Now, allow Nullar to help the bright maned female."

"Okay," she breathed out a shaky breath. "She's my best friend. You're sure New-lar can help her?"

"I'm sure."

"Her name is A-mee," my female said to Nullar, who looked to me for translation.

"The bright maned one is called A-mee," I told Nullar.

"How can you understand me, but he can't?" my female questioned.

"I'm the only one with a translator."

"That's really strange," my female murmured while keeping a close eye on Nullar when he placed a naturolyzer on A-mee's forehead.

Aggar dragged the alien from one cage after another, releasing all the females. They warily skirted around me to swarm around my female, clinging to one another, some crying, while others peered around with wide eyes set in shocked faces.

The last female Aggar freed was the dark maned one who hadn't stopped glaring daggers at him. "About time." She launched herself out of the cage as soon as her electro-bars dissipated.

"Wait!" My female turned to me when Aggar dropped the alien to the floor. "There are more of us. Will-o is trapped inside that pile somewhere. She said there was another girl trapped in front of her. And, we have to get all of them out, even the dead. I'm not leaving a single person behind."

Spoken like a true warrior. My female... Wait. Why had I not asked her name? "What are you called?"

"Lily." She touched her chest. "I'm Lily."

"Lil. E."

She shook her head. "Lily. Only one word."

"Lily." She told me that before the translator. I hadn't recognized the word as a name—her name. "I am Jakkar."

"Jack-car," she repeated with a smile playing across her full lips.

I shook my head. "Jakkar."

"Jakkar."

I nodded at her pronunciation, and she coyly ducked her head.

"Enough with the pleasantries," the dark maned one complained. "Let's get the other women out."

"Wee-mahn," I tried out the unfamiliar word. That was what species they must be, wee-mahn.

"Women," Lily corrected. "It's only one word.

"Women," I tried again.

Lily smiled, and I watched my female with her companions. She was a natural leader, just like me. Aside from our one commonality, I had a lot to learn about my new spirit mate.

Aggar and I worked fast to move the bulky cages. Haphazardly stacked, we took great care to move them without toppling over the others. The electro-bars were deadly with prolonged contact. As fragile as these women appeared, it wouldn't take much to kill one of them.

Some of the cages we found empty, others with more females inside. The one named Will-o was in the center near the bottom of the pile. My Lily was especially pleased to see her.

We found eight women alive in all. Two remained unconscious, and Nullar worked feverishly to repair the damage inside their skulls.

Respectful of the dead, we carefully laid them on the far side of the room: such a tragedy, this loss of life. Aggar and I took a knee and bowed our heads.

"May the Gates of Eternity open and the Spirits embrace you," I humbly prayed. "Hail to the Spirits."

"Hail to the Spirits," Aggar chanted.

When I turned back to face the watery eyes of the living, I was struck with the memory of our last war with the Nuttaki that very nearly wiped us out. I had to say goodbye to many of my kinsmen that suns-rise. The funeral pyres were stacked so high that the flames scorched the clouds, licking at the sky in great sweeping gusts.

I took stock of the newcomers while Nullar continued to set up a hasty triage, treating the more seriously injured first.

With a hard swallow, I shifted my stance to accommodate the weight of responsibility that now settled on my shoulders.

Chapter Seven

LILY

I watched as the one Jakkar told me was named Aggar, dragged the lifeless body of the gray alien out of the hole in our wall and back out into the hallway, followed by a sickening crunch that turned my stomach. I felt no remorse over the alien's demise. If it were up to me, I would have made that piece of shit suffer for what it did to all of us.

The medical elf named Nullar finished treating a snippy Marie's wounds, then moved on to the next girl, Willow. She was shaking like a leaf, quietly sobbing, but bravely allowed Nullar to treat her injuries.

All of us girls were huddled together in the center of the room. Everyone was silent, including Layla, which was a blessing. Probably from shock over the situation we found ourselves in.

I dutifully kept my eyes averted from the line-up of bodies. Morbidly, I envied the dead. At least their worries were over. Most had never woken up to discover their nightmares had been real and died in the crash.

Aggar returned and approached us with caution, holding a cloth bag. He reached inside, and all the girls shrank back except for Marie. She narrowed her eyes as if daring him to make one false move.

"What do you want?" Marie stood her ground even though I could feel her slight trembling.

He smiled at her with a cocky upturn of his mouth.

"Take the translator," Aggar said. Marie jerked away from him, not understanding. "Place it behind your ear." He touched his device then held another out for her to take.

I watched the exchange between them. Aggar knelt in front of her, his face a mask of expectation. She didn't scoot away but held and returned his steady gaze. Fear and curiosity played across her face.

Marie quickly took the device from Aggar's hand, placed it behind her ear, and held back a yelp when I knew the thing had sucked itself to her skin.

"What are you looking at?" Marie snapped.

"Marie," I chastised. "What is wrong with you? Stop acting like such a bitch."

"Sorry. I'm not so sure about these guys," Marie shivered and nodded at Aggar. "He's looking at me like he wants to eat me. And maybe not the good kind of eating."

I choked on my laugh. Marie had no filter, blurting out whatever crossed her mind. I could tell she was scared, and sarcasm was a wall she hid behind.

Aggar stood when Marie didn't return his smile and moved on to the next girl.

Willow plucked the device from his palm like a good girl and ducked her head sweetly. She placed the device behind her ear, and Aggar gifted her with an approving nod before moving off to converse with Jakkar.

"See how he smiles at all the girls?" Marie tsked. "He's a player. Reminds me of my ex-boyfriend, always hitting on anything with a vagina. And it pisses me off that I'm attracted to him."

I smirked over Marie's comment. "I think he's just trying to be nice, Marie. I don't think he's trying to get into anyone's pants," I said, then tried to catch Jakkar's words through the drone of the girls chatting around me.

It was odd how the translator device worked. It was his voice, but his mouth wasn't always in sync with the words. It was like watching an English version of a foreign film.

From what I could gather, they were strategizing a way to get us off the spacecraft using a flat device that looked a lot like an iPad.

The girls hadn't moved from where they initially huddled together but were beginning to feel more comfortable around the huge males helping us.

For the life of me, I couldn't keep my eyes from straying back to Jakkar. There was something that felt familiar about him. I couldn't put my finger on what it was. I knew nothing about him or where we crashed. Everything had happened so fast. There hadn't been time to ask all the questions flying around inside my head.

Once we were all outfitted with translators, the only information we exchanged were names and the correct pronunciation.

Marie shifted next to me. She sat close to my side, her hand holding mine in a loose grip. I couldn't decide if she was reaching out to me for comfort, or if she was offering it.

I was grateful for Nullar, who kept close vigilance over Amy, and the girl with short blonde hair, who remained unconscious. I was optimistic that whatever machine he wrapped around their foreheads was working. Their color had brightened, and they no longer held the gray pallor of death.

My eyes followed Jakkar as he moved off and spoke into some kind of box. It reminded me of Captain Kirk's tricorder. The voice that came back was too low for me to hear, so I only got half of the story.

My big bad elf was concerned about our location, which worried me. I had never seen him in action with those gigantic twin blades he had strapped across his back, but judging by all that muscle and deadly hardware, I would bet he was a one elf wrecking machine. I sure as fuck wouldn't want to mess with him. And if someone that looked like him was nervous, that made me nervous, too.

"What do you think they're wearing under their skirts?" Marie asked, a naughty glint in her eyes.

"I would say it's more along the lines of a kilt, Marie," I answered her and passed the waterskin Jakkar gave us to Willow.

"Did we crash-land on a planet full of Scottish elves?" Marie cackled. I was relieved she was beginning to relax. "Can you ask your boyfriend if he's got anything to eat? Not that I'm ungrateful, but whatever that liquid was, it isn't water, and I'm freaking starving."

The girls that were huddled around me were in agreeance. Honestly, I'd been floating in such a state of shock since Amy was freed that I hadn't been paying much attention to my own needs, but I was pretty hungry too.

I pushed myself up from the floor and looked down at the bubble cast around my ankle. Nullar said I could bear weight on it. Given that it looked like it was made of bubble wrap, I was leery, so I hopped over to where Jakkar stood guard in front of the jagged hole.

"Hi." I dropped my eyes, suddenly feeling self-conscious, hanging onto his tremendous forearm. We just met, yet he looked at me like he already knew me.

"Greetings, my heart."

I had never felt the need to swoon before now, and I was totally blaming my breathlessness on the exertion from the hop over. I had no idea what all this "my heart" was about, but it made my insides feel all wonky. "I, um... that is, the girls and I wondered if you had any food. I don't know the last time any of us ate."

"I promise to provide everything you need when we get you to a more secure location." Jakkar's admission sent shivers of fear through me.

"We aren't safe here?"

"We are for the moment," Jakkar looked down at the device in his hand. "Aggar has almost completed his search of the remainder of rooms on this floor. As soon as he returns, we will be leaving. Save your strength and wait with the others. We will have to move fast."

Yeah, I didn't like the sound of all that, and I wasn't so sure I liked him carrying me back to the group of girls like I was a naughty kitten out of its pen.

He gently set me down next to Rose and returned to his post, but not before brushing fingertips down my cheek in a smooth caress.

"Hey, Starry Eyes," Marie coaxed. "What did he say?"

"That we were going to a secure location soon, then we could eat."

"What location?" Isobel chimed in.

"Hell if I know," I shrugged.

"You should have questioned him more," Marie griped.

"Sorry. I didn't want to push. I don't think pissing off an elf-wielding swordsman would be a good idea," I quipped.

Marie stuck her tongue out at me, and I returned the childish gesture.

"You know, he's freaking hot for an alien," Rose whispered. "You could do a lot worse."

"I'd rather not do at all. I didn't get abducted to enter into a relationship with an alien no matter how hot he is," I whispered back. "Finding a way back home is priority number one."

The girls all mumbled, nodding their heads.

Jakkar's pointed ears twitched. His piercing eyes narrowed and touched me for a split second before flitting away. I wondered how much of that conversation he'd picked up on.

My shoulders slumped. If I could melt into the floor, I still wouldn't have felt any less like an ungrateful asshole.

Jakkar and his friends had been our heroes. They'd freed us, given us medical care and the alien equivalent of water. I did not doubt that if it weren't for Nullar's medical treatment, Amy and the unconscious blonde would be lined up with the other corpses.

Here I was rebuffing Jakkar's advances if that was what all the caressing and googly-eyeing meant. Then there was the strange warmth behind my sternum like a magnet pulling me toward him.

What do I know about extraterrestrial courting? He mentioned getting us to a secure location. What does that mean for us? Hopefully, aboard another ship bound for Earth.

The way his eyes had settled on me in that needy, hungry way, I didn't think returning me from whence I came was what he had in mind.

I shoved my interest aside. I just found out my fiancé had been cheating on me right before I was abducted, so rebounding with an alien wasn't on my list of things to do. Really, it wasn't. No matter how much I was drawn to him.

Aggar poked his head inside the room. He uttered a few rushed words and motioned for Nullar to join him out in the corridor. They were gone for only a few minutes before we were rounded up.

Jakkar gathered an unconscious Amy in his arms, and we were systematically filed out of the room through the jagged hole.

At first, I balked at the floating table on which Nullar instructed Jakkar to place Amy. Then, the flashback of my bestie being brought in and dumped into that cage hit me like a head-on collision.

The elf guys were taking great care with her, unlike the horrid way the gray aliens mistreated her, so I clenched my fists and forced myself to calm.

The blonde was laid out on a second floating table. Finally, I came to terms with the fact that this was the way they had to be transported.

They carried four backpacks full of God only knew what, between the three elves while herding eight injured girls down a battered hallway on a crashed alien spacecraft. These guys had their hands full.

Aggar led our group with Nullar to one side and Jakkar bringing up the rear. I was glad for the visual break. It gave me time to clear my head of all things Jakkar. The guy was too much of a distraction. When he was in my field of vision, I had difficulty tearing my eyes off his half-naked body.

"I'm scared," Layla clung to my arm and helped support me while I hobbled along on my bubble cast. It was the first words she'd spoken since she was freed. Gone was her earlier snippy attitude. She'd been so quiet I almost forgot she was there.

"Me too," I admitted, wild-eyed and nervous about being back out in the hallway.

Aggar turned and placed a finger across his lips for us to stay quiet. He looked weighted down with two huge, duffle-sized backpacks slung over each shoulder.

The doors I couldn't access were standing wide open. Aggar must have used that alien's hand to open all the doors like he had the light bars. Why the severed hand hadn't worked for me,

I didn't know. It wasn't like I hadn't lopped it off the same freaking alien.

Our direction of travel was toward the black end of the corridor. With Aggar in the lead, I could barely see around his girth and the duffle bags at what lay ahead. I was glad because this ship scared the fuck out of me.

Aggar suddenly threw up a hand, and our group came to an abrupt halt. Jakkar split our group as he moved his way to the front. The girls' whispers weaved a net of uncertainty that made my skin prickle as the males conversed.

We were at their mercy—dependent solely on them for our safety. I didn't like it. I'd rather be in charge of myself, but everything around us was alien, so what other choice was there?

"How far away are they?" Jakkar answered the elf voice that sounded out from his tricorder thingy.

All the guys shifted their stances, indicating something was terribly off.

"The Nuttaki horde is coming this way," Jakkar told the others. "They're headed for the same entrance we used."

"We turn around now." Aggar swept his hand in the opposite direction.

All of us girls huddled together as the alien elves conversed in a rapid and clipped conversation. Apparently, our way out was compromised by something these big, strong elves seemed to be concerned over. Jakkar's use of the word horde nearly sent me into a spiral of anxiety.

"We need to move fast. We'll have to clear the opposite end of the hallway before proceeding," Jakkar told us before we turned around and trekked in the opposite direction.

Once we reached the train wreck of boxy equipment, the elves worked together, clearing the way for us. As strong as all three of them were, it wasn't long before the wrecked hallway beyond was revealed.

The girls all stuck together as we moved in a group. I helped steer the floating table Amy used as a gurney while Marie guided the blonde down the debris-littered corridor. Nullar remained close by, checking the medical devices attached to Amy and the blonde.

The going was slower in this direction and made much worse because of machines and equipment strewn everywhere. The walls were more crumpled than torn, giving the impression the ship had sustained more damage on this end.

The elves pushed us to move faster, which wasn't a problem since we were all scared shitless. I decided to trust Nullar and put all my weight on my bubble cast to keep up the pace.

Aggar easily pushed aside the larger pieces of wreckage to clear the path that was beginning to feel endless. As I glanced back, the black hole at the end of the corridor looked far away. How much longer before we were off this ship?

All eyes shot to the ceiling. A scurrying sound washed over us in a terrifying wave as if a thousand cockroaches weighing a hundred pounds each just ran overhead. The noise reached a bone-chilling intensity before it died off in the distance.

The elves pushed us harder until we were practically running to keep up with their lunging strides. Then, a crash sounded out behind us. I looked back at the dark end of the corridor and wished I hadn't.

Like a swarm of man-sized locusts, the creatures I assumed were the Nuttaki horde, Jakkar spoke of choked the corridor with segmented arms and legs. Each had a long, tubular body and a head like a praying mantis. They came after us at an impossible speed.

"Take these." Jakkar removed his duffle bags and tossed them to Nullar. "Now go! Run," Jakkar yelled at us. "Get the women to safety. I will hold them off for as long as I can."

Swords drawn, Jakkar rushed the horde head-on with a fierce roar. He fought like a savage, slicing through one insect creature after another with lethal swings. The white walls were soon bathed with the thick blue blood of his attackers.

I hadn't realized I stopped moving until Aggar grabbed my arm and tried to pull me away from the carnage. I fought his hold, not wanting to leave Jakkar behind.

"Come on!" Aggar scolded me. "We have to get out of here."

"We can't leave him! We have to help him! He can't fight those things by himself." I pulled free of Aggar's grip. "Look at how many of them there are."

Aggar slung me over his shoulder without further ado and ran in the opposite direction, leaving Jakkar behind. My struggles got me nowhere except sore ribs from bouncing across his shoulder.

"No! Jakkar!" I shrieked. "Jakkar!"

Jakkar was a berserker, cutting down the creatures with wide swings of his blades, cutting body after body in half to land in a grotesque pile at his feet.

No matter how magnificent his fighting skills were, the numbers were too great. The horde soon overtook him, the things crawling over their dead to close in around Jakkar until he was swallowed whole in a mesh of segmented appendages.

"Jesusfuckingchrist," I gurgled. No one could have survived that.

Something inside me twisted, a gathering of something hot just behind my sternum. It banged against my bones, wanting to be set free. The farther away Aggar carried me from the teaming bundle of insects covering Jakkar, the more I felt like I'd just left an important piece of myself behind.

I didn't know how far we ran. All I knew for sure was that it had been far enough that I could no longer see the place where we left Jakkar.

My heart shrank with sickness. My throat was sore from screaming. My eyes blurred with tears. I would swear, my soul was fractured into a million pieces. And all over a stranger. An alien I barely knew anything about.

I wasn't this torn up when I busted Kyle cheating on me the day of my abduction, which was why Amy and I were together that night. She had been working a double shift at the lab when I went to Kyle's apartment unannounced. Supermodel Barbie had answered the door ending my fourteen-month engagement.

Yet this loss felt different. More intense. A bone-deep sorrow for something that should have been but never was. And that was totally fucked up. First of all, Jakkar was an alien with elf ears and scales capable of camouflage. Secondly, I just met him like two hours ago. How could I possibly be attached to him after that short time?

I was not one to believe in love at first sight. Lust maybe, but not bone-deep, I-will-die-without-this-person kind of feelings. So, where was this heartache coming from?

We reached the end of the corridor when there was no more hallway to run through. The passage was crushed like a tin can.

Closed doors flanked us, and none looked like an exit. Gaining access to a room held no appeal; the goal was getting the hell off this spacecraft. We all started to look around for another way out. Aggar hadn't brought the gray alien with us, so unless he had another way to open doors, we were screwed.

I checked on Amy, then slumped against the wall, torn between anger toward Aggar for leaving Jakkar behind and heartbroken over losing my alien elf before I ever got a chance to know him. It was a sour mixture that churned low in my belly.

Nullar pulled out a device that looked like an iPad. He panned it around the hallway and tapped on the screen, "This room is void of life."

Aggar nodded and did some tapping on his iPad thingy. "It appears to be close to the outer hull, too. I found a laser cutter in the room where the lone female was hiding, so it might be possible to cut our way free."

"Wait," Marie spoke up. "What lone female?"

"There was one of your kind in a room across from the cargo hold where you were being held," Aggar explained while rummaging around in one of the duffels to pull free a metal square with blinking lights. "She stayed hidden. I caught her, but then she slipped out of my hold and bolted through the open door."

"I'm sorry, what?" Isobel piped up. "There's another girl, lost, on this ship, and you didn't go after her?"

Aggar landed a hard stare on Isobel. "She would not be lost had she not run. I tried to catch her, but she took off down the hall and disappeared before I could reach her."

"Poor thing," Rose sniffled, looking up at Aggar through her lashes. "You probably scared her to death. No offense, but you guys look pretty barbaric with those swords and kilts. Like angry alien Scotsmen. I would have run away too."

Aggar blinked, sobering. "Alien?"

"Yeah," Marie said. "You're aliens. Take a look in the mirror. Humans don't have pointy ears and shimmering scales."

"Hue-men?" Aggar repeated and ran a critical eye over Marie. "You look nothing like a Valosian female. It would appear you are the alien here."

Aggar turned his back on a fuming Marie and placed the metal square to the blinking panel next to the door, and it opened.

Aggar tore off a piece of his kilt and attached it to the panel while Nullar checked the space. Then we were ushered inside. The room was in complete disarray, just like the rest of the ship.

"How are you doing?" Marie asked in a hushed tone.

I shrugged off Marie's arm. "Tired, scared, and pissed off."

My anger had bristled beneath the surface with every step that took me farther away from Jakkar. Marie's attempt to comfort me only pissed me off more than I already was. She wasn't the reason I was seething mad, though. Just as soon as Aggar closed the door behind us, I was on him.

"You motherfucking piece of shit!" I railed, beating on his chest with fists that looked tiny compared to his massive frame. "How could you leave him back there to fend those things off?"

He took my abuse without moving a muscle. His eyes spoke volumes, downcast at the loss of his friend. I should feel bad I was taking my shit out on him, but I couldn't stop the boiling rage consuming me.

"Sia Jakkar made me swear to the Spirits I would protect you at all costs, even with my own life," Aggar told me. "The only chance for us to escape was to slow down the Nuttaki horde, and Sia Jakkar was the most logical choice."

"Logical?" I scoffed. "How is leaving one man behind to hold off hundreds in any way logical?"

"I don't know what a maayn is. Sia Jakkar is a warrior of Valose. One that is newly awakened. The beating of his spirit mate's heart inside his chest comes with extraordinary strength," Aggar explained. "There is a good chance he made it out of the horde. None followed us, so that is a good sign."

I didn't know what all this mumbo-jumbo was about spirit mates and extraordinary strength, but it all sounded like total bullshit to me. "How do you figure he made it out? You didn't see those things crawling over him. He was completely covered in minutes. How could you leave him to die like that!"

A feminine hand touched my shoulder, and I let Marie drag me into her arms. She shushed me, smoothing circles on my back as I wet her clothes with my tears. Wracked with sorrow, I was close to hyperventilating when pounding on the door exploded out into the room.

I turned my head just as Aggar opened the door.

Chapter Eight

JAKKAR

I lurched forward and was caught between Aggar and Nullar before I landed face down in front of my spirit mate. There was nothing valiant about collapsing to the ground at the feet of the one you were meant to protect.

My Lily rushed to stand before me, wide-eyed and expectant. I stayed solid, adjusted my rebreather that managed to remain on my face while I fought, and waited for her approval. I must stand on my own two feet to prove my fortitude in battle to her. A spirit mate needs to know her male can keep her safe from any danger, even if it *had* killed him in the process.

"I knew you would come out the victor." Aggar helped to steady me without being obvious.

"Leaving the scrap of kiltus was smart." I swiped away a dribble of blood from my eyelid. "There are so many doors in this section. It would have been difficult to find you. Is this room secure?"

"Yes, Sia," Aggar reported. "Secure enough for a brief rest before we can move again."

"The Nuttaki threat has been exterminated for now. More may follow, but Draggar reported what's left of the horde has tucked tail and headed back to their hives."

"That will buy us some time," Aggar nodded. "Thanks to you, the females are safe."

"For now."

"How are you alive?" Lily finally addressed me. "I saw those things cover you like a blanket."

She stepped forward and touched the center of my chest. I immediately began to thrum, singing to her spirit while vibrating the palm of her hand. My ancillary heart, the one that beat solely for her, pounded against my sternum at her touch.

Clear fluid streamed from her eyes. I started to brush away the wet from her cheeks but dropped my blood-covered hand, not wanting to dirty her.

"I would kill every Nuttaki on Valose to keep you safe," I declared. The weight of my injuries threatened to list me to the side, but I held steady.

"I can't decide if you're the bravest or stupidest man I've ever met." Lily threw her arms around me to the gasp of many women. "You were like a crazy person, hacking up those things into little pieces. Then they swarmed you, and I was sure you were done. I can't believe you're alive."

I didn't know what to make of her strange words. She complimented and criticized me in the same breath. Covered in my enemies' blood, I didn't want to soil her, yet the temptation to return her embrace won out.

"Come on, my silver savage, let's get you patched up." She led me over to where Nullar had set up his medic devices. The two unconscious women remained on their floating pallets in the corner where Lily directed me to lie down on a third pallet Nullar had fashioned out of fabric squares on the floor.

Lily knelt at my side and began to wipe away the carnage from my battle with the Nuttaki horde. The cloth she used was quickly saturated with my blood as well as my enemies. I enjoyed the flutter of her hands as she fretted over my wounds, even giving orders to Nullar on how to tend me. Just like me, she was a natural leader among her people.

"I never thought I'd see you again," she whimpered. "Don't ever do anything like that ever again. Promise me."

That was the one promise I could not make. "A Valose warrior vows to protect, and the beating heart inside my chest that belongs to my spirit mate demands it."

"You're gonna have to explain to me what all this spirit mate talk is about." She shook her head as if to clear it. "First, let's get you cleaned up."

Aggar held out his loodskin for me to drink. As I looked around the room at all the females' faces under my protection, I pushed it away. "Don't waste your drink on me, Aggar."

"You're right, Sia. The females are more fragile than we are."

"Fragile," Marie snorted. "After everything we've been through, I wouldn't exactly classify us as fragile. And what kind of name is Aggar anyway?"

"A warrior's name. What kind of name is Marie?" Aggar challenged.

"I don't know." Marie popped her hands on her hips, clearing gunning for a fight. "An American one. And what is that contraption that keeps on beeping?" Marie flicked her hand at the device Aggar held.

"It's called a tragore." Aggar puffed out his chest with pride. "It detects usable power sources."

"What happens when you find this usable power source?" Marie clucked her tongue skeptically.

Aggar launched into a technical explanation that was sure to impress. He'd shown an interest in learning the ways of technology from Zikkar, but to hear the excitement in his voice and see his face brighten, was telling of just how much.

Ever since my crown was stripped from my head, the world I once knew had begun changing around me. The lines between the warrior and scholar classes blurred more and more with every suns-rise.

"Huh. You're smart for a pretty boy." Marie huffed, then held her hands up to her ears. "Why do you have those pointy Mr. Spock ears? You look like an extra right out of the Hobbit."

"And you look like … nothing I've ever seen before," Aggar volleyed back with a crooked grin. "Get some rest, alien female. We will be covering a lot of ground in a few hurs."

"Marie!" Isobel took the loodskin Aggar offered and tried to silence her. "Stop trying to pick a fight with him. He got us out of those cages and saved us from those things."

The women ushered Marie away from an amused Aggar and cleared a spot on the floor to rest.

These alien females were so confusing. With every praise came vilification, yet my female fussed over me. Fretting and cooing every time she found another cut or scrape as if tending my injuries was more important than anything else. Her actions spoke more than her words ever could.

"I apologize for Marie," Lily whispered. "The girl has no filter, and I think she's lashing out because she's scared."

Aggar's ears twitched. His eyes swung to Marie and softened in understanding before scavenging what he could of the scattered contents in the room. With our sensitive auditory systems, there wasn't much we didn't hear.

"I think you're right," I whispered back. "I can't imagine how I would act if I were taken from my world against my will."

Her face was so close to mine; I could count the dark blue flecks sprinkled in her eyes. They were the same color as the churning waters of the Caspeen Sea. My spirit mate held mysteries like what lay beneath those dark waves.

Lily stared back with the same intensity. At that moment, I would give my dominant sword hand to know what was going on inside her head.

Aggar approached, breaking our intimate connection. I could have throttled him for the interruption.

"I think we can cut our way out of this room, Sia," Aggar indicated the far wall. "The laser I found will create a disturbance that will most likely alert Sakkar's men. Once we cut our way through, we will have to move quickly away from the crash site before they pick us up on their scanners."

"Agreed." I nodded. Leave it to Aggar to find a secondary escape route. "Let the females rest for a few hurs, and then we will be on our way. This ship is a death trap."

"I couldn't agree more." Aggar moved on, stopping to pick up a disc of some sort, and examined it before shoving it inside his pack along with all the other alien technology he'd gathered.

Nullar swept the sanitary beam over my dirty flesh before sealing the legion of cuts and gouges from the Nuttaki's beaks covering my body. The blood and gore from my battle were erased in secs.

"It's like magic." Lily looked on, astonished.

I didn't know what it was she spoke of, but this may-jack must be a good thing where she was from.

"Who is Sakkar? Is he your enemy?"

"Yes, as well as my brother." To her piqued interest, I found myself telling the story of my exile—however, I left out the part about being stripped of my crown—and hoped she didn't judge me too harshly. "A few munthis ago, Sakkar brought back an alien germ that wiped out our females. Before the coal of the pyres had fully extinguished, Sakkar was already planning another mission to the stars. He'd learned nothing from his foolhardiness. Valosian feet were meant to stay on the ground."

Sakkar had no business venturing beyond the stars. He had never brought back anything but death.

"Val-o-c-ans?" she asked. "Is that what your people are called?"

"Yes." I liked the sound of my species on her lips. My eyes drifted to her mouth, imagining her taste.

"I'm... well, we,"—she swept her hand toward the other women — "are humans."

"Hue-mahns." I nodded. "I thought you were women."

Her giggle set my blood to a slow simmer.

"We are women. Human women. Females of our race."

"Aw." That made sense. "Well, human, you are lovely, in the most unique way."

My hand found the way to her silky cheek. She flushed a darker shade than her odd skin tone. A camouflage reaction to my touch? Perhaps, my spirit mate was shy.

She nuzzled my hand before dropping her eyes from mine. Shy, indeed.

"So, if you have a spaceship," she hedged, light danced in her eyes, "does that mean you can take us home? Back to Earth."

"Err-rth. That is the planet where you're from?"

"Yes. Earth." She scooted closer. "Will you take us back there?"

My hand fell away. I wanted to be her champion in all things but not give her the means to leave now that I just found her. There was no unhearing her words as she'd spoken to the other human women back in the storage room. Finding a way back home is priority number one.

"For one, the vessel belongs to my brother, and for another, I would not know how to fly it, nor do I care to learn," I pushed through clenched teeth. "Nothing good has ever come from the stars."

Yet, from the stars was where my spirit mate derived.

I peered into her crestfallen features and cursed. "Except for you, of course."

"Why do you hate space travel so much?" She cocked her head. "NASA would give their left nut to be able to travel to other planets."

"Who is Nassha?"

"Not who, but what," she corrected. "It's an agency full of smart people who study space."

I grunted. "Not too smart if they risk their people to the unknown. Traveling beyond the clouds is the same as sending out an open invitation for catastrophe."

"You said that I wasn't a bad thing, and I came from the stars."

"Yes, but how did you get here? Abduction. Stolen from your home by gray creatures before crashing on Valose."

Lily opened her mouth, then shut it. "Okay, well, you have a point. But then again, I never would have met you if none of that had happened. That's a good thing. Right?"

"Are you always this optimistic?" I could use some optimism in my life.

"Um... not normally. I mean, I'm not one of those sunny people that always looks on the bright side, but I guess under the circumstances, I'm glad to still be alive given everything that's happened to me," she grinned. "By the way, thank you for helping us."

"It was my pleasure." Her humbling words warmed me, causing a riot of colors to ripple across my scales.

"That's really cool how you do that." Lily smoothed a soft hand over my healing flesh. "You heal fast, too. Are you like a chameleon?"

"Aren't you?"

Lily's eyebrows popped high. "No. Our skin doesn't change colors to match our surroundings."

"Then how do you survive in your world if you can't hide from the creatures that would eat you?"

"Well," she nervously laughed. "We are pretty much on the top of the food chain where I'm from. What kind of planet is Valose?"

"A dangerous one."

She paused before asking, "If you're not taking us to another ship, where are you taking us?"

"To my settlement."

"Is that where your home is?"

"Yes."

"Is it far from here?"

Not for warriors on rovers. Now that we had extra bodies, some with injuries, I couldn't guess how long it would take to get back. We would have to go slow and careful through the thick of the jungle and protect the women along the way. "It will take many suns-rises now that there are more of us."

She nodded inquisitively. "Aggar called you Sia. What does that mean? Is it like a nickname?"

My mouth opened, but I snapped it closed to give myself time to think of a definition that wasn't a complete lie. "Sia means leader."

"I sort of figured you were the one in charge. You have that look about you."

"What look is that, my heart? My nula." The term of endearment slipped easily off my tongue.

"You know, all authoritative and bossy."

A rare laugh escaped me. "You think me bossy?"

Lily quirked a brow. "Don't you have to be if you're the one in charge?"

"I suppose so."

"So, back to what you said about your brother." She fiddled with the hem of her dress. "That he brought back a germ that wiped out all your women, er... females. Did you mean that literally?"

"Yes." I tugged Lily down and cradled her in the crook of my arm. "Enough talk for now. Time to rest."

"Okay, but we'll talk more later."

"Yes," I soothed. "Later. Rest now."

She snuggled into me with a heavy sigh—sweet and trusting. My ancillary heart pounded a contented rhythm, knowing my spirit mate accepted my comfort—for now.

I had made her no promises of aligning myself with my brother for the use of his spacecraft. I didn't even know if it were possible after all that had happened between us. Lily's raw hope sorely tempted me to at least try.

Soon, her breathing was deep and rhythmic. I closed my eyes, taking advantage of this moment to savor the feel of my female.

I could not predict what the next suns-rise would bring with my hearts waging war inside my chest. One beat with hatred for my brother, the second beat with the sole purpose to serve my spirit mate.

To which cadence did I yield?

Chapter Nine

LILY

Jakkar was gone when I opened my eyes. I'd only meant to rest for a few minutes, but the warmth from his scales and firmness of his muscled arm made for too good a place to snuggle.

I peered around the room to find him huddled up with the other two elves—correction, Valosians—their whispered voices not carrying far enough to hear.

Movement caught my periphery, and I glanced over to find a wide-awake Marie, sitting up in the center of the nest of girls that still slept surrounding her.

She smirked, motioned between Jakkar and me, then made a lewd hand gesture like she was giving a blow job. I flipped her the bird, and she held back a laugh with her hand.

"Jealous?" I mouthed.

"Whatever," she mouthed back, forming a W with her fingers.

A soft moan sounded out beside me. I leapt to my feet to find a lethargic pair of bright green eyeballs looking back.

"Oh my god, Amy!" I touched her cheek. "You're awake. How're you feeling?"

"Shitty," she groaned. "Weird dreams. Cottonmouth and my freaking head hurts."

Nullar rushed over and began a medical assessment, tapping on the device spread across Amy's forehead.

"Who the hell is that!" Amy recoiled, wide-eyed and shaking.

"That's Nullar; he's a medic," I spoke gently to calm her. "He saved your life."

"He sure as fuck doesn't look like any medic I've ever seen."

"He's a Valosian, Amy." I tried to keep her from scrambling off the floating table. "Nullar won't hurt you. Amy, please stop fighting, or you're gonna hurt yourself."

Amy was so focused on Nullar; she wasn't listening to anything I had to say. Gripped with panic, she fought my hold. Just before she flopped off the table, Nullar was there, gathering her in his arms. He may not have been as large as Jakkar or Aggar, but the guy was way larger than any human man.

"Be calm, female," Nullar spoke softly.

Amy kept fighting his hold, not understanding his words. Worried she would hurt herself, I removed the translator from behind my ear, fought her flailing arms, and managed to place it behind hers.

"I'm not going to hurt you, Amy." Nullar kept his voice as calm and steady as any good physician would. "You're safe."

Amy instantly stopped struggling. "I don't… I don't understand what's going on. What are you? Where am I?"

My heart squeezed at the mask of real fear obscuring her strong demeanor. Amy had never been one to back down from anything, always standing her ground. To see her trembling with fear made me sick.

"Amy." Her eyes flitted over to meet mine. "Nullar has been taking really good care of you. Please don't be afraid."

Not that I completely trusted these Valosian guys, but they were all we had. After seeing the giant insect creatures Jakkar fought to keep us safe, I was glad they had come to our aid.

"Lily." Amy struggled, and Nullar settled her on the pallet I had shared with Jakkar. "Lily, where in the hell are we?"

"We're still on the ship that crashed, remember?"

She nodded and rubbed at her temples.

"You fell unconscious, and these guys,"—I gestured to the three Valosians now staring at us— "rescued us. We're getting ready to cut our way out of here thanks to Aggar finding a cool laser thingy."

Amy eyed me incredulously before wetting her lips and scrutinizing the Valosians. "I feel like I've woken up on the set of the Lord of the Rings. They look like elves."

"Yeah, they kinda do. We crashed on a planet called Valose, and these guys are Valosians—"

"And the biggest one, Jakkar, is Lily's new boyfriend."

I whirled around to find Marie and her unfiltered mouth right over my left shoulder. I ignored her comment and made introductions. The other girls began to gather around, and Amy started to relax.

Nullar's approach was cautious, talking to Amy as he ran scans and made adjustments to the device covering her forehead. It was all mumbo-jumbo, and I looked to Aggar for a replacement translator.

I stuck the device behind my ear and cringed when it sucked itself to my skin. These things were nice, but if we were going to be here for any length of time, learning the language of the natives would be wise instead of depending on these devices.

Now that all the commotion had died down and Amy was settled, the guys got back to work assessing the wall they planned to cut a hole through. Aggar held up some sort of plate-like technology, and I couldn't resist peering around his shoulder.

It worked like an X-ray, showing the twisted skeleton of the broken spaceship and the terrain beyond. Thick vegetation surrounded us, and I couldn't wait to get out there and breathe air that didn't taste of burnt metal.

Packed up and ready to go, Jakkar checked the corridor before ushering us to wait outside the room while Aggar cut through the spacecraft's hull. Jakkar stood with swords drawn, guarding us against anything that might happen down the corridor, while Nullar watched over Amy and the unconscious blonde still lying on the floating tables.

The screech of metal was a scream born from a nightmare, vibrating the air around us. We were warned the laser cut would be loud, yet none of us had expected anything like that. We shrank together in a tight knot of trembling uncertainty. Even Jakkar flinched.

I hoped Aggar was okay. Before I could finish the thought, the door opened.

"We need to move fast." Aggar stepped aside, revealing a huge hole leading outside. The precision edge of the laser cut still glowed hot.

Jakkar and Nullar ushered us into the room. Huddled in our little group, the guys surrounded us. Aggar gave us directions on staying in a tight group, moving only when they did, and keeping as quiet as possible. Staying focused on Aggar's instructions was difficult with an eyeful of blue vegetation.

The jungle beyond was thick and lush. Huge prehistoric-looking leaves waved lazily in a perfumed breeze. It smelled as if the jungle had come straight from the dryer, all Downy fresh. All of us sucked back huge gulps of the fragrant air.

A balmy breeze stirred my hair around my shoulders. Fine dust swirled through the shafts of sunlight spilling in through the hole, making me even more ready to get out of this tin can.

"We're not in Kansas anymore, Toto," Marie whispered.

"You got that shit right."

Aggar pulled off his clear mask, his chest expanding with deep breaths. I looked back to find Jakkar doing the same. With his mask removed, I got an unobstructed view of sculpted lips and a hard-cut jaw covered in a thick five o'clock shadow.

"I will take good care of you, Lily," Jakkar said, flashing fangs. Fangs! He leaned down and whispered close to my ear. His breath, a warm caress, sent tremors down my spine. "This is my world. I will see to it nothing bad happens to you. Of this, I swear."

My mouth went dry, and my knees went weak. I wasn't sure if it was because of the fangs or his protectiveness. For once in my life, I wanted to bask in the safety he offered, to feel cared for and cherished by a man other than my father. I shook off the temptation. Jakkar was a virtual stranger, and we were on an alien planet. Earth rules didn't apply here.

Aggar led the way through the hole. We were careful not to touch the glowing edges as we passed through. It was hard to keep our gasps down as we entered a spectacular blue and silver world.

Nothing could have prepared us for this!

A hand squeezed my arm. I tore my eyes away from the stunning scenery to find Marie clutching my arm, her face a mask of wonder as she peered up into the lush canopy.

I followed her gaze and had to blink twice at the silvery sky featuring two suns that peeked through the split in the leaves above. "That's impossible," I murmured.

"Stay together and move fast," Aggar whispered. Swords drawn, he cut a path through the dense jungle.

I kept my eyes front, trusting Jakkar had our backs. The jungle floor was littered with crunchy debris, and I tried to keep my steps light despite my fat bubble cast.

Staying watchful and cautious was paramount to these guys. All our nerves were on edge. Sweet-scented or not, the jungle had a scary vibe to it.

I pushed aside a spiky leaf that reminded me of a palm frond. My peachy skin was a blotch against the vivid blue. As Aggar's broad back came into view, he was nearly invisible against the backdrop of vegetation, and I recalled Jakkar's confused look when he learned my skin couldn't camouflage.

He'd said his planet was a dangerous one. Now that we were in the thick of it, I felt the press of trepidation. Fear of the unknown dogged our every step as we pushed through the jungle at a fast clip. We all stayed silent, afraid of what might be lurking.

We slowed and huddled under a single, gigantic leaf—Aggar telling us to hold there.

Holy shit, the leaf was so large. It was like looking through a magnifying glass without the magnifier. Every vein, every hairy fiber was visible to the naked eye.

A great shadow swooped across the ground. Curious, I looked up to find a dragon circling overhead. A dragon! My skin shrank tight to my bones, a sinking feeling settled in my belly.

Now I knew what a small woodland creature felt like hiding from a bird of prey.

The creature dove down before making another pass. Unfortunately, I got a better look at its twenty-fucking-foot wingspan. The thing looked familiar for some odd reason, and I realized it was the same winged animal featured on the buckle of Jakkar's kilt.

The dragon's colossal head swung toward us but focused on a point far away. Aggar threw up a hand for us to hold in place. The tension thickened, and I felt we were getting ready to make a run for it.

In a tremendous downward plunge, the dragon dropped from the sky, diving down just above our heads. Its wings pitched a gust of wind that blew back my hair, leaving the earthy scent of the animal in its wake. The dragon changed direction, soaring high in the air before dipping into the canopy a few hundred feet away.

The screech of some poor creature was our cue to haul ass. Aggar threw his arm forward, and our group rocketed across the ground. A spike of adrenaline-fueled my legs to pump fast beneath me. Foliage slapped at my arms and legs, and I kept one hand up to shield my face and used the other to push Amy's floating table.

The jungle was infinite, an unyielding wilderness that blocked out the rays of the twin turquoise suns high above us. I felt like we would never stop running, my lungs burning with the exertion. The air here felt thinner than on Earth, my head grew light, and I was afraid I might pass out.

Like a blue curtain, the foliage ahead of us suddenly split open, held back by three enormous Valosian guys that looked just as shocked to see us as we did them.

More guys equaled more protection. I was all about the additional escorts the remaining way to their camp, which was circled by strange floating machines that looked like jet skis, only longer and thinner.

Once inside the protective ring, the new males couldn't take their eyes off us. I stared back, getting a good look at our latest protectors.

All three were as imposing as our rescuers, built like tanks and armed to the teeth. The one covered in slashing scars terrified me the most. His eyes were even more cunning than Jakkar's as if he missed nothing.

Another gave me the creeps as if he were silently scheming. A wolf in sheep's clothing, for sure.

The third was remarkably handsome with a kind face and a smile at the ready as soon as my eyes landed on him. I returned his smile with a wobbly one of my own.

Marie leaned in close as I held tight to Amy's floating table. "We should have stayed on the damn ship."

Chapter Ten

JAKKAR

I should have told Draggar we were bringing females from another world, but I was worried we would be overheard on the comm. These women were a rare, precious gift from the stars who needed to be protected at all costs.

"Sia?" Not a greeting but a question from Draggar.

"We need to find a safe place for the dark hurs. Preferably, in the direction of the settlement," I said, measuring the drop of the suns. "We have several wounded. The humans can't move as fast or for as long as we can. I fear it will take us twice as long to return to the settlement. They need food and rest."

Draggar's mouth hung open before he regained his composure, staring the longest and hardest at Marie. It had been a long time since we had seen a female. Alien or not, these women were a sight for starving eyes.

The males sprang into action. It was comical to watch them bumping into one another to make the females at home. Draggar made them a suitable place to sit from our sleeping pallets while Vallon offered them dried chiksin meat and noobian berry rations. Rayyar pulled extra loodskins from the rovers and passed them around to the females.

The females whispered among themselves, sniffing at the rations before warily nibbling on them. I wished it were more. If I were still living inside the palace at Huren, they would have had a feast laid before them, not a sack full of dried food.

We would need to hunt, and soon with more mouths to feed on the journey back to the settlement. Maybe a deerth or an elkson. That would make a more acceptable meal for my spirit mate and the other females.

Lily sat with the other women, yet her eyes sought me out as I moved around the camp. My ancillary heart fluttered with warmth, knowing my female's eyes were upon me.

"Who are they?" Draggar asked in low tones. Vallon stood shoulder to shoulder with him, wearing the same expression of awe.

"They are human women from Earth," I began. "They were found in a cargo hold locked inside metalliodic cages with electro-bars."

"They were an alien's cargo?" Vallon hissed.

"For what purpose?" Draggar seethed.

"I don't know. Many died in the crash, and I promised my spirit… the female, Lily, that I would make every effort to go back and honor her dead," I explained to my warriors. "She agreed to the Valosian way of a funeral pyre for the ones lost."

"So, the spacecraft is not theirs?"

"No."

"Then whose?"

"A spindly, gray freak with the power of mind control," Aggar butted in with a sneer. "It claimed to be of a mighty race called the Gretolic. We found only one with a missing hand, compliments of Jakkar's spirit mate."

All eyes snapped to me. I wasn't ready to divulge that information to my males. Simply having females present for the first time in munthis was enough of a shock, but to know they were compatible would create a distraction the settlement couldn't afford.

"It was not an intentional pairing." I widened my stance defensively.

"Spirit mates never are," Vallon replied and turned to scan the group of females. "The soul recognizes its life-companion. The choice of who we mate is made for us."

"I never thought to have one of my own." My gaze landed on Lily.

"A spirit mate is an unexpected treasure never to be taken for granted," Draggar added, his eyes drifting over the females.

His saddened expression tore at me—the loss of his spirit mate, a tangible tragedy.

"This camp isn't sufficient enough—"

The patooga came out of nowhere, careening through our circle of rovers.

One moment, the females were finishing off the rations, and the next, they were scurrying away from the hairy beast with high-pitched screams sure to alert other creatures to our presence.

My warriors and I acted fast, swords drawn and circling the sleek, powerful beast. Nullar and Rayyar herded the females away from the danger and tried to keep them quiet. Their shouts of fear would only draw more of the jungle's creatures to us.

"We must put the patooga down fast." My concern for the females' safety had me lunging for the beast's legs, knocking the thing off balance.

Draggar, Vallon, and Aggar followed my lead, swinging their blades in sweeping arcs at the patooga's tough hide before the beast regained its balance. It growled and hissed, baring enormous fangs dripping with paralyzing saliva. We dodged the shake of its head that slung the dangerous mucus in thick, slobbering strings onto the ground at our feet.

It would take all of us to bring it down. The patooga was too large for one warrior to handle. I nodded to my warrior's and the four of us attacked in a practiced move. Draggar feigned left, distracting the beast with his movements, giving the rest of us a clear path to stab while its head was turned.

Aggar slashed low while Vallon and I stabbed our blades into the back and neck. Bright blue blood spurt from its wounds. The patooga roared, rounding on us in an angry snap of jaws and saber teeth. We dodged most of the mucus, which landed harmlessly to the ground except for a single strand that wrapped around Draggar's forearm.

The effects were instantaneous, and the warrior dropped his sword from a limp hand. Draggar was not deterred and kept fighting one-handed, slashing and stabbing.

Angered by the punctures to its neck and head, the patooga swung its backside around, knocking us off our feet with its slashing tail. The air was driven out of my lungs from my hard landing. I gasped for breath and watched in horror as the beast gained the upper hand.

Rearing back on its hind legs, it prepared to pounce. I rolled away and readied to spring to my feet when a rexose stormed through the foliage. Jaws opened wide in a killing roar, the rexose scooped up the patooga in a single mouthful and plowed through to the other side, taking one of our rovers with it.

Dazed, we looked around at each other and took stock of our disheveled camp. The females had formed a tight group, holding onto each other in a knot of trembling bodies. Nullar and Rayyar stood guard, swords up and at the ready.

Two rovers lay on their sides, pieces of their gravity disruptors littered nearby. Not a good sign.

I sprang to my feet and ran to the females. "Everyone all right?" I spoke to the group, yet my eyes traveled over my spirit mate.

A few wobbly nods came from shocked faces. Now was not the time to remain still. "We must move fast and away from this place before more beasts come this way."

"The blood of the patooga will attract more rexose." Draggar stood up one of the downed rovers with his good arm. "Looks like we're minus a rover."

"Make that two." Aggar leaned over the other rover toppled by the attacking patooga. "I can salvage the gravity disrupter, but the thruster is badly damaged. Looks like it will have to be rebuilt, and I don't have the time or the tools to do that here."

"We salvage what we can, but quickly." I helped the women to their feet, taking extra care with Lily. "The women will all have to ride inside the hauler. We'll double up on the rovers. Aggar, take the lead and scan the area. Find us a safe place to pass the dark hurs."

"Yes, Sia." Aggar removed an alien device from his pack that he salvaged from the ship and began scanning the area.

The rest of us moved quickly, gathering up what we could carry and formed up in the camp's center. Pride welled within me as the females jumped in to help. Still shaking from the experience, they overcame their fears and aided my warriors in packing what they could inside the compartments on the rovers. There was barely enough room for eight in the bed of the hauler, but with Vallon's help, the women managed to squish together without complaint.

I repressed a growl when Vallon helped Lily inside the open bed of the hauler. Every fiber of my being fought to mark her as mine, yet I held my spirit in check. There would be time for coupling later after we were all safe. That was if she accepted me as hers.

"We go north and then cut to the east." Aggar pointed out the directions. "There are caves along the Sien river where we can replenish our loodskins and camp during the dark hurs. I think I can fashion a barrier with the nutrillium from the gravity disrupters and the fibrous tubing from the ship."

"Then, let's be on our way."

At my command, we took off through the jungle, not as fast as I would have liked with a loaded down hauler, but at least we were moving in the direction of the settlement.

Chapter Eleven

LILY

I was so not feeling this cave. It was super eerie and dark as sin inside. But this looked like where the guys were planning on setting up camp.

Vallon and Aggar had already been inside and deemed it safe. Who was I to question them? This was their planet, and they knew the dangers better than any of us.

After seeing those guys in action, fighting off a saber-toothed cat … thing before a T-Rex crashed the party and ate the damn cat in one gulp, my trust was with these guys. So, if they said the cave was safe, then my ass was going in, even if I was scared shitless of dark, creepy spaces.

Jakkar helped me out of the bed of what they called a hauler. It looked like the bed of a pick-up truck had been affixed to the back of an elongated jet ski. That same stretched out jet ski without the bed was what the males rode on called rovers. The machines somehow hovered above the ground with no wheels, using thrusters to propel them forward.

I placed my palms on his bulging shoulders when he grabbed me around the waist. I was lifted, up and out, as if I weighed nothing to slide down all that strength before my feet touched the ground. My skin tingled, energized from the contact.

My bubble cast lopsided my stance, so I used the excuse of instability to hold onto him for a bit longer than I should. My gaze slid up to meet his. There was something so compelling within the swirling depths of his silvery eyes. The fight to step away was lost. The pull I felt was odd and unexplainable.

If I could, I would just hang onto this moment and figure out why I was so drawn to him. I reluctantly dropped my hands and moved away so he could help Amy out. Amy's arm went around Jakkar's neck for support. When he cradled her in his arms, a spear of jealousy knifed me in the chest.

Gawd! What in the hell was wrong with me? Amy wasn't fully healed from her head injury. She'd probably fall flat on her face if she tried to walk on her own. Of course, Jakkar would have to carry her, yet I wished so badly it was me in his arms.

With the rovers and hauler parked close by, I followed Jakkar and my best friend into the cave now lit with stones that Vallon had pulled from a sack. They were like a child's phosphorescent toy, giving off a soft glow.

I helped spread out heavy blankets and sleeping pads the guys brought in off the rovers. There weren't enough to go around now that us girls had joined their party. I felt terrible knowing the guys would be surrendering their sleeping pallets to us.

Despite the crude living situation, we were treated like queens. They looked at us as if we hung the moon, especially the scarred one, Draggar. He was ever attentive and attuned to our every need. Earthmen could take a few lessons from these guys on how to treat a lady.

Jakkar settled Amy on a pallet where I joined her. I stretched my legs out before me, taking an expressed interest in my bubble cast. I couldn't look at Jakkar. He was too close, and I didn't trust myself not to fling myself at him.

I wasn't a clingy girl. I could take care of myself. I didn't need a man to feel complete, so why did I feel so empty when he wandered off to talk to Draggar?

"I'm going out to hunt, Sia." Draggar checked his weapons.

"What of your arm?" Jakkar gave Draggar a stern look.

"All better." Draggar flexed. "See. It's as if nothing ever happened."

Jakkar grunted, a glimmer of amusement shining from that silver gaze. Too easily caught up in him, I tore my eyes away and turned my attention to Amy. "How are you feeling?"

"My head is swimmy, but I'll take that over the pounding inside my skull." Amy rubbed at her eyes. "I don't know what that medic guy gave me, but it seems to be working."

"His name is Nullar. He saved your life." I laid back on the pallet that held Jakkar's scent and resisted the urge to shove Amy off it.

"What is up with you and Jakkar?"

"Nothing."

"Nothing doesn't undress a man with her eyes, Lil," Amy scoffed. "You like him, don't you?"

"He's an alien on a strange planet." I rolled to my side and gave her my back. "I don't even know him."

"And yet you look at him like he's your long-lost love or something."

"Yeah," Marie chimed in. "Or something."

"Gawd, will you two stop?" I snapped, shoving myself up to a sitting position. My friends were hitting too close to the truth.

I was feeling Jakkar and not just in the new-crush-butterflies-in-your-stomach kind of way. There was an inexplicable tug deep down I couldn't shake.

Nullar joined us and ran his weird devices over Amy's head and then my ankle. I had no clue what any of his medical gizmos did, but they seemed to be helping all of us.

"Thanks, Nullar."

"You're welcome," he nodded, his pleasant demeanor a soothing balm we were all in desperate need of.

He smiled at us before heading over to the pallet Isobel and Willow had claimed. Once he checked the girls over, he was off to treat a sobbing Layla, who was being comforted by Rose. The bitch Layla had presented herself to be had melted down into a slobbering mess.

For the time being, we were stuck here until Jakkar talked to his brother and secured a spacecraft to take us home. We were just going to have to make the best of it. And Layla would have to toughen up despite the unlimited anxieties this planet had to offer.

The last girl Nullar checked was the blonde that had yet to regain consciousness. My heart went out to her. I couldn't imagine her reaction when she woke to a blue planet with silvery elf dudes all around her. Then again—my eyes traced over the muscles on Jakkar's naked back while he spoke with Aggar—these guys were some *serious* eye candy.

As if he felt me watching, he turned and nailed me with a hot stare. The shock of it melted my core, and I was horrified to feel wetness pool between my thighs. Our shapeless dresses were all we wore. No panties. No socks or shoes. Just these white, sack-like garments. So, my sudden arousal would leave a wet spot on my alien attire.

I laid back and groaned, squeezing my thighs together tightly. I braced for a sarcastic remark from Marie. When nothing came at me, I turned to catch her glaring at Rose, who'd left Layla's side to join Aggar at the cave's entrance. Rose was helping him set up some kind of contraption with that fiber tubing stuff I recognized from the ship, along with a part he salvaged from the wrecked jet skis.

"What does she think she's doing?" Marie slung her hand at Rose. "She doesn't know shit about alien technology. Like she can help him or something."

"Why do you care if Rose is helping him?" I asked.

"I don't," Marie said, then completely changed the subject. "Did you know Draggar went out to hunt alone? Do you think he'll be okay?"

"He's a total badass." I tried to sound optimistic. Truth was, I didn't know. "He'll be fine."

Amy and I exchanged a surprised look before I relaxed back and searched the cave for Jakkar. At the far end of the cave, I found him talking into his tricorder.

I hoped he was calling for reinforcements. From what I had seen so far, Jakkar hadn't exaggerated when he called this planet dangerous.

Something flashed then dimmed, gaining everyone's attention. Over by the cave's entrance, Aggar and Rose's little science project had turned out to be a wall made of translucent, white light. It glowed and shimmered in waves.

"Oh, wow." Isobel, followed by Willow, approached with caution. "What is it?"

"It's a lumi-nee-tric barrier." Rose looked to Aggar to see if she had gotten the pronunciation right.

Aggar nodded as we all gathered around. "Close enough."

"It's like the shield technology used on the Enterprise," Rose added all smiles. "We pretty much made a forcefield from the nutrillium, a mineral mined on this planet which powers the gravity disruptors on the rovers, and the fibrous tubing from the alien spacecraft to channel and expand the energy into a solid sheet."

For two beats, we all just gaped and blinked at Rose's explanation.

"Oh Lord, spare me from Trekky nerds," Marie grouched and stormed off to the back of the cave, clearly worried over Draggar.

"Did I do something wrong?" Rose looked at the girls gathered around.

"It's not you, honey. Anger is how Marie deals with stressful situations. My little sister acts the same way." Willow patted Rose on the back. "She'll calm down."

"Drop the shield!" Draggar's shout was heard before we ever saw him barreling out of the jungle.

In one hand, he clutched a sword, and in the other, some kind of dead animal. His arms and legs pumped hard and fast as he sprinted toward us.

Jakkar sprang into action, directing all the girls away from the entrance to the back of the cave. I didn't miss how he paid extra attention to me with lingering looks and brief touches.

Jakkar squatted down and placed his palm on the cave floor, and that was when I noticed the increasing tremors vibrating up through the soles of my feet.

"It's big. Whatever is chasing him." Jakkar's comment prompted a group huddle.

"Probably a tondru." Vallon joined us, carrying Amy.

"Oh, no," Marie breathed out.

Layla whimpered and tucked her head into a much smaller Rose. "Why can't these things just leave us alone?"

I'd read her all wrong when we first met in the cargo hold. She was just scared like the rest of us, and being a bitch was her way of dealing, the same as Marie's angry sarcasm.

Aggar wasn't immediately reacting to Draggar's shout but crouched low at the entrance and waited until Draggar got closer before deactivating the barrier. Once the light fizzled out, the cave was open to the jungle.

And what a jungle it was!

Now that the twin suns had dropped and the shield no longer obscured our view, everything was illuminated. The giant, prehistoric-looking foliage was trimmed out in various glowing blue, white, and silver shades. The tufts of silver grass that sporadically grew from the navy dirt shimmered from within. Even Draggar himself had radiance patterns on his chest and arms like backlit tattoos.

Draggar launched himself head-first through the entrance at the last second, executing a perfect dive roll. The moment his feet cleared the threshold, Aggar engaged the barrier.

Marie ran to Draggar's side. The scarred warrior lifted one side of his mouth in a curving sneer that I decided was his version of a smile. The grim expression he always wore softened for Marie.

Not a second later, an enormous wolf crashed into the light wall. It rippled in angry white waves before settling into a placid, see-through shield.

Light should not be able to keep anything out. Forcefields were the invention of science fiction. Yet, it was doing just that. The giant wolf circled outside as my huddled group of girls swallowed back our squeals and screams. Its bright eyes leered in at us, a meal just out of its reach.

My tense body relaxed as the wolf appeared to have given up and headed back into the jungle, but I'd lowered my guard all too soon. Head down, the animal charged the forcefield, having backed up to get a running start.

The ground shook from the wolf's incredible weight as it headed right for us like a freight train. The girls squeezed in tighter, bracing for impact.

The resounding boom as it hit our translucent wall resonated throughout the cave. The light wall absorbed the impact and held. Aggar arrogantly moved to stand in front of his creation, casually placed his hands on his hips, and watched the wolf back up and ram the light shield again and again.

"That damn thing must be bulletproof," Isobel mumbled.

"See, Layla," Rose coaxed Layla to unhide her eyes. "It's perfectly safe in here. Nothing can get us."

We all disbanded and resumed our respective pallets. Vallon deposited a pale-faced Amy next to me. "You okay?"

"I think I might have peed myself a little."

I giggled at her. "I think I did too."

Draggar and Jakkar began to field dress the animal Draggar had hunted. I had to look away. I was by no means a vegetarian, but my meat came prepackaged from the grocery store. Killing something out in the wild and eating it wasn't exactly my thing.

The guys made quick work out of preparing and spitting dinner over a fire they started close to the entrance. The smoke billowed out, somehow passing through the forcefield to the outside. The scent of roasting meat filled the cave, and my stomach wasn't the only one rumbling.

Meat was cut from the animal and passed around on large leaves used as plates.

"I can't eat this." Layla pushed hers aside. I noticed she'd only eaten some of the dried berries that the guys had given us back at the camp.

Rose picked it up and tried to get Layla to eat. "You have to keep up your strength, sweetie."

Layla shook her head and turned away. I noticed the other girls sniffing at their meat with hard swallows. Apparently, none of us had ever lived off the land. Eating mystery meat wasn't my fave thing, but I felt like I needed to set the example and took a tiny bite off mine.

I felt Jakkar's eyes on me—I met his stare. His face was a mask of expectation, like when someone cooks for you and was waiting to see how you liked the food.

My teeth sank into the juicy meat. The texture was nothing like what I expected, which freaked me out a little. All eyes were on me, and I needed to give the alien food a fair shake. It wasn't so awful, more along the lines of a portobello mushroom, meaty yet different.

"Does it taste like chicken?" Marie snorted.

"No. More like pork loin." I took another bite and nodded happily at Jakkar, who beamed back at me. "The texture is a little off from what we're used to, but it's delicious."

"That's good enough for me." Willow bit into hers.

"Me too," Isobel joined in.

All the girls except for Layla followed suit, and soon we were all lounging on our sleeping pallets with full bellies. Vallon passed around waterskins full of what they called lood that he'd collected from the small river outside the cave. Soft snores began to fill our camp. I turned to chat with Amy, but she was already out like a light.

I closed my eyes to a zillion questions buzzing inside my head about what tomorrow would bring. This cave was only a temporary reprieve from what awaited us outside in the jungle. Big, strong warrior dudes aside, the thought of going back out there scared the shit out of me.

I gave up trying to fall asleep and glanced around the cave to find the one for who I was searching. As quietly as possible, I hobbled my way to the cave's entrance.

"Hi," I said with a nervous lilt.

"Hello, Lily," Jakkar returned my greeting. "You should be resting with the others. The next suns-rise will be long and arduous."

"I know," I shrugged, "but I can't sleep. Too much going on inside my head. How come you're awake?"

"The same as you. Sit with me?" He gestured to the square cushion of animal hide where he was sitting.

Jakkar helped me to the floor at my nod, seating me on the hide while he scooted to one side. The dampness of the cave floor seeped into the hide, and I could only imagine how uncomfortable he must be sitting directly on the cold ground.

"We should share your cushion. Maybe I could sit on your lap or something—"

He stood so suddenly and swung me into his arms, and I was settled on his lap before my heart could pump its next beat. The guy was massive, enveloping me in an immense embrace, which I immediately snuggled into. His body temperature was higher than a human's, chasing away the cool temperature of the cave's interior.

He began that strange internal vibration that put me at ease.

"How are you already healed?" I touched him longer than necessary, running my fingers over his newly healed scales and down the bumpy ridges of his abs.

"I'm healing at the rate I should be." He shifted around, rubbing my arm and knee. "Nullar said your species' healing process is incredibly slow. *I* worry that you're in pain."

"Not at all." I relaxed, making his shoulder my pillow. "Nullar rubbed some sort of cream on my ankle before he put on the bubble cast. It feels good as new."

"I'm glad to know you're not hurting." The rumble of his baritone moved through me in shock waves.

"Are you born with these, or are they tattoos?" I smoothed my hand over the glowing patterns marking his arms and chest. Now that the fire inside the cave had dwindled, all the guys had begun to glow. "They're so beautiful."

Jakkar looked down at what I was referring to. "I don't know what a tat-too is, but yes, we are born with these markings. They help camouflage our bodies during the dark hurs."

My palm then found the source of his vibrations. "What does that mean when you do that?"

"Thrumming?" He laughed a little. "It's my spirit singing to yours."

"That's a beautiful thing to say."

"It is a song only for my spirit mate." Jakkar peered down at me with such reverence I could swear I was the only person left in the world. "Each is a unique serenade of courtship. Once the spirit finds its match in another, the male thrums to let the female know he is ready to couple with her."

By the time he was done explaining, my face was on fire, and there was a heavy fluttering low in my belly. This guy had a serious way with words, and the blistering look he was giving me made my girl parts tingle. That spicy, fresh scent of his had amplified, knocking me off-kilter.

We sat cuddled together in companionable silence. Him thrumming up a storm and me staring up at him like a lovesick teenager. Yet, the questions banging around inside my head wouldn't let up, dampening the mood.

"You mentioned spirit mates. What does that mean?"

"Spirit mates happen when the spirits of a male and female recognize each other as companions. Coupling is the catalyst for them to coalesce for the first time." His eyes raked over me in a hungry way that left me squirming. "After many couplings, the spirits become amalgamated, so much so, one doesn't know where the other begins or ends. It's a merging of the spirits that lasts for all eternity. Not even death can tear them apart."

The word coupling spoken in his husky voice was like fuel thrown on a fire. My thighs clenched together to stave off the urgent need to straddle his hips and grind against the massive erection pressing against my backside.

"Spirits as in souls?" I licked my suddenly dry lips. He tracked the movement with a darkening swirl in his silvery gaze. "You believe in soulmates?"

"Yes. Don't you?"

"I don't know." My voice dropped to a husky whisper. "Seems more like a romantic fantasy."

Up this close, the man... er, male elf... Valose warrior... was breathtaking. His shimmering scales sparkled in the wake of my palm, and he was smoother than the finest leather. I couldn't stop touching him, smoothing my hand over the expanse of his bare chest.

His scent burrowed into me, rich and potent—all-consuming. Fierce and captivating. Exotic. When my eyes coasted down to his sculpted lips, my breath was coming out in shallow pants. All I could think about was kissing him.

Then it happened. Jakkar leaned down and brushed his lips across mine. I was lost to the sensation—every question I wanted to ask dissipating like smoke on a strong breeze.

My lips parted on a moan, granting him entrance. Jakkar slid his tongue across mine, deepening the kiss. He plundered every inch of my mouth—savage in the tasting of me.

The ground fell away as Jakkar stood with me in his arms. He set us down in a private nook away from the prying eyes of the others, and I was again cradled on his lap. Leaning against one brawny arm, his other was free to stroke and touch me everywhere.

I turned into his body, wanting to do some touching of my own. Our sensual kisses turned frantic, and what began as a hungry exploration turned into an all-out grope session.

In the furthest reaches of my mind, I told myself I shouldn't be making out with an alien in a cave full of people. I mean, what in the hell was I thinking giving a virtual stranger liberty to touch me as if he owned me?

Yet, I didn't want him to stop, especially when his large hand smoothed up the inside of my thigh. And I definitely should have put on the brakes when his fingertips grazed the petals of my sex, not part my legs, granting him greater access.

Oh Lord, when the cool air of the cave hit my exposed sex, I felt how wet I was—soaked. For him.

Jakkar plunged his tongue inside my mouth as he glided a thick finger between my slick folds. His thumb worked my clit into a frenzy. Electric jolts shot down my spine and crested into a pinpoint of painful pleasure. My abdomen tightened before I could process the exquisite sensations, and I came on a crashing wave that swept me away.

Jakkar swallowed my moans, lazily pumping through my orgasm. His gaze seared me to the core when his lips lifted from mine. My fingers were still clawed into his shoulders as I worked through the tremors of my release.

He wasn't done with me. Not by a long shot. Jakkar slid out only to return with a second finger. His thick appendages slipped easily inside my drenched sex. My back arched from the invasion, my body stretching to accommodate him.

I followed his inward stroke, my pelvis tilting up as I ground my ass into the stony ridge of his enormous erection. I wanted that inside me now!

I tried shifting around, wanting to straddle his lap, but he held me tight, whispering in my ear, "Not here. Coupling is to be done in private."

Well, yeah! Of course, it was. One good orgasm, and here I was, ready to toss up his kilt and get down to business. *And* in a cave full of other people.

"Let me pleasure you." Jakkar's words brushed hotly over the hollow of my throat. "Feeling your release is enough for me until I can get you alone."

Who was I to argue with the logic of talented fingers? I shouldn't have allowed this to happen, but this was a pleasant diversion from all the crazy shit I'd been through, so I gave myself over to my warrior's capable hands.

Chapter Twelve

JAKKAR

My spirit mate melted at my hand for a second time. The scent of her awakened sex was intoxicating. I could stoke her desire for the whole of the dark hurs and never tire, but she looked exhausted, her eyes drooping with satisfaction.

"Rest now, nula." I held her close, tugging her garment back into place even though my cock was harder than the stone at my back. I brushed a kiss across her forehead. Her eyes leisurely closed, her lips parted slightly in her early repose.

The cave had grown quiet. Gentle snores from the women were mixed with the harsher breaths of my warriors. I carefully shifted my position inside the small, private nook to see the cave in its entirety.

I wasn't surprised to see Aggar asleep with his back to the gravity disruptor pod he'd converted into a luminetric barrier. New to all things tech, the warrior proved to be a quick study under Zikkar's tutelage. Like a nursling with a coveted toy, Aggar was fiercely protective of the equipment he built.

Vallon had bunked down near the pale-maned female, Layla as if to offer her his protection. I feared it would be some time before she fully recovered from the shock of her abduction. She reminded me of the mentally worn females fresh from the stresses of wars with the Nuttaki. Some had proved stronger than others. I was afraid that would be the case with the human females.

My Lily was strong. A natural leader. I took pleasure in watching her sleep. So lovely, yet so very different from a Valosian.

I wondered what my sire would think of me finding my spirit mate in another species—one from the stars. A place neither one of us looked favorably upon. My brother, Sakkar, was the only stargazer in my family.

My eyes were drawn to Rayyar. The traitor in our midst was stretched out on the cold ground at the back of the cave. He remained fully awake, staring me down as if he wanted nothing more than to cut my throat while I slept.

His eyes narrowed on Lily bundled in my arms. Given a chance, Rayyar would run to Sakkar and tell him of the females we found. The longer I pondered Lily's request to be returned home, the deeper I sank in distrust for my brother.

Sakkar proved to be a reckless ruler, and as Sia of Clan Huren, he could demand the females be handed over and kept inside the safety of the city's dome. I didn't trust him to keep them safe or fly them home.

As an exile, Sakkar was no longer my ruler. That wouldn't stop him from marching an army to my settlement and demanding I hand them over. I would never willingly give my spirit mate over to anyone.

Lily's request to be taken back to her home planet weighed heavily upon me. I wanted to do as she requested with every fiber of my being, but that would mean alerting Sakkar to the female's presence.

As my eyes touched every feminine face, I couldn't shake the impression that these human women could be the future Valose needed for our dying race.

And Sakkar could *never* know of their existence.

SLEEP NEVER CAME. I waited out Rayyar, but his eyes never closed. Twin pools of silver swirled, brewing with trickery. I knew it in the marrow of my bones that it was only a matter of time before he made his move.

Even now, as we packed up camp, Rayyar's eyes were prowling over the females, sizing them up for the Spirits only knew what, proving Rayyar was too much of a danger.

Draggar stayed close to Rayyar's side as I'd ordered. Unfettered, there was no limit to what havoc he could wreak. I didn't need any more reason than that to have him shackled.

"I want him taken into custody. I tire of his vile expression." My sharp tone left no question for Draggar as to who I was referring. "Search and strip him of any devices."

"My pleasure, Sia."

To the gasps of the females, Draggar tackled Rayyar to the cave floor before he could flee. I watched as Draggar moved with quick, purposeful movements, binding Rayyar's hands and feet.

The male was trussed up like a fresh kill before he could even blink.

Nullar looked on, wide-eyed and confused. The scholarly male was oblivious to the traitor who lived among us.

"Sia?" Nullar looked at me with wide, astonished eyes.

"He spies for my brother."

"How long have you known?" Nullar gulped.

Therein lay the difference between the classes. Warriors had instincts beyond those of ordinary males. Abilities that were embedded in the genes passed down from warrior sire to son. One of them was sensing who protected your back and who was eyeing the best spot to plunge their sword.

"Since before, my crown was ripped from my head." I forced a smile of reassurance for Lily, who had stopped tending to Amy and looked at me with panicked eyes.

All the women had stood in wild-eyed confusion, huddling together as they tended to do when frightened.

"If it would not offend, why did you allow him to join you in your exile?"

"Sometimes, it is better to keep your enemies close," I replied with a friendly clap to the male's back. "Let's get the females ready to travel. We have a long way yet to go before we reach the settlement."

Nullar nodded and moved to the cave's center to help the females.

Aggar disengaged the luminetric barrier, and we were now vulnerable to the jungle's creatures. It was safer to travel in the light, given the majority of creatures were nocturnal. There was always a chance of an encounter, like the patooga attack from the last suns-rise.

The rovers and hauler were brought to the cave's entrance, and Vallon helped load the females into the hauler's bed.

"Can that luminetric barrier be made larger?" I asked Aggar while readying my rover.

"It could." He nodded to Rose. "With the female's help, I think I can create a perimeter large enough to hold all of us, including the rovers. What have you got in mind?"

"The pool just past the floratrap field skirting the Nassbian cliffs. We would have the coverage of the carnivorous plants to our backs and the rocky outcrops surrounding us. If you could provide us a shield, we could make camp there and refill our loodskins. Maybe even allow the women a bath."

"The females would like that," Aggar smiled.

"Very good." I clapped him on the shoulder and sought out my female.

Lily was about to climb into the hauler next to Amy when I approached. All the females were fawning over the pale maned one called Layla. She would hardly eat anything, and when she did, it was nuts or berries. Her weeping was continuous.

My spirit mate excused herself, leaving Marie to look after Layla.

"How is she?"

"Not any better." Lily dipped her head sadly. "I think she's getting worse the longer we're out here. To be honest, this planet of yours is scary as fuck. You know all the monsters that live out here, but we don't. It's a bit unnerving not knowing what will come at us next."

"Aggar has plotted a route outside the heaviest traffic of the jungle's creatures," I said, and her tense expression softened. "The next place we make camp will be as safe as the cave. Everyone can rest without fear, plus there is a pool for bathing."

Her face lit up brighter than both suns combined. "Did you say a bath? Seriously?"

I nodded, and to my utter shock, she lunged at me, her arms wrapping around my neck. I gladly returned her embrace, lifting her off her feet and breathing in her heady scent from the hollow of her throat. She was so light and fragile, my human, yet her curves were generous, and her body—oh so—responsive to my touch.

In this moment of calm, with her scent filling my nose and her pliant body pressed against mine, I would have fought a legion of Nuttaki, a hundreths tondru, and a herd of rynose for the feel of her. When she pulled away and gazed up at me as if I were the conqueror of all her fears, I would have done anything to capture and hold her adoring regard.

I reluctantly let my spirit mate go, helping her into the bed of the hauler. I left her chattering with the other girls about the pool. The females' dour mood lightened as if the clouds in the sky had parted to reveal a perfect suns-rise.

Draggar tightened the last strap, binding Rayyar to a rover he would share with Vallon with hard pulls. Rayyar winced but kept quiet. The combination of their foul moods was a toxic mix.

Once done, we were ready to travel, moving slowly on the outskirts of the thick jungle. It was safer travel for the women, though it would take us many suns-falls longer to reach the settlement.

I bristled with the urgency to deliver the females safely behind the settlement walls. My jaw ached from gritting my teeth as the thick foliage passed by at a painstakingly sluggish rate. Every milose we put behind us had been excruciating laborious. Fucking Helios! I cursed the Realm of the Wicked. I could run faster than this.

At the end of the suns-rise, the Spirits had shown us favor. There were no encounters with creatures of the jungle along our exhausting journey, only a brush with a herd of migrating rynose that was easily avoided. I silently thanked the Spirits for the uneventful journey as Aggar scanned the area where we intended to make camp.

Chapter Thirteen

LILY

The girls were skeptical about the possibility of a bath. I couldn't say I blamed them. There was nothing out here but giant trees and plants and scary as fuck monsters, making it difficult to imagine what we were all gawking at right now.

It's an infinity-edged swimming pool carved out of stone, with the infinity part being a cliff's edge. The water was crystal clear with a blue tint from the reflection of rocks surrounding it.

There was no vegetation growing around where we would be making camp, only rock, so there was no chance something with large teeth lurked behind a mammoth leaf waiting to eat us for dinner.

I climbed out of the hauler and stretched my stiff arms and legs. We girls were pretty squished the entire journey, but no one complained because we were all together. We held each other tight in the small bed of that floating alien contraption, eight strangers thrust together in the most extreme circumstances, drawing strength from one another.

Now that we were somewhat safe inside a deep valley made from solid rock, we had stopped moving and worrying about every little unseen snapping twig and animal grunt, I took the time to look around. This planet was beautiful—blue skies with fat, silvery clouds floating overhead, lazy and carefree. The land was covered in lush foliage in every shade of blue and silver mixed in with white touches that grew out of royal blue dirt.

Our new camp buzzed with activity. Rose had already run off to help Aggar recreate the forcefield thingy they'd made back at the cave while Marie stood nearby trying not to look crestfallen as Draggar helped Amy out of the hauler and offered her his arm to help her walk around the camp. She'd improved by leaps and bounds, thanks to Nullar, in the hours since we left the cave.

Draggar shuffled his steps, allowing Amy to set the slow pace. I suspected the fiercest looking of all the males was a giant teddy bear on the inside. A smile spread across my face as I contemplated the two of them as a couple.

I quickly shook the idea loose. We weren't staying. Just as soon as I could convince Jakkar to talk to his brother about a ride home in that spaceship of his, we were off this scary assed planet.

The prospect of leaving Jakkar carved out a hollow ache in the center of my chest. I glanced over to where he was guarding the entrance to the valley, both blades out and ready to chop anything into tiny pieces that may pose a threat. So strong, so courageous. I would never forget how he put himself in harm's way to save us from that horde of insect creatures back on the ship.

I jumped in to assist with setting up the camp much the same as we had last night, laying out sleeping pallets and making a special place for Nullar to oversee his unconscious patient.

Rayyar, the guy Jakkar claimed as his enemy, was led away and staked to the ground in shackles and turned, so he faced away from us. I was relieved not to deal with his piercing stare prickling my skin. My instincts told me he was devious.

A careful hand landed on my arm, startling me. I turned to find Nullar. "The female is beginning to wake. Better for her if it's your face rather than mine she sees first."

It took me a second to comprehend his words, and then I followed him over to where the blonde lay on a pallet on the ground. I crouched down beside her as she slowly blinked awake. Her eyes were blurry and unfocused until they landed on me.

"Hi." I kept my voice low. "I'm Lily. You've been asleep for a long time. How are you feeling?"

At first, she just blinked, then raised her hands, making sloppy gestures. I looked to Nullar for guidance. He stood apart from me and out of view of the girl. Smart idea. No need to unnecessarily freak her out. There'll be plenty of time for that when another one of those over-grown wolves, Jakkar called tondru, comes barreling down on us.

"I don't think she understands," I said to Nullar, then I felt a tug on the front of my dress. It was the blonde, and she was making more hand gestures that were becoming less messy and crisper.

And it dawned on me. She was using American Sign Language.

"Do any of you girls know ASL?" I shouted out to the women milling about the camp.

Every head moved back and forth, and my shoulders slumped. Well, shit. This was a real issue.

"Anybody got anything to write with? A pen and paper?"

"I'm fresh out," Marie shrugged, pulling at her dress.

"Here,"—Aggar slid a tablet-looking device across the ground to me— "use this."

Out of complete ignorance of how to use the thing, I touched the screen, and it flared to life. I was met with bizarre hieroglyphics, none of which I could make heads or tails of.

"Sorry, not tech-savvy." I slid the device back at Aggar.

The warrior took it, tapped it a few times, and made some marks before sliding it back. "Use your finger to write on the blank screen."

I studied what he wrote. It looked more like symbols rather than letters.

"You can erase it with a swipe down the side." I noticed the glossy track on the side and ran my finger the length of it. It worked just like he said, clearing the screen.

I handed the device to the girl trying to crane her head around to see who I was talking to. I moved in her line of sight, giving her the device.

"You can hear me, so you're not deaf."

The girl shook her head and touched her throat.

"So, you're mute, then?" I asked, and she nodded. "Can you write on this with your finger? Sorry, I don't know ASL."

She took the tablet and awkwardly held it in one hand while using her finger on the other. When she was finished, I read what she wrote. "Where are we?"

"What do you remember?" I drug my feet, unsure how to tell her that aliens had abducted her.

"Nothing."

Great! How to break this to her gently?

"What was that language the man spoke to you?"

"Um... not English."

The girl looked at me as if to say, duh.

"What's your name?"

"*Elise Grant*."

"Hi, Elise. I'm Lily Macintyre. Okay, so,"—I wet my dry lips—"try not to freak out." Probably not a good way to begin. "But you, along with a few other girls—and me, of course—were kidnapped."

"More like abducted," Marie was suddenly behind me, "by these creepy gray alien guys. Do you remember anything from the spaceship?"

Elise shared a look between us, then burst out in silent laughter, then sobered, looking around at her blue and silver surroundings. She started to sit up, weaving heavily. I grabbed to steady her into a seated position.

She fumbled with the tablet and scribbled a few words.

"Not a dream?"

"I'm afraid not." My smile was sympathetic.

"What planet is this?" Elise wrote.

"At least she's accepting it. But wait until she gets a gander at Spock." Marie thumbed over her shoulder where Nullar patiently waited to examine his patient.

I cut my eyes at Marie before answering Elise, "We crashed on a planet called Valose. We were rescued by these guys that are Valose warriors. They won't hurt you. And one is a medic that's been taking excellent care of you while you've been unconscious."

The girl tried to look around my shoulder.

"Are you ready to meet him?"

She nodded at me and swallowed hard.

"Now. They don't exactly look human," I began. "They sort of look like elves from the Lord of the Rings. Did you ever see that movie?"

Elise nodded.

"Except they're huge, have fangs like a vampire, and are covered in silvery-blue skin that camouflages," Marie added. "And they're super fit like bodybuilders and hot as fuck. Jakkar is off-limits, though, because that's Lily's boyfriend."

"Seriously, Marie. TMI." If I could strangle someone with my eyes right now... "Jakkar is not my boyfriend."

"Bitch, please." Marie looked at me sideways. "Going by the sounds you were making last night; you claimed his ass as yours."

My face erupted in flames. The selfless orgasms Jakkar had given me echoed with tingles between my thighs.

I cleared the knot of embarrassment from my throat. "Be that as it may—"

Sniffles grabbed my attention. Elise was silently sobbing into her hands.

"Sorry," I rubbed her back to comfort her, "we're being assholes arguing in front of you."

I turned to find Nullar easing forward. "Is she ready for treatment?"

"Let me introduce you first," I told him and turned back to Elise. "This is Nullar. He's a fantastic medic."

Elise looked up and recoiled but calmed right away when Nullar smiled. The guy had the best bedside manner of any physician.

"I'm just going to take a few scans," Nullar explained. "Make sure you're healing properly."

"Nullar is just going to scan the injury to your head. Okay?" When Elise nodded, I moved to the side, giving Nullar room to work.

Marie sidled up to me. "You think she's gonna be okay?"

"I hope so."

Draggar ambled by in the distance, carrying in bundles of sleeping pallets.

"Draggar looks like he needs help," Marie said, taking off after him.

As afraid as Marie had been when we'd first met the warriors, I still couldn't fathom why she was crushing on the scariest one in the bunch.

I stayed by Elise's side while Nullar looked her over. He spoke to her in that professional way of his that seemed to put a patient at ease. When he treated my ankle, I remembered something comforting and trusting about his gentle tone and kind eyes.

"What's he saying?" the girl wrote to me.

"We need to get her a translator," I told Nullar. "He's just saying that the bleeding from your subdermal hematoma has stopped, but you should still rest."

Nullar motioned for Aggar. The two males talked, and before I knew it, I was handed the translator I asked for.

Elise jerked back when I went to attach the translator behind her ear. "It's okay." I showed her mine. "It'll allow you to understand what they're saying."

She reluctantly allowed me to place the tiny device behind her ear. I made sure to keep a smile on my face so she wouldn't be scared when the thing sucked to her skin.

"Okay, Nullar, chat away."

The medic cleared his throat. "Are you feeling any dizziness? Headache?"

Elise looked at Nullar, wild-eyed, and touched the disc in wonder. She went for the tablet, scribbled her answer, and showed it to Nullar.

He studied it a moment and shook his head at me. "I cannot read your language."

"So much for breaching the language barrier, huh?" I took a look and read it to him. "She says no dizziness, but her head hurts, mostly on the right side."

"I'm not surprised. That's where you sustained the most damage," Nullar explained to the girl.

Elise agreed to a pain reliever, which Nullar administered, and relaxed back on the pallet.

A splash and giggles drew my attention to the pool. Willow and Isobel played in the crystal-clear water while a reluctant Layla dipped her toe in the shallow end.

I longed to immerse myself in that sparkling water, but Elise had taken ahold of my hand while Nullar rubbed that magic cream on her temples. She needed me, and I couldn't in good conscience leave her to enjoy a swim.

I noticed the guys had all turned their backs when the girls peeled off their white sack-like dresses and slopped them up on the bank, giving them privacy. Layla eventually eased into the water, and I swear I saw a hint of a smile play across her lips.

Rose, now finished assisting Aggar, helped Amy to the pool. They slid into the water with delighted expressions. Jealousy hit me hard until I glanced down at Elise and knew this was where I was needed.

Elise was fighting sleep, looking around at the unfamiliar and catching glimpses of the guys as they moved around the camp. Together, we watched the twin suns set over a glistening horizon, the bright blues of the dying rays a sight worthy of poetry.

Eventually, her eyes fluttered closed, but I waited until her breathing became heavy and rhythmic before I freed my hand from her gentle grip and joined Jakkar, where he was patiently waiting for me.

His eyes roamed my face as if he hadn't seen me in years and was trying to memorize every nuance. It was exhilarating to be the sole focus of a guy's attention, but at the same time, it made me feel all quivery and shy inside. My smile was bashful as I sat with him.

Jakkar handed me a pouch filled with all different kinds of small leaves. The Valose version of a salad, I supposed. I pulled out a thin leaf and nibbled on it. It was a little bitter but good.

Next, he gave me a pouch of dried meat. I didn't shy away from it like Layla. It was white and tasted like turkey jerky, so I convinced myself that was what it was.

"You didn't bathe with the other women." Jakkar pointed out. "Instead, you watched after one of your own."

"She was scared and needed me."

"Sacrifice is the trait of a good leader," he nodded sagely. "What leadership role did you play on your world?"

I chuckled. "Well, I was vice-president of my high school's science club. Does that count?"

"I'm certain that it does."

"But, seriously,"—my hand fluttered through the air— "I'm just a lab rat at my local hospital."

"What does a lah-b wratt do?"

"I... well, me and Amy are both laboratory technologists. We look at tissue samples under a microscope and determine if there is anything there that shouldn't be. You know, like cancer or viruses."

"So, you are a learned human? A civilian scholar in your world like Nullar?"

"Hmm..." I mused. "Not exactly like Nullar, but I suppose I qualify since I did go to college."

"I would have thought you a warrior." His full, sculpted lips perched, and all I could think about was the taste of his kiss. "When I first saw you in the cargo hold defending the women despite your injury, your ferocity spoke volumes to me."

I waved away his assumption. "Please don't mistake unadulterated fear with courage."

He assessed me then casually leaned against the rock at our backs. "A natural leader always stands strong for the people that follow," he stated.

I had never thought of myself as a leader, but how to convince Jakkar of that? I squirmed, never having been very comfortable talking about myself. Time to change the subject. "So, I know you said you don't get along with your brother, Sakkar, but under the circumstances, do you think it would be possible to talk to him about giving us a ride home?"

Every hair on my body stood at attention from the growl rising from Jakkar's throat. Fuck! I shouldn't have said anything. The rift in that relationship must run deeper than I thought. I just wanted to find a way home. Pissing off Jakkar was not my goal.

"Sorry, I didn't know that the two of you were completely on the outs." I touched his arm for emphasis.

"There is a great deal of strife between Sakkar and I having a conversation that doesn't involve swords. I cannot promise the use of his ship, nula."

I pushed aside the unexpected relief I felt, knowing that the perfectly good spacecraft capable of taking us home might be off-limits. I was glad now that I hadn't mentioned a possible way home to the girls.

There had to be another way off this planet. The girls wanted to go home, and I was just going to have to find it with or without Jakkar's help.

We finished our meal in awkward silence. The guys kept watch over the camp while the others took a dip in the pool. Once again, I was envious of their splashes, knowing how good it must feel to be clean.

I glanced around the darkening camp. The girls looked refreshed, lounging on their sleeping pallets and wearing fresh dresses we scavenged from the ship.

"You're not swimming?" I asked Jakkar when he remained by my side.

"Now that the others are finished,"—he stood and held out his huge, silver palm for me to take— "it is our time."

Lust rode me hard. Skinny dipping with Jakkar was an unexpected treat. Nervous flutters swarmed my belly, and I didn't hesitate over the possibility of more than just the heavy petting that hung between us.

Jakkar snagged a small pack, and we headed to the pool I'd been dying to dive into ever since I laid eyes on it. I sat on the water's edge and started to dip my toes in when my bubble cast reminded me that submersion might not be possible.

Jakkar pulled off his boots and sat next to me. "There's nothing to fear. No creatures live in the lood."

"I'm not worried about that." I gestured to my bubble cast. "Can I get this thing wet?"

"Yes." Jakkar unbuckled his kilt, leaving it on the bank next to me before diving in. His tight ass made a brief appearance before disappearing below the water's surface. His head broke the water, and he swam back with sure, even strokes. "I've had plenty of broken bones. The splinth is completely submersible."

Bubble cast forgotten at the sight of Jakkar rising out of the water like a slick, silver water god. His arms opened invitingly, and I accepted the invitation but not before the pervert in me took a quick peek at what was going on below the waterline.

Holy mother of monster cocks!

He was completely erect, a girthy temptation my pussy wanted intimate knowledge of. The water rippled around his waist, obscuring my vision, so I couldn't be sure if the bulges and ridges I was seeing were entirely accurate, but I aimed to find out.

He gathered me in his arms, holding me as close as his skin. The hot probe of his cock pressing between us was a promise of more mind-blowing orgasms. I shouldn't want an alien's cock inside me, but I didn't look at Jakkar that way. His differences were beautiful to me.

I wrapped my arms around his neck and my legs tight around his waist, squeezing his fat erection against my belly. He growled, so I did it again. His eyes narrowed on me in warning.

He could have had me back in that cave. I was so drunk on lust; I would have let him do damn near anything to me. So why did I get the impression he was holding back?

Jakkar playfully swished me around in a wide circle before walking us back to the bank, where he left his small pack. He fished around inside then pulled out a rough-looking bar of what I suspected was soap.

He gently set me back and handed it to me. The crush of his rejection was a sharp sting I didn't understand. There was no hiding he wanted me, so what was the problem? Was I too alien for Jakkar?

Jilted for a second time, the rawness of Kyle's transgression rubbed me hard. I hadn't had time to process that my future marriage was over since I'd been so busy being abducted by aliens and all.

Was I trying to rebound with Jakkar? Maybe I was reading the situation with him all wrong. When he held out his hand for me to join him in the pool, perhaps it was an invitation for bathing only.

Jakkar leaned back in the water, his eyes still on me, and pushed off the bottom in a backward surge. He turned and swam the length of the pool, putting distance between us. I ignored how fluid his powerful body looked moving through the water. Crestfallen, I turned my back to wash.

It felt amazing to peel off my dress. I created a rich lather rubbing the crudely made bar of soap between my hands. With quick hands, I scrubbed the sting of Jakkar's rebuff away.

I shouldn't compare Kyle to Jakkar. The two situations couldn't be more different. Kyle cheating on me with Swimsuit Model Barbie and Jakkar denying me the sex I craved was in no way comparable, yet rejection was rejection. No matter the nature of the dismissal, it all hurt the same.

I dipped down in the tepid water, letting it soothe me. Hair washed and skin cleaned, I shut my eyes only for them to fly open at the skim of large hands around my waist. Fingertips grazed my belly, an erotic flirtation to travel lower.

Jakkar stood so close behind me, the heat from his body radiated into mine. I tilted my head back to rest against his chest and widened my stance, an unspoken challenge for him to explore all of me.

Tingles drifted over my skin, his tantalizing touches drawing out a moan. I arched back in anticipation of his hand between my thighs, yet he merely skirted across my mons—so close to my clit that I wanted to scream—then up to brush the fullness of my breasts.

Jakkar snagged the soap and left me in burning agony. I swirled around just in time to see the knowing lift to his lips and the flirtatious glint sparkle in his eyes.

The big, silver bastard was a tease!

Well, two could play at that game. I watched him swim a few feet away. He stopped to take his turn with the soap and rinse routine. Then it was my turn to do some teasing of my own.

I raised up out of the water just enough to show him what he was missing. I had been told on more than one occasion that I had a nice rack. A tear dropped, full C-cup with pale pink nipples, not too small, not too large, but just right for Jakkar's perfect mouth.

My brazenness shocked me. I'd never acted this way, but something about the hell I'd been through pushed me outside my comfort zone. So, I went with the moment and cupped myself, thumbing my erect nipples to the intensity of his stare.

Come on, big boy, take the bait, I silently pled. *I could use a good dickstraction.*

Now that I had his undivided attention, time to cross the line. I kept one hand at my breast and let the other drift beneath the lapping water at my waist and thighs. My arm began to move, leaving no room for misinterpreting what I was doing to myself.

He scowled and barreled down on me like a freight train. His face was a mask of hunger. I should have run, not allow this stranger to ravage me. That was exactly what I wanted him to do.

As soon as he reached me, his lips slammed down over mine. He licked his way into my mouth, and my lips parted to greet his questing tongue. His mouth was an inferno—his tongue slick and seeking as he devoured me.

My arms flew around his neck, holding on as he moved us to a more private location. I clung to his massive shoulders when he deepened the kiss, holding on so I wouldn't fly away. Breathless, he pulled away and dropped his head to the base of my throat, breathing in my scent.

"You are a naughty female, my Lily," Jakkar's words thundered through me. "To tease me this way. You leave me no choice but to finish what you began."

"Please..."

Jakkar placed me on a smooth rock and stepped between my open thighs before dipping his head to latch onto one nipple. He sucked me in, rolling his tongue around the peaked tip. My body writhed against his, seeking more contact, craving to be pressed against every inch of his hard body.

His hand dove between my thighs, cupping my sex most deliciously. I ground into his touch and was rewarded with the invasion of his thick finger. His palm rubbed my clit, the friction robbing me of breath while I clutched at the release barreling down on me.

Just as I was about to fall off the edge, he disengaged, denying me what I needed. My hips curled, seeking relief only to jerk back and groan at the hot nudge of his cock. Solid rock sheathed in silk; my sex bloomed against the bulbous tip.

Jakkar was right. I was a naughty girl to crave a stranger's cock. If this should feel all wrong, then why did it feel so right? I was too far gone to care, so I widened the spread of my thighs, inviting him inside.

"Are you certain this is what you want?" Jakkar's voice was so hoarse, I hardly recognized it. "Once our spirits coalesce, it will be for all time."

The tip of his cock rubbed along my slick folds. Pleasure jolted through my veins, muddling the meaning of his words. I bucked and rolled against the tip, wanting him inside, needing him inside. Jakkar barked out a curse, tremors wracking his big body.

"Lily!" he gritted out through clenched teeth. "Yes, or no, female, I can't hold back much longer."

My clit got in on the action as I rocked against him. So close to coming, so close, I could see the rising storm behind my tightly closed eyelids.

"Yes!" I answered on a harsh exhale. "Hell, yes."

Every thick inch of him slid home in a single smooth stroke, stretching and burning his way inside until I felt the slap of his heavy balls against my backside.

Breathing was impossible. Holy shit! I'd never been this full.

Jakkar went still, letting me adjust to his invasion. Something warm and tingly culminated behind my breastbone. A sharp pinpoint of light crested, heating my blood and setting my sex on fire.

The very second Jakkar pulled back and thrust again, the dam broke free and sent me flying, soaring outside myself. All I could feel, and smell, was him. At this moment, we became one. Him plunging deep in a perfect rhythm, me meeting him thrust for thrust.

I could feel more than just his body pleasuring mine. I could feel him inside me. My soul rejoiced as if I'd been waiting for him my whole life—a lost companion finally found. As I climaxed repeatedly, it was more than just a release; it was a celebration, a union of more than just two bodies coming together.

We were one.

Jakkar seated himself fully and swelled inside me. His balls grew firm before hot jets of his release filled me. The spurt of his climax caused my inner muscles to contract. I clamped down around his thick cock and orgasmed again from the wicked sensation.

Jakkar held me close as I floated down from my orgasmic high. The water in the pool, disturbed by our lusty movements, lapped at my waist. Strong arms held me tight against the heat of solid muscle. A blissful peace settled around me. And for the first time in my life, everything felt as it should. My puzzle solved. My purpose found.

Mmm... I could stay like this forever.

A small sound of protest squeaked from my throat when he pulled back. I smiled up at him; his eyes were a warm silver as he smiled back. Usually so stern in his demeanor, the softness of his expression took me by surprise.

"You should do that more often." I brushed my fingers along his cut jaw, marveling at the silkiness of his beard stubble.

"What's that?"

"Smile." I kissed his chin. "You have a really nice one."

"I never had a reason until you."

His compliment curled my toes. "That's the nicest thing anyone's ever said to me."

"I am only speaking the truth," Jakkar whispered at my throat. The brush of his lips tingled down my spine. "My most precious spirit mate."

That romantic endearment no longer sounded over the top to me. He'd called me his spirit mate so many times before. After what we just shared, it matched the swell of tender affection I felt shifting inside me.

He pressed his cheek to mine while gently caressing the other. A hint of possessive pride drifted through me, mixing with my feelings of contented happiness. When he pulled away, I saw the same in the swirl of his silver gaze and somehow knew his feelings were intermingling with mine.

"The hur is late, and we need to rest for our journey on the next suns-rise." Jakkar lifted me from the rock and walked us over to the bank, where he left his pack.

I was reluctant to get out of the pool, knowing I might never come back here. I used the cloth he handed me to dry off. Mid-swipe, I paused.

There was a florid circle over my left breast that hadn't been there before. It was like a swirling tattoo of silver that glowed from within.

"What the hell..." My voice trailed off, and my eyes lifted to Jakkar in question. There, between his pectorals, was an identical mark.

His earlier words banged around inside my head. No longer drunk on lust, I examined his words before I had welcomed him inside my body. He said our spirits would coalesce.

At the time—inside my lust-saturated brain—I thought it had been pillow talk, Valose style. I thought Jakkar had been speaking metaphorically as a hopeless romantic talking about spirit mates and eternal love. I hadn't figured his words to be literal!

Jakkar's eyes flipped up to meet mine. "What is it, nula?"

Could he feel my turbulent emotions? Because something hot and possessive was churning inside my gut, and it wasn't me.

"Oh, shit!"

Chapter Fourteen

JAKKAR

I knew what was bothering Lily. There was no need for her to speak the words. I could feel that piece of her spirit now living within me, spinning in turmoil.

Her distress was my fault. I had heard bawdy talk of how sex with a spirit mate could blind a male to all else around him, that the urge to mate was crippling. I dismissed it as a perverse talk by males infatuated with the act. Now I knew firsthand what they described paled compared to what I felt with every fiber of my being.

I should have been stronger and resisted the urge. All I could think of was being buried inside her tight sheath. Even now, my cock lengthened with want.

I should have explained further. Of how coupling would initialize the bond between our spirits and make certain she understood all that was involved before I claimed her. She was not of Valose. How could she know our ways?

My gaze flitted to where she sat, huddled with the other females in the back of the hauler. Her eyes were shut against the wind whipping past as we journeyed. My rover brought up our formation's rear and in perfect line of sight to my spirit mate.

I would never in my life forget the horrified expression on her pretty face when she saw the shawra, the mark of the spirit mate that matched mine, over her heart. At the pool, she'd looked up at me through clouds of distrust.

When I explained again what it meant to be a spirit mate, her knees had buckled, the weight of understanding taking her to the ground. I caught her in my arms, and that was where she slept. She asked no questions, only tossed and turned as she processed the first sharing of our spirits. It had been a fitful sleep for the both of us, making this suns-rises journey even more taxing.

We were in the infant stages of the bonding. It was still possible to sever the connection. It was all my fault. I should have explained more, made her understand what it would mean when I claimed her. Coupling with a spirit mate was more than just rutting for pleasure. It was a communion of life essence between two kindred spirits.

It was selfish of me to take what she didn't understand from her. Now I must make amends with my female. Even though it went against the grain and would hurt worse than chopping off my hand to let her go, the only way to make this right was to request an audience with Sakkar and convince him to take the females back to Earth.

For now, I had to deliver the females safely to the settlement. Every milose that passed brought us closer to my home and relative safety. Outside those antiquated walls and with only a few warriors to protect the females, the jungle was that much more dangerous. We were all in favor of remaining close to the cliffs and traveling on the jungle's edge where fewer creatures roamed.

Lily's essence paled. I experienced her exhaustion as if it were my own. We had already ridden half a suns-rise. I had to remember these human women weren't as resilient as Valosian females.

"We stop in the next clearing," I called up to Aggar, who led our formation.

He glanced back at me with a pinched brow but didn't question. "Yes, Sia."

Once we reached the clearing, I dismounted my rover and rushed to Lily's side, lifting her out of the hauler and swinging her into my arms. She tensed, then relaxed against me in relief. I sat her on a spongy patch of grass and handed her my lood-skin, but she pushed it away and collapsed back.

I waved Nullar over. The medic immediately began scanning my female.

"I'm fine." Lily's hand fluttered in the air. "Just exhausted."

"How does your ankle feel?" Nullar inquired.

"Good." I helped Lily sit up. "The air here is just a little thinner than what I'm used to. Makes me lightheaded and hard to catch my breath sometimes."

Nullar nodded in agreement explaining how humans required only twenty-one percent oxygen to survive while the breathable air on Valose was higher. What she was feeling was normal for her. I studied my female's face and marveled at the differences in our species. I had so much to learn—

The swoop of the wetlock caught everyone off-guard. On silent wings, the beast flew low overhead with a squirming rynose clutched in its curved talons.

The rynose herd that had been quietly grazing nearby was now unsettled. Thundering hoofs vibrated the ground as the heavy creatures scattered in all directions.

A group of them was on us in secs. I barely had time to grab Lily and whisk her to safety. She wrapped her arms and legs around me in a constricting squeeze as I quickly climbed the closest tree.

Nullar followed. We clung to the branches as the herd raged below. Some had run headlong off the cliff, while others skidded to a halt on the loose dirt, kicking up dust clouds that hang heavy in the air before thinning out.

"We're safe up here." I hugged a trembling Lily to me. "The wetlock came for what it was after. It won't be back."

The tree we climbed began to list to one side. I exchanged an alarmed glance with Nullar as my words to Lily were proven wrong. The ground wasn't as stable as we thought. It cracked open in great crevices from the herd trampling so close to the edge, crumbling away in great chunks over the cliff and into the deep gorge below.

"If we climb down, we'll be trampled by the startled rynoses," I yelled to Nullar over the commotion below. "If we remain up here, we'll fall to the ground along with the tree."

"I'm not in favor of either scenario," he yelled back, moving to another branch when our tree tilted more.

Neither of us moved to climb down, taking our chances up in the canopy rather than risk certain death below under the hooves of the startled beasts.

Lily was stuck to me like a second skin. She hadn't spoken a word since the rynose stampede, but I could feel the echo of her fear inside me. She was terrified.

"Sia!"

Draggar yelled from below. He and most of the others were on the opposite side of the devastation.

"Go!" I yelled down at him with a great sweep of my arm. "Get out of here and get the females to the settlement."

"What of you?"

"We will find a way down and meet you there," I said with more confidence than I felt. "Now get out of here before the herd changes direction."

Draggar cursed. I watched the play of indecision cross his scarred face before he gathered the remaining group, loaded the hauler, and sped off on the remaining rovers.

A coldness settled around me when I didn't see Aggar among them. My head swiveled in all directions, peering at the ground until I caught movement on the edge of the panicked herd.

It was Aggar, and he was trying to muscle his way between the beasts. He was after something—more like someone. My heart sank when I saw a flash of a curly, bright mane and what Lily called peach skin tone.

"No. Rose!" Lily spotted the female at the same time I did. "We have to help her."

I held Lily tight when she started to squirm. It appeared Aggar was going in after her. It was foolhardy. He would be trampled to death the same as Rose. There was no way she had lived through a stampede of rynose, but the warrior looked determined.

Our tree groaned with great pops. Nullar and I exchanged a look. The beat of my ancillary heart sped up, pushing adrenalyne through my veins to increase the strength and endurance I would need to protect my mate.

"Hold on as tight as you can." I glanced down at the gorge where mountains of dirt were already piling up. "That's where we're headed. As large as this tree is, with any luck, we can ride out the landslide."

Nullar repositioned his hold on the thick branch he was perched. I did the same while Lily clung to me with a whimper.

The herd of rynose began to lose their footing, and one at a time, they fell over the edge with high-pitched howls. The world shook around us as the ground disappeared at an alarming rate. Our tree's thick roots were revealed, sticking out in a tangled web with nothing to latch onto.

"This is it!" I announced as our tree gave itself up to gravity.

Chapter Fifteen

LILY

In my periphery, I caught sight of Nullar's silvery hair flagging behind him as we toppled over the edge, slow at first and then frighteningly fast. From vertical to horizontal in a single breath, the tree Jakkar had climbed like a spider monkey, with me clinging to his front, turned into a log ride down a dirt waterfall.

The wind screamed past my ears as we plunged into the gorge at immeasurable speeds, riding out the landslide like a carnival ride gone wrong. The sudden stop was so jarring, Jakkar lost his hold, and we went sailing before landing in a hard, sliding heap.

Jakkar moved below me, his breath hot and raspy against my neck. Nullar sputtered from someplace nearby. The dirt clouded the air into something so thick and soupy; it would have been easier to chew than breathe.

"Everyone all right?" Nullar coughed.

"Good, I think." Still clinging to Jakkar, I moved my arms and legs, testing to see if everything still worked.

Jakkar did the same. "I'm good too."

"Well, that was fun," I lifted my head and laughed weakly, "but let's not do it again. Anyone see Rose?"

"Or Aggar?" Jakkar added.

"No," Nullar coughed and spat.

Gloomily, we tried not to think of the ones we lost and focused on climbing out of the tangle of broken branches caging us. Clear of the tree, it was hard to believe what we lived through with only a few scrapes and scratches.

From what I could tell, we rode the tree down about a hundred feet; I could barely see the top of the cliff. All around us was devastation. A new mountain of dirt and trees lay before us, blocking the gorge at one end. Going up didn't look to be an option. Behind us was our only path out. Unfortunately, it was back the way we'd come.

"Looks like we will have to backtrack—" Jakkar words seemed to get stuck in his throat.

Off in the distance, the silhouette of a male carrying a limp body appeared through the powdery debris. Jakkar raced towards him, Nullar close on his heels. I followed at a slower pace, my legs cramping with fatigue.

"Is she... is she okay?" My voice was thin at the sight of Rose's limp body.

Aggar's face was a frozen mask of fear. "She breathes, but barely." He looked to Nullar. "Save her?"

"I will do everything I can." Nullar motioned for Aggar to lay her on the ground.

Nullar reached to the side only to grab at air. I guessed he was reaching for his medical bag that wasn't there. His empty hand curled into a fist before he assessed Rose by touch, peering into her eyes and palpating her abdomen.

"She has several broken bones, including her ribs. I suspect by her wheezing exhalations she could have a punctured lung. I can't be sure without the proper medic equipment." Nullar's assessment made me weave on my feet.

"What can be done?" Aggar spoke calmly despite his frightened eyes.

"We can splint her bones and wrap her ribs." Nullar began looking around for anything to use for suitable splints. "That's all unless we can locate my medic bag or a comm to get us out of here."

The males all checked the pockets of their kilts. Three lood-skins and two pouches of rations were all they had between them.

"Wait. Maybe." Jakkar felt for something under the wetlock buckle on his kilt. "Fucking Helios! We have no comm. Not even the tracker Nekko attached to my buckle. Looks like we're on our own."

We scattered and searched the debris field for anything useful. I lifted a broken branch, and pain lanced through my left shoulder.

"Shit!" I hissed in pain, cradling my arm close to my body.

"What's wrong with your arm?" Jakkar gently questioned. "Are you hurt?"

"My shoulder. It's just sore from the wild ride down."

"I will have Nullar look at it." Jakkar turned to call out for Nullar, but I grabbed hold of his forearm, stopping him.

"It's nothing. It can wait," I spoke softly. "Rose needs him more."

"If you're certain." Jakkar placed his hand over my much smaller one. I liked the feel of his touch, even one this chaste.

My eyes drifted from his too handsome face to the matching swirling tattoos he called shawras in the center of his chest. "We need to talk... about what happened last night. After we help Rose."

I tugged my hand out from under his and moved away to keep searching. I wasn't prepared for the loss I felt from his touch. It was as if winter had bitch-slapped my soul. His echo which now lived inside me was contrite yet churned with determination.

After an endless search, Nullar's medical bag was nowhere to be found. The medic had already used small branches as splints and strips of fabric torn from Aggar's kilt to immobilize Rose's broken bones. He was finishing wrapping her ribs when the dragon's screech, which Jakkar called a wetlock, cut through the air like a warning.

"We can't stay here." Jakkar looked to the sky. "With so many dead rynose lying about, they are an easy meal that will soon attract many predators."

Aggar gathered a limp Rose in his arms. "The suns-fall will soon be upon us. We should run until we find a cave to shelter inside during the dark hurs, then figure a way out of this gorge."

I gasped in surprise when Jakkar scooped me into his arms. I held on tight as he took off through the gorge at the speed of a gazelle. On both sides of us, the sheer cliff walls became a blur. Still, I tried to keep an eye out for anything cave-like where we could take cover for the night.

The twin suns had traveled across the sky and touched the horizon before finding a small crevice in the wall. None of the males were breathing very heavily from their marathon run once we wriggled inside the tight space.

"I don't think this qualifies as a cave, but it will have to do," Jakkar mumbled.

We were cramped, having to line up like sardines, but the air was cool, and my skin was hot from the twin suns beating down on me. We'd been out in the open for hours, following a deep gorge of solid rock, with no giant jungle leaves to shade us.

I'd worried about Rose the entire way, worried about all of us, literally, running for our lives, worried if I'd ever see Amy again. Beautiful or not, what could be so appealing about living on a planet where everything counted us as an entrée?

The answer to my question blocked the entrance to our small cave with a boulder. Jakkar's body rippled with strength as he effortlessly shoved a massive rock in place to hide the crevice we'd squeezed into. The liquid silver of his gaze caught mine, and I flushed. I'd been pressed against his amazing chest for what felt like days, but one glance from him and my heart sped up, skipping a beat.

What was wrong with me? I'd never been one of those women that fell all over themselves because of a guy.

Warmth swirled and spread from my new tattoo in a soothing glow. I placed my hand over the mark expecting it to be moving, but it was still and only mildly warm beneath my palm.

The warmth I felt came from within, like being hugged from the inside.

Whatever it was I experienced with Jakkar needed to be discussed. Sex shouldn't physically change a person, and I was definitely changed.

I scooted over as Jakkar approached. He crouched before me, handing me the waterskin attached to his belt. I took a few sips and gave it back.

"You need to drink more." Jakkar pushed the skin back at me.

"If that's all the water we have, it needs to be rationed." I held up my hand to ward him off. "When Rose wakes up, she'll need it more than me."

"Aggar and Nullar have loodskins as well." Jakkar wagged the skin at me again. "Drink."

I wasn't one to be told what to do, but I took the skin and made a show of drinking more. Once Jakkar's scowl turned pleased, I gave the skin back. "Happy?"

Jakkar nodded briskly and settled in next to me. We were seated closest to the entrance, with Nullar and Aggar caring for Rose in the far back.

"How is she?" My soft words echoed off the dense walls.

"The same," Nullar stated gravely.

"In one of the rooms on the ship, I saw medic equipment," Aggar began. Cold chills washed over me with where he was going with this. "My scanners were lost in the landslide, but as far as we've already run, if I follow this gorge, I believe I could make it back to the crashed spacecraft by the next suns-rise."

"It is too dangerous to travel during the dark hurs, Aggar," Jakkar warned.

"I can't just sit here and do nothing, Sia." Aggar's heartfelt plea brought tears to my eyes. "Rose is so much like the sister I lost to the alien germ. I won't let another sister die."

"And what if you make it back to the medic lab, Aggar?" I was surprised at Nullar's challenge. "Even if I tell you what to look for, you'll have to run all the way back here for me to treat her. Now you're looking at another suns-rise, maybe two, and that's if you're lucky enough not to be eaten by nocturnal beasts. It's better for all of us if we stay together. You won't be doing her any good if you're dead, and I need your help to carry her."

Aggar's pleading eyes meet Jakkar's. When his leader didn't dispute Nullar's sound reasoning, he spat a flurry of curse words then slumped back against the rock wall in defeat.

"We will continue at the twin suns first light," Jakkar swore. "As a group, we will return to the alien ship so Nullar can heal Rose."

Aggar's face ran through a myriad of emotions until settling on resignation. He wanted so desperately to help Rose. She was special to him but not as a love interest as I'd first thought.

We all wound down for the night. The cave grew eerily quiet with only the occasional rustle from Nullar at the far end as he regularly took Rose's vitals.

Jakkar and I moved closer to the entrance with Jakkar on the side of our huge rock door.

"Can we talk about this?" I touched the silver tattoo over my heart.

Jakkar glanced to the back of the cave before focusing on me with a brief nod.

"Tell me what all this spirit mate stuff is about. What does it mean for us?" The others could probably listen in on our whispered conversation, but I needed answers.

When Jakkar began to thrum, I could feel the rhythmic vibrations dancing inside me as if I were making the sounds myself. "Spirit mates are complementing spirits. Once they find each other, the need to couple becomes an urgency impossible to ignore."

"Couple, as in sex?"

"Yes." His heated expression burned. "Mating is the catalyst needed for the spirits' first bonding."

"And this?" I swallowed hard at the implications and touched my tattoo.

Jakkar placed his hand over his identical mark. "These are shawras, the portals from where our spirits can coalesce."

This guy was talking about literal soulmates. Soul. Mates. Something back on Earth only realized in romance novels. It wasn't like I didn't believe in love because I loved many people. My dad, Amy, at one time, Kyle... but love was a feeling, not a tangible thing that could come out and play.

With Jakkar, I could feel a part of him inside of me. It wasn't creepy like a parasite or something but a gratification as if the thing I'd been looking for my whole life was finally found. I still felt like me, only more complete.

He was waiting for me to process what I'd just been told. I could hint the calm of his patience. I was gaping at him like a fish because what else could I do? An echo of me was now living inside him, which meant he had an inkling of what I was feeling.

I shook myself out of my stupor. "And what happens if we continue to... couple?"

I really wished his beautiful eyes wouldn't swirl and dilate in that provocative way. It was like he was trying to take all of me in at once. I felt stripped raw yet vulnerable in the most powerful way. And none of that made any damn sense.

All I knew was Jakkar could see all of me, even inside my soul. I was his, and he was mine. It was as simple and complex as that. I craved him like no other. I wanted to crawl under his scales and wallow in his essence.

"The more we mate, the stronger our bond becomes." Jakkar placed his hand over my shawra. "Do you feel a heated tug here as if some part of you is reaching out to me?"

"Yes." I felt the tug. It was more like a yearning, a calling that drew me to Jakkar like a moth to a flame. I was powerless to stop it.

"When I first saw you back on the ship, I was terrified." I laughed nervously. "Then there was something... oddly familiar about you. I couldn't understand why. I still don't understand it, but for some strange reason that I don't want to admit, I feel like I'm where I'm supposed to be. Yet, I want so badly to go home. It's all so confusing. I don't know..."

Jakkar ran gentle fingers along my jaw and tilted my chin to peer into my eyes. "I'm truly sorry for the position I've put you in. I swear, I will speak with Sakkar about returning you and the others to Earth. No matter how painful it will be for me to let you go, if I keep you here, I will be just as guilty as the ones that abducted you from your home planet." He smoothed his hand over my cheek and tunneled his fingers through my hair. "I should have explained to you fully about the bond. My only excuse is that I was impatient to make you mine. You see, I've been waiting for you the whole of my life."

"Wow." The electricity of his words zinged through my veins. "If we were in a bar, that would be the greatest pick-up line ever."

I was half-joking, but, in all seriousness, this spirit mate stuff was the real deal. It was too soon to honestly say I was in love with Jakkar. It'd only been a couple of days since we met, but there was no denying the solid connection between us.

If I could find a way home, that connection would be severed. And I had a feeling; it would be more painful than mourning the death of a loved one.

Chapter Sixteen

JAKKAR

Aggar's body vibrated with urgency. Just as soon as the first rays of the twin suns had peeked over the horizon, the warrior was bouncing on the balls of his feet at the entrance of our tiny cave.

Nullar made Rose ready to travel, and I pushed aside the boulder we used as a barrier between us and the outside. As soon as I gave Aggar a nod to exit, he gently gathered a still unconscious Rose in his arms and impatiently shuffled his feet as he waited for the rest of us to leave the cave.

"Let's be on our way." I swung Lily into my arms, and we all took off at a fast clip.

"If we keep up a fast pace, I think we can make it to the space-craft before the end of the suns-rise." Aggar looked to the sky, assessing our location to that of the fading moons.

Lily's grip around my neck tightened, her spirit shrinking into a tight, little knot. I wasn't eager to return to the ship either, but what choice did we have? It would take many suns-rises to double back toward the settlement, and Rose didn't look like she had that much time. And the safest place from the jungle for Lily was inside the shelter of the spacecraft.

We hadn't covered much ground before Aggar skidded to a halt. I looked overhead in anticipation of a wetlock attack, only to find a clear sky. When I looked down—at first, I didn't notice it. The object blended so perfectly with the cliff wall where it rested.

"What in the Spirits is it?" Nullar's jaw hung loose in disbelief.

"Looks like a shuttle." Aggar cautiously walked around the spherical craft.

"Does it belong to Sakkar?"

Aggar flicked me a glance before carefully handing Rose off to Nullar. "No. It's not Sakkar's. I've never seen anything like this before. Has to belong to the Gretolics. Maybe it was flung from the craft on impact."

The crash replayed through my mind. I recalled how the ship had bounced before skidding to its final resting place. Aggar could be right.

"If I can find a way inside,"—Aggar ran his hands over the sleek hull— "maybe we can fly it back to the settlement."

"When was the last time you flew a spacecraft, Aggar?" I asked.

"Never, but I'm willing to try if it means fast-tracking Rose to where she can get medic care."

I had never flown before, and I wasn't keen on it now, but Rose looked severely injured. I wasn't even sure if she was still alive.

To Aggar, she was the younger sister he'd lost to the alien germ. If a few milose of discomfort meant saving another female, I was not going to interfere.

"Let me down." Lily patted my chest. "You guys sure don't believe in pee breaks. My bladder is about to burst."

My head whipped to Nullar at her complaint. "You must see to my female. Her bladder is going to rupture."

"No. No. Just a figure of speech." Lily waved me off while walking away. "I'll just be behind this rock. And, no, I don't require an audience."

I pulled my swords free from the straps at my back and guarded over her and the others. Nullar knelt on the ground with Rose, and to my surprise, I saw her move. Just the flutter of her fingertips, but that was enough to assure me she lived.

After finishing with her business, Lily all but collapsed on the ground to hover over Rose while Nullar did what little he could to help her.

Time was ticking, the twin suns had moved across the sky, and I was about to give up hope and suggest we move on when Aggar let out a whoop. "Over on this side." He careened around the hull. "I found a door."

Aggar gently lifted Rose from the ground, and we followed in his easy steps. The door to the vessel was narrow but wide enough for Lily. My males and I had to turn sideways to wedge ourselves through.

Inside, it was a strange contraption. There was a sky's worth of twinkling lights on every surface. When the door whispered shut behind us, I forced myself not to flinch. Lily stuck close to my side as we lapped the interior of the small vessel, looking for anything useful. It warmed me that she sought out my protection.

"Strange how none of this is visible from the outside, yet we can see through the hull as if we're still standing outside," Nullar marveled.

"If I can get this thing to fly, we could be back at the settlement in no time. Maybe pick up Draggar and the others if we can find them on the way. It would be better if Nullar could treat Rose at the settlement. And we would have a ship." Aggar's eyes sparkled at the prospects.

"Is there a comm we can use to notify Nekko and Draggar?" I asked, hopeful.

"None that I can use," Aggar's fingers tapped several lit buttons. "Their frequencies are nothing I can decipher."

I wasn't in any hurry to have my feet leave the ground, but there was merit in what he suggested. "Fly it, if you can."

Aggar managed to squeeze into a seat designed for the thin form of the Gretolics and immediately went to work figuring out what all the lights and switches on the console did while Nullar made Rose comfortable on a platform that slid out from the wall. Lily and I explored the small craft, searching for anything that could be of help.

"I'm so thirsty." Lily pressed her lips together in a thin line.

I handed her my loodskin. "You should not have relieved your body of precious fluid if you were dehydrated."

"It's not like I'm given a choice," Lily snorted. "When you gotta go, you gotta go. So, you guys don't relieve yourselves?"

"We do, but only when certain conditions warrant."

Lily eyed me strangely before drinking, then popped open a compartment in the wall. "No food. No water. Only a bizarre thingy that kind of looks like a medic scanner. Hey, Nullar, is this something you can use?"

The medic turned. His eyes widened when he saw what Lily held up. "Yes! What else is in there?"

As Nullar barrelled over and sifted through the compartment, Lily moved out of his way. He pulled out a small pile of items and carried them back to where Rose rested.

The next compartment Lily opened held an array of materials in shocking colors. "Oh my god! No fucking way." Lily marveled. "This," she shook a garment at me, "this is what I was wearing when I was abducted. And this is my purse… Oh my god, I never thought to see any of this stuff ever again."

I joined her when she sat in the center of the pile, looking at each garment before carefully folding and setting them aside in neat stacks. She found more of those ornate pouches that appeared to be made from animal skins. Tears streaked down her cheeks as she pulled out little cards with strange writing and a small picture of a female.

"These are driver's licenses," she sniffed. "This girl was among the ones that didn't make it. She died in that fucking cage."

I pulled her into my arms and thrummed. "I swear on my honor as a Valose warrior, I will see to your dead, Lily. First, we must help the living, and getting you and the other women to safety is my first priority."

"Thank you," she hiccupped and relaxed against me. "If it weren't for you and the other guys, we would've never gotten out of those cages. You saved us."

I wasn't worthy of the admiration reflected in the pools of her watery eyes. It was wrong to bind her to me and not tell her the whole truth of my exile.

"It wasn't right of me to mate with you before you realized what it meant."

"It wasn't as if I was pushing you away." Her face flushed. "I had instigated it by teasing you in the water. The truth is,"—Lily leaned in so close, her hot breath washed across my scales in a varying display of blue— "I wanted to have sex with you."

If we had been alone, I would have split her thighs and mated her until we both saw stars. I couldn't wait to get her inside my skypod, stretch her out on my bed, and show her just how much I wanted her.

"It isn't fair for you to shoulder all the blame for where we are now," Lily placed her palm over my shawra. "I'm just as much at fault."

"You're not of my world." I dropped my face to her throat and breathed her in. "I should have made it clear we weren't just mating for pleasure."

She shuddered under my questing hands as I gathered her to me and thrummed loud enough to rattle the shuttle. Throats were cleared by the males as the air between us sizzled. I wanted to shout, to Helios with them, and have my female beneath me. As much as my body, my spirit, ached to be joined with hers. But this was not the place for such intimate things.

I brushed her lips with mine before pulling away with great effort. She followed, crawling higher into my lap, wanting more. "I would gladly couple with you, my most precious spirit mate, but the more we mate, the stronger our bond will grow. It will be that much harder to break if I can convince Sakkar to return you home."

Lily's gaze was wide open. "You would make amends with your brother to help the other girls and me, even though I can feel how much you would loath doing it?"

"Yes. It won't be as simple as what you think. I will have to request an audience with Sakkar. He may not accept."

"Request an audience?" Her brows pinched together. "You make it sound like he's some sort of monarch."

My hearts sped up as she guessed the truth. "He is the... Sia of Clan Huren. Their ruler." I paused a beat before adding, "As once was I."

I studied her face as my words sank in. "You were a king?"

I bobbed my chin, nuzzling the top of her head. "Sakkar is my twin. Our sire wanted the two of us to rule together. He said that having twin rulers on different ends of the spectrum would be complementary." Lily pulled back to look me in the eye as I told my truth. Her admiration never wavered. "I was trained as a Valose warrior while Sakkar was schooled as a scholar."

"Brains and brawn."

"Exactly. Our sire thought, together, we would make a more complete ruler. Sakkar had a different plan than I for the future of Huren." I fiddled with the hem of her dress where she was seated in my lap, reflecting on that day when Sakkar's males escorted me to the gate as if I were a criminal. "Our difference of opinion came to a head, my crown removed, and I was exiled."

"That was a shitty thing for him to do to you."

"There's more. If I'm granted an audience with Sakkar, I will have to make your presence known to him. He could insist all females be placed under his protection since I am an exile."

"We're Earthlings. He can't tell us what to do."

"Technically, you and the other females were found inside Huren territory. I'm no longer a citizen of Clan Huren. I have no rights, and being the Sia of Huren, Sakkar can lay claim to anything found within his territory."

"None of that sounds very promising." Her much smaller hand squeezed mine. "I'm glad I didn't mention Sakkar's spaceship to any of the girls. I was afraid of getting their hopes up. Maybe, we should find another way and skip Sakkar altogether."

"That might be our wisest choice." I skimmed my fingers along her jaw. No matter how hard I fought the urge, I couldn't stop touching her. "I swear on my honor as a Valose warrior, I will help find you and the other women find a way back to Earth."

"I can feel how much that hurt for you to say," Lily rubbed her sternum. "If you don't want me to go, how can you promise that?"

"Because you are my spirit mate, and I can deny you nothing, even if it means giving you up." My throat constricted as I choked out the words.

"That's the most selfless thing I've ever heard."

"I'm only speaking from my hearts." I pressed her palm over where my life's blood beat through me.

Lily gasped and moved her hand around my chest. "Wait! You have two hearts? How is that possible?"

"This one beats to give me life." I took her hand and placed it over my primary heart and then over my newly awakened ancillary heart. "And this one beats only for you."

Chapter Seventeen

LILY

You could have knocked me over with a feather. Never in my life had I ever heard words like that spill from a guy's mouth. If he was trying to woo me, it was freaking working.

Something inside me gathered, swirled hot, and pressed against my breastbone, wanting to get out to be with him. It was the tug Jakkar had spoken about.

I'd never been this conflicted in my life. I wanted to see Earth again, where everything was familiar. To see my dad. To get back to my boring ole routine of working for the weekends. To hang out with Amy or go to dinner with Kyle.

Amy was here, and Kyle was no more. Even though this planet was full of scary monsters that wanted to eat me, I had this incredible silver elf with uber-sword skills who had declared it his job to protect me.

Whenever I imagined myself on a ship bound for home, a hollow ache would bloom in my heart, and the warm swirls that swam behind my breastbone would become a torrent of anguish.

Every time I pictured my dad's face, it would crush me to think of never seeing him again, of him not knowing what had happened to me. He would never know if I was dead or alive. I didn't want him to worry unnecessarily. If I could just get a message home, I wouldn't feel so torn if I stayed. I knew it in my soul that my heart belonged to Jakkar.

Decision made, relief slammed into me so hard, I listed to one side. Or... maybe that was the floor.

Still seated in Jakkar's lap, we slid with the tilt of the shuttle. Aggar's hands flew over the twinkling dashboard, righting us before we left the ground in a silent hover.

"A warning next time, Aggar," Jakkar cursed.

"Sorry, Sia." Aggar threw an enormous grin over his shoulder. "I'm as surprised as you are."

We left the gorge behind in a gentle ascent. Nullar threw himself over Rose's prone form as we took to the sky.

It was a woozy up and down as Aggar figured out the controls. If the shuttle weren't cloaked, I imagined we would look like a stray soap bubble bobbing through the sky.

The craft was completely transparent from the inside looking out. Jakkar was focused on the invisible floor, his eyes huge inside his skull as we climbed above the tree line. He held me so tight I thought my bones would crack.

Aggar rolled some sort of ball embedded in the console under his palm, and we shot forward, the jungle speeding beneath us. Valose looked incredible from up here. The lush, tropical valley with sapphire mountains off in the distance pierced the clouds.

"There they are!" Jakkar shouted, pointing at slight movement off in the distance. "Can you land this thing?"

"I believe so." Aggar's answer did nothing to boost confidence. "Maybe that slight clearing up ahead."

Our descent was anything but smooth. It didn't matter. I was too excited to see the flash of Amy's fiery head to care about all the sudden drops and nauseating swoops.

Our landing went unnoticed. Their vehicles zipped through the jungle like the speeders in Star Wars. They kept coming fast until they were nearly upon us.

Jakkar ran to the door just as Aggar opened it. The sweet jungle air rushed inside as Jakkar jumped out to a surprised Vallon, who was in the lead and towing a rover with Rayyar strapped to the seat. The warrior all but cartwheeled to a stop, the shocked look on his face almost comical.

I raced past Jakkar to the hauler. Amy lunged out of the bed, tackling me to the ground. Marie was right behind her. We hit the jungle floor in a tangle of arms and legs.

"I never thought I'd see you again," Amy wailed.

Marie talked over her, "I'm so sorry for being a crazy bitch."

"I'm so happy to see you all!" I cried.

It was an all-out blubber fest as all the girls crowded around us. Even Elise, who looked to be recovering nicely from her head injury, got in on the hugs.

"We need to go." Jakkar broke up our reunion. "It will be safer for the women to ride in the shuttle the rest of the way to the settlement."

"Okay," I stood and brushed the blue dirt off my hands. "All right. Come on, ladies. Follow me."

The warriors were crowded around the shuttle, poking at it with puzzled expressions as we made our way to the door. No one was happy about boarding an alien vessel, so I had to coax the girls inside—especially Layla, who looked shellshocked, all bug-eyed and trembling.

I had the perfect distraction. Once everyone had seen that Rose would be okay, I handed over the bundles of clothes and personal items to the squealing girls. Their eyes danced over the clothes, and garments switched hands until the items had been returned to their owners.

Layla was especially pleased to see her Gucci handbag. A long-awaited smile glided over her face.

Too many garments were left unclaimed, including purses and belts of the dead whose bodies we had to leave behind in the cargo hold. Jakkar had sworn he would send a squad to honor them as soon as we reached the settlement, and I believed him.

He was my hero, my silver savage, who could conquer anything. He appeared at the door as if called, and I flung myself into his arms. The door closed behind him, and the shuttle began to lift off the ground.

"Are we just gonna leave them?" Marie pointed down through the transparent floor to the warriors mounting what was left of the vehicles after the rynose stampede.

"Draggar and Vallon will take the rovers and hauler back to the settlement," Jakkar said. "The shuttle can't carry the vehicles and all the supplies from the alien spacecraft. Worry not, Marie, Draggar is a capable warrior."

"I know." Marie nodded, misty-eyed as we lifted off the ground, the males growing smaller and smaller until the heavy foliage of the jungle swallowed them from sight.

My heart bled for her. If the roles were reversed and that had been Jakkar left on the ground, capable warrior or not. I would be freaking out too. This planet was too dangerous by far.

I squeezed Jakkar, thankful to have him in my arms. He brushed his lips across mine before setting me back. "Once we reach the settlement, I will need your help to look after the females." His fierce mask of authority back in place. "You're a natural leader. They will look to you for guidance."

"Of course."

"Wow!" Layla's shout startled everyone. Her palms were pressed to the transparent walls like a little kid on her first airplane ride. I went to sit among the girls crowded in the back of the shuttle. "Is that where we're going?" Her apprehension forgotten, she pointed to a giant, shimmering dome poking up through the dense jungle a vast distance away.

"That is the City of Huren," Jakkar grumbled, going to stand behind Aggar's seat at the console. "We won't be going there."

"Oh." Layla slumped down with her back against the wall, shrinking back into her shell. Isobel and Willow flanked her, chatting away to try and cheer her up.

"So, what's up with you and the big guy?" Amy whispered close to my ear. "And don't say nothing because I'll know you're lying."

A goofy grin stretched across my face before I grew serious. "Listen, I need you to do something for me when we get all of you back home."

"Wait just a damn minute, Lil." Amy tossed up her hand. "You aren't going back with us, are you?"

"That must be some serious cock to get you to stay on this fucking death planet," Marie blurted out.

I shot Marie a dirty look and turned back to Amy. "I need you to give my dad a message. Tell him I'm okay and that I found... my soulmate."

"Lil, you can't be serious?"

I tugged the neck of my dress down to show her my shawra.

"Oh my fucking god, he branded you!" Amy gasped.

"No, Amy, it's not a brand," I rushed to explain. She looked ready to pounce on Jakkar. Once I told her about spirit mates and the bond created from the coalescing of souls, she went from ready to kill to ready to have me committed. "I'm not crazy, so stop looking at me like that."

"You actually believe all that bullshit he told you?"

"I do, Ames, and it's not bullshit. It's true," I implored. I glanced over at Jakkar, but he was deep in conversation with Aggar. "I can feel his emotions as if they were my own. He's a part of me now. If I leave this planet, I will never feel whole again."

"Oh, sweetie." Amy tilted her head at me, unbelieving.

"Promise me, if Jakkar can find you a ride back home, you'll tell my dad that I'm okay." When Amy gave me an exasperated look, I pleaded, "Please, Amy. I've made my decision. I haven't been brainwashed or coerced. What I feel for him is real. Our souls were meant to be together."

Amy shook her head with a small smile of disbelief. "Lily, you're a smart girl. I can't even..."

"I'll tell him for you, Lily," Marie offered.

I was glad I had already been sitting down because you could have knocked me over with a feather. Marie, the most unlikely person on the planet, was supporting me. No sarcasm. No smart assed comment to follow. Just pure understanding, as if she knew exactly how I felt.

"You believe me?" I gawked at Marie.

"Yeah." Marie lifted a shoulder. "Yeah, I do."

"Thank you." I squeezed her hand.

"What did you guys do to Aggar? He looks so intense," Marie bobbed her head at the warrior flying our craft. "Not his usual smiling self."

"He's very upset about Rose," I said. "She reminds him of the sister he lost when the alien germ wiped out all their females."

"I'm sorry, what?" Amy grabbed my shoulder and pulled me around. "What germ, Lily? What females are you talking about?"

Shit. I'd been so preoccupied trying to survive. I hadn't had a chance to tell Amy what I had learned from Jakkar. After seeing her reaction to my shawra, I was reluctant to tell her anything else.

It wasn't fair of me to withhold information like this. So, I gathered all the girls around and explained the alien germ Jakkar's brother had brought back from one of his trips off the planet that had infected and killed all the females from Clan Huren. I told about Jakkar's exile for standing up to his brother and how a small group of males had joined him.

"That's where they're taking us. To the settlement where Jakkar and the other exiled males live." The girls all stared at me with unhinged jaws. "I know it's a lot to take in, but we'll be safe with Jakkar and the others until they find a spaceship to fly everyone back to Earth."

"We are the only females on this planet?" Willow eyed me suspiciously. The shock of being abducted was wearing off, and she was presenting to be a force of nature. "What makes you so sure they aren't going to do something … horrible with us."

Isobel audibly gulped. "They could pimp us out."

Chattering chaos ensued. Jakkar and Nullar's eyes swung to meet mine. The echo of Jakkar's concern swirled in my gut. I had to put a lid on this before panic could take root. "Ladies, listen to me." I raised my voice above theirs. "They aren't going to hurt us. If they were going to force themselves on us, they would have already."

"They did get us out of those cages and saved us from the giant insect things," Isobel reasoned, glancing at Aggar with shy eyes.

"And they fought off that saber-toothed cat," Willow chimed in.

Elise eagerly nodded, her hands flying to form words none of us understood.

"Lily's right," Marie said. "They gave up their sleeping pallets for us. They hunted and fed us. If they were going to rape us or something, they already would have. They've given us no reason to be afraid of them. We should feel perfectly safe."

"And Nullar has healed every one of us," I added for good measure. I left out the part about my shawra and spirit mates. It was all too fresh and felt too personal. Besides, once Jakkar found a ship, they would be on their way back home. What was the point in telling them? They weren't staying.

"You and Jakkar are a couple?" Layla's candid question stunned me into silence.

"It's not exactly a secret you guys have been messing around," Isobel giggled. "You and Jakkar got pretty noisy at the pool. The rock walls echo."

My face was on fire. Everyone knew about us, so what was the point in hiding it now? "Jakkar and I are spirit mates." I tugged the neck of my dress down to show them my shawra.

"Holy. Shit." Willow leaned forward for a closer look.

"It's called a shawra. Jakkar has the same mark." All eyes swung to Jakkar, then back to me. "It's a port where our spirits can join, creating a bond between us."

"A bond, how?" Isobel cringed.

"It's sort of personal," I blurted out defensively.

Willow's eyes widened, and her mouth dropped open. "You bond through sex?"

Elise, full of curiosity, frantically scribbled on her tablet and flashed it at me. "Oh my god, you had sex with an alien!"

This conversation had quickly gone sideways. "All you need to know is that we're safe with Jakkar and his people and that they are going to find a way to take you all home."

"What about you?" Isobel asked. "Are you staying here with your new alien boyfriend?"

"How soon can we go home?" Layla asked, hopeful.

I ignored Isobel's question in favor of Layla's. "I don't know for sure yet, but Jakkar will do everything he can to find a ship. I promise."

The shuttle went quiet as everyone ruminated over the facts before them. I looked around at all the expectant faces with a knot in my gut and prayed that the tether of hope I had extended wouldn't come up short. I promised Jakkar would help them get home, but what if he couldn't?

Willow stared hard at me as if she were trying to read my mind. Isobel chewed on her lower lip, deep in thought. Elise studied the tablet in her hands, and Marie stayed quiet, glancing at Aggar every few seconds, where he sat at the console flying the shuttle. Layla just stared longingly out of the clear-walled shuttle at the glittering dome covering Huren as it passed by in the distance.

"I want to get a look at that germ." Amy broke the silence.

"Me too, Ames," I said. "I want to see what killed the female population on this planet. What kind of germ is it? A virus? A bacterium? I don't know."

"I'm curious as hell." Amy shifted and whispered in my ear. "What if this germ can kill human females?"

I didn't want to think about that, yet it was a real possibility that needed to be explored. "I'll ask Nullar as soon as we reach the settlement if we can take a look at it."

"Yep," Amy eyed me. "And we'll be discussing this spirit mate nonsense and you not going home."

"I've made up my mind."

"We'll see," Amy said curtly. My bestie was pissed at me. I didn't want her to leave mad, so I had to find a way to make her understand.

"Is that it?" Willow asked, pointing to a wooden wall tall enough to keep out King Kong. "Is that the settlement?"

"Yes," Jakkar answered.

I left the girls to join Jakkar, where he stood behind Aggar at the shuttle's console.

As we flew closer, more of the settlement came into view. It was apparent it had once been a war zone. There was nothing left but a footprint of crumbling structures and cracked roads, a skeleton of a city that had once been prosperous.

My heart lurched and sank to my toes. A sense of loss significant enough to buckle my knees washed over me. The wave of grief inside me belonged to Jakkar. I squeezed his hand and instantly felt the comfort I extended. He smiled sadly. I willed him to know how sorry I was for his loss. In response, he squeezed back.

Collected in the center were strange metallic balloons floating in a group. Besides a lookout tower, it was the only thing that appeared intact. "What are those?"

"Skypods," Jakkar said. "Temporary housing until we can create a protective dome over the settlement. It's safer to be off the ground during the dark hurs."

"Your house is a balloon?"

Jakkar glanced down at me. "I don't know that word, bay-loon?"

I opened my mouth to explain when Jakkar tensed at my side. At what looked like the main gate, a chock of males stood facing each other in typical stand-off fashion. With all the posturing, it looked like shit was about to hit the fan.

"We've got company," Aggar growled.

"Go around for a pass," Jakkar ordered. He dropped my hand to move closer to the forward-facing hull.

Aggar swept the shuttle around. I was impressed by how quickly he learned how to maneuver this thing like a pro.

"What is Sakkar doing leading an army?" Aggar cuffed. "He never leaves the luxury of the palace unless it's to board his spacecraft."

"Or unless there's something he wants." Jakkar turned and pierced me with fierce eyes.

Chapter Eighteen

JAKKAR

"Can you land us in the clearing next to the skypod field without detection?" If my brother thought he could waltz in and take what was mine, he was sadly mistaken.

"Consider it done, Sia." Aggar set us silently on the ground.

"Remember what I told you if we are overrun?" My eyes never left Sakkar, standing so arrogantly at my gates.

"Yes, Sia."

"Fly the women out of here and don't look back." I kept my voice low to not reach Lily's ears and shifted my weight between my booted feet. I was bristling for a fight. "Protect them at all costs."

His lips twitched to argue, but instead, Aggar gave me a brisk nod. I could see Nekko standing in my stead with my warriors at his back. I needed to get out there and find out Sakkar's intentions.

My eyes flitted to Lily. I promised to find her a ship home. It irked me to think I would have to ask Sakkar for his help to make that happen. As Lily stared back at me with soulful eyes full of trust, my ancillary heart pounded against my ribcage, and I knew there was nothing I wouldn't do for her, even if it crushed my spirit.

I had to confront my brother. As much as I despised him, I would first need to discover why he was at my gates before I announced the presence of the women. My biggest obstacle was trust. I had no idea how I would request the usc of his ship when I didn't even trust him with the knowledge that I found females aboard that crashed vessel.

He proved himself an irresponsible leader by bringing back that germ from the stars and then making plans for another journey without a beat of hesitation. He learned nothing from his mistake.

Though my walls were made of wood rather than a complex technology, Lily and the other women were safer with me. I would make sure nothing happened to them. I could not say the same for Sakkar.

"Stay with the females on the shuttle until I come and get you," I gently gripped Lily's shoulders. "Aggar and Nullar will remain here to protect you and the other females."

"What about you?"

"I need to meet with my brother." I felt Lily's trepidation like a swarm of mothis in my belly. "Don't worry. I will have capable warriors at my back."

"Be careful."

My scales flashed blue and silver, singing with the warmth of her concern. With a nod, I planted a hard kiss on Lily's lips before storming to the shuttle's door. "Open it, Aggar." I was anxious to discover why it was Sakkar felt so important to leave his throne. Did he already know of the women? Had Rayyar found a way to communicate with him without us knowing?

As soon as my feet hit the ground, I raced to the gate and shouldered my way through my trusted warriors to the front. Nekko stepped aside but remained close.

"Aw, my former brother has seen fit to grace me with his presence," Sakkar scoffed.

"What is it that you want, Sakkar?" I tried hard not to sneer.

"Don't you mean Sia Sakkar?" Sakkar stepped in close. "I am above you, Exile. You are no longer my equal."

"Not from my perspective." A few inches taller, I looked down my nose at him and held my ground. A posture I knew he hated; I couldn't stop myself from goading him. At this moment, I despised him more than the Nuttaki.

His army surged forward, as did mine. Blades scraped and sang against their sheaths as swords were drawn on both sides. It was not my nature to yield, but I had never had eight human females under my protection. Or a spirit mate.

I reached down deep and scraped the bottom of my humility. The step I took back was excruciating, as was the slight bow of my head. "Sia Sakkar," I pushed through gritted teeth and gestured to my warriors to ease their stances.

Sakkar chuckled, as did the males behind him. I knew all their faces. I had been the one to train them as Valose warriors. Yet what stood with my brother was little more than a band of decadent, sloven shadows of the males they once were. The age of technology had taken its toll as I knew it would.

They had the numbers, but we had the skills. They were no match for us.

"Well, well, well, Jakkar, I didn't think you had it in you," Sakkar gloated. "Here I thought I'd be leaving this place with your blood splattered on my kiltus."

I swallowed his bait, my scales bristling in a wave of contempt. In what world could Sakkar ever best me? "Seems like we've both changed, brother." My palms itched to free my swords from their sheaths. "I never thought to witness you dirtying the soles of your boots to walk among the civilians. Yet here you are."

Sakkar seethed and began to pace. His desire to attack was tangible, yet he held back.

"Your settlement is primitive." Sakkar scowled at his surroundings. "How do you think to keep it secure from the jungle's beasts? From where I stand, you have multiple repairs needed to your walls."

His insults rang true but pissed me off. "Surely you did not lift your royal ass off your beloved throne to walk all this way because you're concerned with the safety of my settlement."

Nekko shifted behind me, choking on his laughter. I was in desperate need of tact, but Sakkar wasn't in an amicable mood to ask the favor of his spacecraft, and I was itching for a fight. He had somehow found out about the females, and he was here for them; I knew it in my bones.

Sakkar rushed me. His face was so close to mine I could count the silver flecks sprinkled in his eyes. "What did you find on the crashed vessel?"

"What crashed vessel?" I stood defiant. "We were merely investigating an asteroid that crashed near here."

"I want the cargo you took from that vessel." Sakkar's pupils narrowed. I'd never known my brother to be so aggressive. It was not in his nature to fight. He was a politician; words were his swords. Yet he stood before me, teeth bared, fists clenched, and ready to brawl.

This male was not the Sakkar with whom I was raised.

"What has become of you, brother?" I peered deeper into his pupilless eyes.

A spark of recognition flashed, Sakkar's face softened for only a sec before a mask slammed down over his familiar features making him a stranger to me once more. I recoiled from the effect.

Something was very off. As I glanced around at the group of Sakkar's males, they all wore the same narrowed-eyed expression. They were not themselves. I'd never seen anything like it.

"Give me all you found on that vessel, Jakkar, or I will mow down your minuscule squad and burn what remains of this settlement to ash."

Sakkar's words set my blood to boil. An image of the females huddled together in the cramped space of the shuttle and the thought of Lily at the hands of these males—strangers to me now—were the deciding factors.

I hesitated only a moment. "Do only what is necessary!" was my war cry, and the fighting commenced.

Sakkar ducked out of the way just before the flat of our swords were met with the dull blades of theirs. A sword was a mere extension of a Valose warrior; it was not the whole. As Sakkar's males used their weapons in an attempt to kill, mine used theirs as tools to lengthen their reach and incapacitate.

I knew I need not explain my war cry further. My warriors knew not to kill Sakkar's males. Exiles or not, we would always be of Clan Huren. None of us wanted to kill our own.

As the unconscious bodies began to pile at our feet, we continued to hold the advantage. We used the chokehold of the gate to pick them off as soon as they entered. It was a ridiculous offensive position, but Sakkar had never been a fighter. Leading warriors into battle were not his forte; it was mine.

A splash of blood whipped across my face. A hand still clutching a dull sword was next to follow. The fighting had turned real, and not all could be spared. I surmised protecting the females was my first priority when my sword hit home. The head of the warrior determined to kill me bounced on the ground, coming to rest a few fates away from his still twitching body.

I trudged forward, swinging my twin blades at my foes, spinning, and kicking my way through the seemingly endless surge of Sakkar's males infiltrating the main gates. Most I toppled off their feet with a swipe of my swords and knocked them unconscious with a well-placed hilt. Others were determined not to go down without bloodshed.

Nekko and Sazzar fought alongside me, warriors with skills to match my own. They swung away at those surrounding them. Eyes rolled back in their heads as Sakkar's warriors hit the ground. The males able to shake off the impact of our sword hilts, determined to fight, were cut down. There was no help for it. We would mourn the dead later.

Out of nowhere, Sakkar rushed me from behind. I heard before I saw him and whirled around to dodge his sword made ready to stab me in the back.

As I prepared to return his swing, Sakkar dropped his sword and clutched his head in both hands. As one, Sakkar and his males fell like flites, littering the ground in writhing heaps.

My males all looked to me for answers I didn't have. I eased myself to the ground, wary of the situation, Nekko and Sazzar watching my back as I assessed my brother.

Sakkar writhed in pain, his feet digging at the dirt as his legs shifted restlessly.

"Brother, what is wrong?" I touched his once pristine white mane, now dusted with blue dirt. "What is happening?"

His mouth was stretched wide in a silent scream. His eyes met mine in a plea for help. Nullar was on the shuttle treating Rose, so I had no medic to offer him.

The glint of a device tucked behind his ear caught my eye. I turned his head to get a better look. As soon as I tried to dislodge it, Sakkar jolted and rebounded to his feet. I was knocked on my ass and plowed over in a trample of feet.

In a few secs, the settlement was cleared of Sakkar's males. Only the dead were left scattered on the ground around my warriors, who stood wild-eyed and as bewildered as myself.

"What in the Spirits just happened?" Nekko lent me his palm and hefted me to my feet.

"Close the gates!" I yelled.

"Hold that," Draggar called out from a distance.

Tekkon, a budding warrior, looked to me for direction. At my nod, he held open one half of the massive gate as Draggar and Vallon blew through as if their asses were on fire.

Draggar—taking longer to slow the hauler's heft—kept going through the settlement as Vallon skidded to a halt, his rover's gravity disrupters kicking up dirt in a fat arch. He dismounted and ran toward me. "Close the gates, Sia! We've got trouble on our tails."

I waved the gates to be closed, my eyes never leaving the ashen face of my warrior. As fearful as his eyes were, I anticipated the boom of a rexose ramming the gate. All remained quiet, making Vallon's raspy breaths that much harsher.

"Gray. Aliens." Vallon grated. "The Gretolics are all around the perimeter."

I felt the mind control from my first alien encounter tickle over my memory, and I cringed now, knowing why Sakkar and his males hadn't been themselves. The device behind Sakkar's ear was some sort of comm used by the Gretolic to control their actions.

I dropped to my haunches over one of the fallen. Behind his ear, I found the same type of device Sakkar was wearing. I tugged at the metal square until it finally gave way, leaving behind a scar where it had been attached to the soft scales behind the dead warrior's ear.

My heart plunged to my feet, knowing Sakkar was under the influence of the Gretolics. He had acted strangely the suns-rise of my exile too. I hadn't considered his actions to be anything but his own, but now that I knew of the Gretolic's existence, I wondered how long those fuckers had been using mind control to rule over Huren.

I had hated Sakkar for all the wrong reasons. Now I had to save him from a new enemy, the Gretolics.

"Secure the gates and guard the wall. Nothing gets inside unless it's one of us," I ordered.

"Draggar caught one. It's in the hauler." All other thought came to a screeching halt at Vallon's announcement.

The warriors around me were clueless about what we found on that ship, but they ran with me to the hauler as Draggar dismounted and strode around to the bed. The body that was lifted out stilled all movement. Not even a breath was taken.

Gray as death, the lithe body of the bulbous-headed alien, wriggled with Draggar holding it up by the back of its neck. Its arms and legs bound tight to its body. He'd gagged the alien's slashing mouth, yet it sneered and seethed, teeth dripping with anger.

"Strip the Gretolic of any devices and secure it in the solitarium. Keep it gagged. Its words can control the mind." I sliced my hand toward Rayyar, still strapped to the rover Vallon had towed. "And lock Rayyar up in the penitentrium until he rots. He is not worthy of a warrior's death. His betrayal has cost him a place among the Spirits."

My warriors gathered around me, palms flashing silver in greeting, as Draggar and Vallon carried out my orders. Grumbles flew in a storm of questions. I had so much to tell them.

"Good to see you home." Nekko returned my plasma gun and presented his forearm for me to clasp. "I think this belongs to you. You had me worried. Zikkar lost your signal near the Nassbian cliffs. I was assembling a squad to search for you when Sakkar and his army of sloggs began to march this way."

"We had a little trouble with a herd of rynose," I said, tucking the plasma gun in the pocket of my kiltus.

"Draggar told me," Nekko said. "He pinged me back to let me know you'd been found, or rather, you found them."

"It was an... interesting journey."

"It appears you've had *quite* the adventure." Nekko motioned to the shawra marking my chest, a deep furrow cutting his brow.

I wasn't given a chance to explain about Lily before Zikkar muscled his way through the crowd of males and rushed me. "Sia! Glad to see you back in one piece." The scholar caught me by surprise with a hard embrace and a clap on the back.

"Glad to be back." I returned the clap. "You and Aggar have your work cut out for you." I gestured to the hauler full of scavenged alien technology and handed him the small device. "I found this behind one of Sakkar's warrior's ears. Sakkar wore the same. I think it's some sort of comm. The Gretolics can control minds with their words."

"That is not good news but explains much." Zikkar eagerly rubbed his hands together before searching the crowd. "I can't wait to get started on all of this. Where's Aggar?"

"Right this way." I bowed with a flourish. "Aggar has something you'll be most interested in."

I motioned for everyone to join us and strode over to where Aggar had landed the camouflaged vessel. "There's much I need to tell all of you." I had everyone's full attention at my raised voice. I told of the crashed vessel, Rayyar's collaboration with my brother, and the Gretolics that used mind control as a weapon.

I didn't miss the fleeting glimpses of eyeballs scanning my shawra. "There's more. The Gretolic's cargo were females stolen from another planet called Earth. They're new to our world and still a little frightened. They'll only be staying long enough until I can find them a ship and return them home."

I signaled for Aggar to open the shuttle's door. The movement rippled the air in an invisible current. Many gasped, tensing up, ready to fight a foreign threat until Aggar was revealed standing in the doorway. The warrior stepped out with the women trailing behind him. Their arms were full of their belongings. Hushed mumbles and gasps of appreciation followed in their wake.

Lily's eyes found mine in the crowd of males, and I immediately went to her side. Splattered with blood from the fighting, she didn't hesitate to twine her fingers with mine. I sensed her nervousness with so many new faces crowded around.

"You're safe here, Lily," I reassured her. "None will harm you."

The males were curious about the human women. They pressed in close as none had seen a feminine face in many munthis. In turn, the females shrank back and huddled behind Aggar.

"The females can have my skypod, Sia," Aggar offered. "Permission to return to the crashed vessel to recover and honor the bodies of the dead and search for the lone female that ran away."

I'd made many promises to Lily. Honoring her dead was one of them, so I didn't hesitate. "Choose a warrior to join you."

"Thank you, Sia." The haunting anxiety playing in Aggar's gaze lightened. "Tekkon? You up for a mission?"

"Always." The budding warrior stepped forward with a straight spine and powerful build.

Tekkon was the last of the youngest generation to join the warrior ranks. He was proving to be a mighty force. His gaze flitted over the females crowded behind Aggar. I couldn't blame him for his curiosity.

Zikkar ran inquisitive hands over the invisible hull of the shuttle. "You're leaving before I can get a look at this flying contraption, Aggar?"

"I promise to return it in one piece," Aggar said. "With all I brought back, you'll be too busy to notice I'm gone."

Zikkar huffed out a laugh and continued inside the shuttle just as Nullar was carrying out a still unconscious Rose. Zikkar stopped in his tracks. His hand rubbed at his sternum while peering down into Rose's pale face.

"Stand by," Aggar told Tekkon. "First, I need to see Rose settled." Aggar followed Nullar to the underground medic lab, where Zikkar opened the metal hatch for all of them to enter.

I shook off the initial shock of Zikkar's sudden shift in interest. There was much to be done. First, the women needed to be secured. Then the settlement cleared of the carnage before the jungle's creatures got wind of the easy meal. "Draggar, give me a hand to settle the women in Aggar's skypod."

One at a time, Draggar climbed the rope up to Aggar's skypod with a female on his back. Lily remained at my side. Her small hand clutched tightly in mine.

She hadn't spoken a single word since stepping off the shuttle. I'd intentionally kept her turned away from the bodies littering the ground at the front gate. The echo of her spirit churned nervously inside my gut.

It was Lily's turn to go up. "Are you ready?"

Her gaze steady yet fearful, she bobbed her chin. I turned my back and took a knee. She hugged her arms and legs around my neck and waist. Lily squeezed me tighter as I took the rope up in easy pulls until we reached the hatch in the floor.

"I don't like heights," Lily spoke in a hushed tone.

"You're safer up here, especially during the dark hurs," I told her as I entered the skypod.

Skypods were by no means spacious, but now that Aggar's was filled with human women, it felt even less so.

"I need you to watch after the women." At my request, Lily's spirit eased its restless churning.

"Amy and I want to get a look at that germ," Lily blurted out. "With both of us being lab rats from another planet, maybe we can lend a new perspective."

"I will set that up with Nullar soon." I brushed tendrils of her dark mane away from her face. "First, I need to check on the prisoners and meet with Nekko." I left out the part where I'd be planning a recon mission to gather information about the Gretolic infestation. It looked like it was up to me to save the City of Huren and my brother.

I showed the women how to pull the rope up in case of attack. No one could reach them in the sky without it to climb. They were up high enough, no beasts on Valose could reach them, and wetlocks didn't view skypods as a meal, so they were safe from aerial attack.

Then I taught them how to use the comm to ping myself or Nullar on the ground. Lastly, I demonstrated the controls for using the sanitate system and how to operate the loodfall for bathing.

"Dibs. I've had to pee since the stampede." Marie rushed past me and slid the door closed.

"Get some rest," I said to the women as they explored their tiny accommodations. "I'll have food brought up soon." I turned to Lily. "I'll return soon."

A small smile played across her lips. "Hurry back."

I made a rapid descent, then turned back to see my Lily peering out the window of Aggar's skypod. Her eyes were trained on me. My palm automatically covered my shawra as she did hers. The bond between us stretched with a painful demand that I rejoin her.

I fought through the pull and followed the broken road to the solitarium, knowing the yearning I felt now would pale in comparison to the excruciating agony from the loss of her spirit when I returned her—worlds away—to her planet.

Chapter Nineteen

LILY

I watched Jakkar go. My decision to remain here with him solidified at the sight of his retreating back. I hadn't had a chance to tell him of my plans with all the excitement. I wanted some privacy, too.

The skirmish I witnessed from the shuttle was evidence Sakkar would not be lending his spaceship as a ride back to Earth. Maybe there were other ships we didn't know about. I knew I was staying, but the other girls weren't. I had to help them find a way home even if I wouldn't be joining them.

Once Jakkar disappeared, I turned away from the window and into the glare of my bestie. I needed to make amends and, most importantly, make her understand why I had to stay.

"Look, Amy," I took a seat next to her on the edge of the large bed, which took up most of the room. "It's hard for me to explain how I feel when I don't totally understand it myself."

"Then how can you make an intelligent decision to stay on an alien planet with an elf dude you just freaking met?"

"Because I love him," I blurted out before thinking.

Amy fell back on the bed with a cynical laugh that ran all over me. "Give me a break."

"Screw you, Amy!" I popped off the bed. Arms crossed tightly over my chest; I couldn't believe my best friend was acting like this. Amy always supported me no matter what. "What's wrong with you, anyway? Why are you being such a bitch to me about this?"

"Because what you're telling me is ridiculous." Amy sat forward. Her voice was growing thinner the longer she ranted. "If there's a chance to go home, you need to be on that ride. You can't stay here, Lily! It's an alien planet." Her eyes swelled with tears, and I dropped to my knees in front of her. "And... I can't leave my best friend behind, Lil. I just can't."

Amy was a strong person, and seeing this raw emotion pour out of her was crushing. "Oh, honey, please don't cry."

The roles of our friendship reversed, and Amy fell into my open arms. I hugged her tightly to me. She was my rock, and I was the one who leaned against her for support. But I wasn't the same person I had been before my abduction. After what we all went through, none of us were.

"Listen, I can't quite put into words what I feel for Jakkar." I cupped her face in my hands. "I just know that it's real, and it's more than just love. Like right now, his emotions are echoing inside me, and I ache to be near him." His current emotions weren't of the warm and fuzzy kind but thunderous and angry. I wondered what it was he was discussing with Nekko.

Amy tried to pull away when I placed her hand over my shawra as if she didn't want to touch it. "A piece of him lives inside me." I continued even as she shook her head. "It would kill me to leave him, Ames. I know it. He's the beat of my heart, the fire in my soul. I will wither and die without him."

Amy's eyes swirled with confusion and anguish. "I want to understand, Lily. I really do. It's just hard to comprehend how you've fallen for this guy in such a short time that you're ready to give up your entire life for him."

"I'm not giving up my life. I've never felt more alive than I do right now."

"Don't confuse the stresses of abduction for emotional attachment to a stranger, Lily." Her tone was tight, authoritative, like a parent chastising her errant child.

Well, I wasn't a child. Even though I could see her point of view, I wasn't going to waver when it came to Jakkar. I understood where she was coming from. If the roles were reversed, and my bestie had declared undying love over a complete stranger, I would have had my doubts too.

Jakkar was drawing closer; I could feel him even before the creak of the rope announced his ascent. The hatch was gently pushed open to reveal his shimmering white head. The girls moved away, giving him room to enter.

So caught up with Amy, I'd nearly forgotten about the other girls crowded around us. Some had changed back into their clothes I found on the shuttle. Others remained in the shapeless dresses from our abductors. They'd all grown so quiet, listening intently, and all eyes were fixated on me. I felt like an alien among my own kind.

Jakkar placed a fat satchel that he had crossed over his body on a small table in the room. "There's plenty of food and drink for everyone. The suns-rise is coming to a close. In a few hurs, it will be dark. For your safety, no one is allowed on the ground after dark. If anyone would like to walk the settlement now, Draggar is below and will watch over you." He turned to me, brushing his hand against mine. The simple touch was an electric shock that zinged through my veins. "Nullar can assist you and Amy in the medic bay to take a look at the germ. If you're ready, I can escort you there."

"We're ready now." Amy stormed to the hatch, tapping her foot impatiently as she waited for Jakkar to help her down the thick rope.

As much as I wanted to wrap myself up in Jakkar's arms and forget the world existed, I still had to do damage control. I didn't know when the girls would be able to go home, but I wasn't about to let my best friend leave this planet pissed off at me.

First, we'd go check out the germ together, and then I planned on pulling Amy aside and finding a way to make her understand my need to remain here. I couldn't let her leave with the way things were between us.

Layla surprised everyone and pushed her way to the front of the group. "I'd like to walk around the settlement."

"Me too," Marie stepped forward.

One by one, the girls expressed interest in having a look around their new temporary home. One by one, Isobel, Elise, Willow, and Layla rode on Jakkar's back down the rope to the ground.

"I can climb down by myself," Marie skirted around Jakkar to the open hatch. "It can't be any different than the rope in gym class. Right?"

"I don't know, Marie. It's a pretty far drop." I peered down the hatch a hundred feet to the hard-packed blue dirt below. The height tickled the soles of my feet and left me lightheaded.

"There's no telling how long we'll be stuck here. I, for one, don't want to be dependent on these guys any more than we already are." Marie smirked and reached out to grab the rope. "Besides, I'm not wearing anything under this dress. I'll be giving Draggar one helluva show. I'm gonna give it a whirl."

Jakkar reached out to steady her as she stepped off the floor of the skypod. She swung in the air, the tail end of the rope flipping wildly. Draggar was there instantly, holding the rope taut and looking ready to catch Marie if she fell.

I held my breath through Marie's entire climb down. Once her feet touched the blue dirt, a cheer rang up from the girls. Even the ever-brooding Draggar looked pleased. Flushed but pleased.

"I'll be taking the elf-elevator, thank you very much," Amy punched out a harsh exhale.

"Me too," I gritted out. "Just watching Marie climb down scared the shit out of me."

Amy and I were the last on the ground. Marie threaded her arm through Draggar's as if laying claim, and the girls headed off in the opposite direction with Draggar guarding them. All the males stopped what they were doing to watch the girls pass by. None appeared aggressive, only curious with intense stares.

Jakkar led us to a heavy metal door I knew was the underground medic lab where Nullar had carried Rose. The heavy door opened without a sound. Inside, we faced off with a set of stairs, rough-cut out of solid rock and dotted with those illuminated rocks Aggar had used to light up the cave.

It was an easy descent, a slight sloping that took us deeper into the ground until we reached a tunnel cut into the earth. I expected the air to be cool, but it remained the same tepid temperature as the outside.

Nullar greeted us at the base of the steps.

"I'll return just before dark to retrieve you." Jakkar's words belied his movements as his feet seemed glued to the ground.

"You're not staying?"

"I have another meeting with Nekko." Jakkar stepped in close. A flicker of heat passed between us. I could stare into the silver swirl of his gaze for a lifetime.

Someone cleared a throat, cutting into our moment. Jakkar stepped away with a light caress to my cheek. The austere mask he always wore softened—just the tiniest bit—but it was there in the tenderest of regards.

The part of him that lived within me expanded, filling every aspect of my being with the warmth of affection that brought tears to my eyes. I couldn't wait to get him alone so we could talk, and I could spill my heart out to him.

Jakkar turned, and I watched him go as he climbed back up the steps to the outside. I hoped he could feel how much I cared for him.

"Is Rose okay?" Amy asked, pulling me away from Jakkar's disappearing boots.

"Healing at a fast rate, thanks to the advanced medic equipment we managed to bring with us from Huren," Nullar happily reported. "She's sleeping now. I expect her to be awake and up for a visit at the beginning of the next suns-rise."

Amy seemed anxious to visit Rose but agreed to wait until tomorrow. I fought the need to run after Jakkar and followed Nullar down the tunnel dotted with glowing rocks until we reached a panel that slid open as we approached.

Inside a room lined with metallic sheets, the environment was cold and sterile. I shuddered from the memories of the metal cage where I'd woken up in what felt like a lifetime ago. There was a single, long table tucked up against a wall with a curved piece of equipment that looked a great deal like the alien microscope I used to bash against the hand scanner.

Amy and I beelined for the microscope while Nullar went to the back of the room to open a panel that reminded me of a refrigerator. The light inside glowed a soft blue. Nullar reached in and lifted out a cylinder with tiny bubbles floating inside.

The lab was nothing like what I expected. I figured we would have had to wear protective suits around the germ. It was contained inside a clear substance that resembled a bouncy ball.

"Here's a small sample of the germ taken directly from the vein of an infected female." Amy and I cringed away as Nullar brought over the cylinder. "Don't worry. The germ is encapsulated. It can't harm you."

We both relaxed, and for the first time since I told her how I felt about Jakkar, Amy smiled at me. I wanted to hug her, so I did. I grabbed her up and squeezed her to me. "I hate fighting with you."

"Me too." Amy wiggled out of my hold to look me in the eyes. "I love you like a sister, Lil, but we still need to talk about this thing going on between you and Jakkar."

"I love you back, and we will." I gave her a firm look. "I promise."

Amy bobbed her chin. She didn't know it yet, but we would have to agree to disagree. No matter how scary this planet was, I wasn't leaving Valose. My place was here with my spirit mate.

Nullar shifted next to us. His face turned awkwardly away from our sudden display of affection. "So, the germ," I said. "Let's have a look."

Nullar popped open the cylinder, captured a single bubble with a large pair of tweezers, and dropped it inside a pocket in the microscope. "You can see the sample by looking through here." Nullar indicated an elongated cup that reminded me of an eye test machine.

Amy and I exchanged a pensive look when Nullar touched the side of the microscope to illuminate the sample inside. It was unprecedented. We were about to view an alien germ. Something no human had ever seen before, and me and Amy were going to be the first to see it. I leaned down and put my face in line with the viewer.

What I saw shocked me in all its familiarity. "What the hell?" Disbelieving, I rubbed my eyes and looked again.

"What is it?" Amy asked excitedly. "What do you see?"

"You're never going to believe it." I stepped aside so Amy could attest to what I easily identified.

Eyes to the viewer, Amy gasped, "It's rubella."

"You know what it is?" Nullar's eyes grew so wide that they took up his entire face.

"It's an exanthemata's viral disease."

"Also called German measles."

"Which cause skin rashes, but it's rare now that most people have been vaccinated." Amy and I talked over each other.

"Human females can die from this?" Nullar asked, alarmed.

"Not typically," Amy said. "It's usually only seen in young children. Were any children infected?"

"Only the females." Nullar rubbed his brow. "The only Valose people left in Clan Huren are young and old males."

"What I don't understand is how it got here. Jakkar said his brother brought it back from one of his space travels. Where did he travel to?"

Nullar shook his head. "I don't know where he ventured."

"This is an Earth virus, which means Jakkar's brother has been there." Amy clapped her hands and bounced on the balls of her feet. "He knows where home is."

"Maybe," I scratched my head, skeptical. "Jakkar said the gray aliens had surrounded the settlement's perimeter when Sakkar attacked. Since they are already here, maybe the virus was brought back inside a host."

"What do you mean, Lil?"

"I mean, maybe there are other girls here that came before us."

Amy paled and turned to Nullar. "Have you seen humans on this planet before us?"

"No. You are the first." Nullar scrunched his brow in thought. "Then again, I wasn't privy to the goings-on with Sia Sakkar at the palace. I lived and worked in the common district."

"Jakkar hadn't known what we were when he first found us. I don't believe he has knowledge of any prior abductees. That doesn't mean there aren't any in the city," I pondered aloud. "The virus had to have gotten here either by a host or Sakkar, and his crewmates came into contact with an infected person."

Was it a stretch to think Sakkar had been to Earth, or was it?

"Why didn't any of the males die from the virus? Why was it only the females?" Amy's question snapped me out of my head.

"None of the males ever fell ill. There aren't any royal medics in the settlement to answer why," Nullar explained. "Maxxon and Kayyot remained in Huren when Sia Jakkar was exiled. Any discoveries would be inside the city's medic lab near the palace."

"Well, shit." Amy paced.

We weren't virologists, but my curiosity begged to be appeased. "I'd love to look at some tissue samples of the Valose people to make sense of why only the females were infected."

I felt more than heard Jakkar return. Like a shot of adrenaline, my heart raced, and my body temperature soared at the sight of him. I wanted to fling myself into his arms and hold on tight, but I resisted. Amy's eyes were drilling into me from behind, so climbing Jakkar like a spider monkey in heat would only worsen matters between us.

"The suns-fall draws near," Jakkar announced. "Are you ready to go?"

"Did your brother ever mention where he went on his travels? Or bring back any people with him? Did you know he was in cahoots with the gray aliens?" Amy's rapid-fire questions shocked me.

Jakkar stared unblinking at Amy. I didn't think he was going to answer until he inhaled deeply and began, "Sakkar never discussed his travels with me, and to my knowledge, no strangers were ever brought back here. I do not think Sakkar willingly allied with the Gretolics. He and his army were compelled to attack us using mind control."

"Gretolics?" I asked.

"That's the gray aliens' species."

"How do you know?" Amy asked heatedly.

"The Gretolic with one hand told me." Jakkar bowed up; the echo of his spirit spiraled into a tornado.

"What else did he tell you?" Amy demanded of Jakkar.

I didn't appreciate her stern tone. "Jakkar isn't on trial here, Amy!" Jakkar's mood fueled my anger from within. "He isn't the one that abducted us."

Amy backed off, but I could see her stewing.

"He told me nothing else." Jakkar relaxed.

"They never used mind control on us," I said. "Whenever anyone would wake up and freak out, they used a noxious gas that reeked of ammonia to knock us out. Marie was awake the longest. We should pick her brain to see what all she knows."

"Why does their mind control work on the elf guys and not us?" Amy asked.

Nullar whipped out a tablet and started tapping the screen. "Human physiology is different than ours. If I could complete a full-body scan of one of the females, perhaps I could solve the mystery."

"I will thoroughly question the Gretolic," Jakkar announced. "There is much to be learned about Valose's new enemy. First, what of the germ?"

"It's a human virus called rubella."

"From your Earth?" Jakkar gaped.

"Yes," I nodded. "The mystery is how it found its way here."

I could see Jakkar working something over in his mind. "We are in the planning stages of a recon mission to Huren. We must determine the size of the Gretolic infestation before planning our attack. The germ's origin is another question that could be answered once we figure out how to penetrate the dome."

"If anyone would be able to figure out by what means the germ arrived, it's Maxxon. If he is under the influence of the Gretolics,"—Nullar shook his head gravely— "then Valose has lost our best medic."

"We will breach the dome, Nullar. Of this, I vow." Jakkar offered his forearm for Nullar to clasp, his features settling into a fierce conviction. "Maxxon will be saved. I know how important he is to you."

"To all of us," Nullar added. "My friendship aside, he is the most educated medic. There is so much I have yet to learn from him."

Amy's scowl withered, apparently moved by Jakkar's gesture. "I'll volunteer for the body scan. I'd also like more time to study the virus. We've barely glimpsed it, and I'd like to solve the mystery of why it didn't infect any of the males."

"Amy can remain here with me," Nullar offered. "There is an extra bunk in the recovery room with Rose she can use."

Jakkar looked ready to balk at Amy staying behind until she shut him down. "That's a great idea. Thanks, Nullar."

"As you wish," Jakkar agreed, looking annoyed. I knew just how he felt. Amy could be severely bullheaded when she wanted to be. "Bolt the door and remain inside until the next suns-rise."

"Of course, Sia," Nullar said.

We said our goodnights. Hand in hand, we climbed the steps to the ground above. Aglow in a silver shimmer, the settlement was bathed in the waning light from the twin suns. We didn't head in the direction of Aggar's borrowed skypod.

"Where are we going?"

"I would have you spend the dark hurs with me," Jakkar paused and turned hungry eyes on me. "Unless you object."

Heat bloomed over every inch of my skin. With Amy staying below with Nullar in the medic bay, there was no one to cast judgmental eyes when I enthusiastically wrapped a hand around Jakkar's biceps and told him to lead the way.

Chapter Twenty

JAKKAR

The heat from my spirit mate's flesh warmed me from the inside out. Lily clung tightly to my back as I climbed the rope to my skypod with an efficiency born from pure need.

Once inside, Lily walked the perimeter, brushing her fingers over what little furnishings I owned. I was struck with a pang of shame over my living conditions. My spirit mate deserved no less than what I could have provided her in the luxury of the palace.

I no longer held a lofty station. Being an exile, I was viewed as less than the blue dirt dusting my boots.

"What's wrong?" Lily whirled around to face me. "Your anxiety just spiked. Earlier, you were stressed about something. Tell me what's going on."

Her tone wasn't demanding but caring. The swirl of her spirit was a soothing concern as she drew near.

"There's no hiding anything from you," I smirked. Having a spirit mate was a new experience for me; she felt all my emotions. "This recon mission Nekko is helping to plan will be dangerous. I don't like putting anyone in danger. Even more, I don't like not knowing the situation with the Gretolics, and the mission will have to wait until Aggar and Tekkon return from the crashed spacecraft. The settlement can't afford to be down any more warriors, especially now." Lily came to stand before me. The top of her head only reached the center of my chest. Petite, she may be, her presence was immeasurable, and I drew strength from it. "The longer we wait, the more concerned I grow for my brother."

"That's understandable." Lily smoothed her small hands over my chest, coming to rest over my shawra. "If he's under some kind of mind control, your exile could have been influenced by the Gretolics."

"I believe that he was. Sakkar has not been himself for quite some time." My thoughts threatened to scatter at Lily's heated touch. "That's why we must infiltrate Huren soon and discover how deeply embedded the Gretolic have become with Sakkar and the Council. I believe they're ruling over the city."

Lily's eyes dropped to my mouth. My spirit jolted and churned behind my shawra, pounding to join with Lily's. Her presence consumed my small skypod. All I could feel was her. All I could see was her. Even the air was saturated with her scent.

My face dropped to the hollow of her throat; my hands curled around her tiny waist, pulling her against the length of my body—the need to mate—undeniable.

"This was a mistake." I tore myself away and paced on the opposite side of the room. "I was a fool to think I could hold myself back. Come. I will return you to the other females."

Lily looked crushed. Her bottom lip trembled, breaking my hearts in two. The echo of her spirit darkened with my rebuff.

"It isn't that I don't want you, Lily." She turned away, shielding her eyes from me. I crossed the room in two long strides, lifting her chin to peer down into her pinched face. "The more we give in to our spirit's desire, the harder it will be when we part. It could be some time before I find a way to return you home."

"Finding a spacecraft is the most important thing." The weight of Lily's words turned my hearts to stone, the importance of them plunging them to my feet. "The girls need to go home. They don't belong here as I do."

Lily brushed soft fingertips over my shawra, tracing the swirled design rooted in my flesh. Lightning sizzled through my veins as the meaning of her words slowly surfaced.

"You would stay on Valose? Even after I procure a spacecraft to Earth?"

Lily lifted her hands to cup my face. Standing on tiptoes, she placed a kiss on my chin. "Yes. On Valose. With you."

She squealed when I lifted her and spun her in a fat circle. "Why? What changed your mind?"

"I love you," Lily blurted out.

I blinked at her stupidly. No one had ever said those words to me before. After the germ, Lily and Amy had identified as rubella, had wiped out every female in Huren, I never thought to hear such a thing.

"My gut tells me I belong with you," Lily continued when I remained silent. "If I leave, I will be leaving my heart and soul behind."

It had been forever since I last smiled that my cheeks cracked from the expression. Lily pulled in a sharp breath and then smiled to match my own, wild and joyful.

"My spirit found its match in you, my most precious mate." I placed her hand over my ancillary heart. "Know that your spirit has awakened mine to animate this heart that beats in my chest solely for you. The boost of power it gives me, and the quick healing it affords are all efforts to keep you safe. I swear on the Spirits that I will love none but you even after drawing my final breath in this realm and journey into the next. My spirit will wait there for yours, even if it takes an eternity."

Lily's mouth parted on a gasp. Tears leaked from her eyes in huge drops. She flung herself in my arms and clung to me tighter than a floratrap's tentacles. I knew her tears were happy ones without having to ask. Her spirit was filled with an over-whelming joy that nearly buckled my knees.

"You say the most perfect things," Lily hiccupped through her sobs. "My dad always said that everything happens for a reason. I couldn't have picked a better reason than you for being dumped by Kyle and abducted by aliens."

"Dumped?" I scowled. "A male from your planet discarded you? Who is this, Kyle? I will crush him beneath my boot."

I was serious, but Lily giggled. "Stop growling and kiss me."

I gave her what she wanted and more. I'd envisioned her sprawled out on my sleeping platform more than once, a meal ready to be devoured. That was what I intended to do.

My lips captured hers as I placed her in the center of my sleeping platform. I wanted plenty of room to show her just how much her decision to stay on Valose meant to me.

Chapter Twenty-One

LILY

Jakkar stripped me of my clothes. Completely naked before him, I felt erotically exposed. My pussy throbbed for his attention, but he took his damn time exploring every inch of me with soft kisses and sweet caresses.

He thumbed my nipples before licking over them one at a time, all while scorching me with the heat of his silver gaze and a sexy twist of his lip. I had half a mind to grab his head, push it between my legs and ride his face into oblivion. Instead, I took a deep breath and tried to relax, letting him have his way with me.

Like a naughty masseur, Jakkar massaged every inch of me—from feet to fingers—spending more time when he got to my girly bits. I stretched out beneath him and arched my back when he palmed my breasts. I spread my legs wider and curled my hips, hoping he'd take the blatant hint.

His hands glided down my sides and over my belly. He skimmed over my thighs with teasing fingers and back up the inside, pushing my legs farther apart. I moaned, ready to receive a tongue lashing or his enormous cock. At this point, I didn't care which.

Jakkar's fingers were within reach of my heated core. I needed his cock inside me like I needed air to fill my lungs. He gripped my legs and rubbed his thumbs inside the creases of my thighs, pulling my lips apart, exposing my slick heat to the air. I should be mortified to be on display, but I wasn't. He was driving me wild with wanting him.

He dipped a finger inside, testing my wetness. I groaned from the intensity. That shouldn't feel so good, but the swirling behind my shawra magnified my pleasure a hundred-fold.

I almost came when Jakkar brushed that same finger over my swollen clit before placing it between his lips to clean it off.

The urgency to be claimed by him reduced me to liquid fire. Eager to get on with the mating, I grabbed the waistband of his kilt—to tear the damn thing off—but he captured my wrist and stilled my hand above my head.

"I wasn't able to explore you properly at the pool." Jakkar leisurely pumped his thick fingers into me.

"Please … stop torturing me…" I curled my hips to the rhythm of his wicked exploration.

His laugh was dark and rich, a promise of mind-blowing orgasms to come. He pulled free, and I felt his fingers trace over the petals of my sex. I wanted to scream from the intensity. I wanted more, and I wanted it now.

His silver head dipped between my wide-spread thighs. The heat of his breath washed my needy flesh in scorching heat as I writhed beneath his erotic perusal. I was aching and swollen and in desperate need of some action.

As soon as I reached down to touch myself with my free hand, Jakkar nudged it aside and dove between my legs with a feral growl. He ate at me, licking his way inside. I cried out when he impaled me on the length of his tongue. He filled me, lapping my intimate walls until no part of me was left untouched.

Jakkar's perfect mouth smoothed over my lips, slick and hungry, teasing the hard nub of my clit with little flicks of his tongue. Every touch brought me higher and higher until I was perched on the knife's edge of pleasure so painful, I was already seeing stars.

Then he sucked my clit into the heat of his mouth, suckling me until my entire body contorted. I arched back on a silent scream to the heavens, igniting in waves of carnal gratification.

My soul spun into a vortex behind my shawra. The echo of Jakkar's joined mine in a primitive dance of lovers that amplified my orgasm a thousand times over. He nuzzled me with a reverence shining out of his bright eyes as I rode out the final tremors wracking my body.

Now that I'd caught my breath, it was time I got a good look at the erection tenting his kilt. I'd only seen it through a distorted view of the water from the bathing pool our first time.

Jakkar didn't stop me when I fumbled with the buckle on his kilt. In the design of a wetlock, Jakkar had said it symbolized his family. There was so much emotion surrounding his father's death and his brother's captivity. I wanted to do something to distract him.

His cock was enormous. Covered in thick ridges. With large bumps lined up like a spine along the top. The base was impossibly wide. The most intriguing feature was the bulbous tip—a perfect silver mushroom that tilted upward.

I wrapped my hand around his turgid flesh. His skin flashed blue and silver. The intricate patterns adorning his chest and arms glowed brighter in the light of the moon spilling in through the single window.

I stroked down and up the length of his erection. I felt empowered when he shuddered at my touch. That wasn't what had me gasping. Maybe I was seeing things, so I did it again.

What I thought were bumps shaped like arrows at the base of his cock lifted, going taut. With all the extra features his cock was sporting, it was no wonder my eyes had rolled back in my head at the pool.

I looked up to find him watching me like a feral beast. He was snarling, almost drooling with those monstrous fangs out on full display. His ferociousness was a turn-on, and I was ready to be taken by my silver savage.

Jakkar was still wearing his boots when I guided his mushroom-shaped tip to my greedy center. His pelvis swiveled and penetrated me, the tip disappearing between my slick folds.

Propped up on my elbows, I watched as, inch by thick inch, Jakkar fed his massive silver cock inside me. I relished the feel of every ridge, every bump, as he filled me. No sex toy on Earth could compare to him.

When he seated himself fully, I felt the stirrings of the arrow-shaped bumps. Jakkar pulled out just enough to expose them. Lined up, one behind the other in ascending heights, they stood erect and ready to please.

He didn't waste any time putting them to good use against my clit. They stimulated that tight bundle of nerves with every stroke until I threw my head back, groaning with pleasure. My mouth was wide open as one climax after another overlapped; I couldn't tell when one ended and another began. It all felt so damn good.

A soft glow bloomed between us, and Jakkar's leisurely strokes turned frantic. The echo of his essence grew, coalescing with mine in a primal and intoxicating mix. Our pleasures combined, erupting into a blustering ecstasy too violent to contain.

I let go of all my inhibitions and held onto Jakkar's muscular forearms as his pelvis rocked wildly. His nostrils flared, his fangs on full display as he rode me like a beast. I took everything he had to give and more until we lay spent in a pool of our mating.

I fell asleep cradled in my lover's arms, with his lips in my hair and his body entangled with mine. Nothing could ever feel this perfect.

Chapter Twenty-Two

JAKKAR

I knew the commotion on the ground was nothing good even before the ping of my comm made me curl up tighter around my spirit mate, sleeping soundly in my arms.

The echo of Lily's spirit was more substantial now that we mated several times in the past few hurs. It floated languidly within me, a cloud of contentment dancing with mine with no care in the world.

I tensed at the second ping and jerked to attention at the resounding crash. Her essence tremored in surprise, and her body tightened, pressing closer to mine.

"What is it?" I answered the comm with a grating voice.

"A pod of rynose has breached the wall near the penitentrium." Nekko sounded winded as if he were running.

Lily shifted but didn't wake. I slammed my eyes shut, giving myself over to the feel of her delicate hands roaming over my back. Her breath washed over my neck and chest. I tried to lose myself in the moment, wanting Nekko's interruption to be a bad dream.

"Sia?"

My fantasy crumbled at the sound of Nekko's voice. "I'll be right down," I snapped into the comm. I wasn't one to shirk my responsibilities, but Nekko was a skilled Valose warrior. He could handle a rynose pod of two males and a female.

"The solitarium has been destroyed, and by the looks of the body, the Gretolic was trampled to death by the rynose," Nekko added, then his voice floated away as he spoke to someone else. "Vallon just reported that Rayyar has escaped during the confusion and taken at least two of the females with him. Amy and Layla."

I was on my feet in secs. Lily sat up, rubbing at her eyes. My gut soured knowing that one of those females was what Lily called a bess-tee. I assumed that was Earth's equivalent of a close friend.

"Any more good news, Nekko?" I scoffed while buckling my kiltus around my waist and strapping my swords to my back. "Where is your location?"

"I'm headed to the penitentrium now."

"I'll meet you there."

I shoved my feet into my boots as Lily started to dress. "Stay here inside the safety of the skypod. Pull up the rope after I'm down. Do not let anyone up except me."

I pinned her with a stern look when she opened her mouth to argue. Now was not the time for a discussion. Now was the time for keeping the most precious thing to me on Valose safe, my Lily.

Lily nodded. I felt the echo of her fear bubbling. I placed the comm in her hand with instructions not to hesitate to use it. "I'll return as soon as I can. Please remain in the skypod where I know you're safe."

"I heard mention of Amy," Lily said in a thin voice. "Is she okay? What's happened?"

The worry for her friend was paralyzing. I could feel that she would balk at having to remain in the skypod if I told her what little I knew, but I wouldn't lie to her. Even if I did, she would know it.

"Rayyar has escaped and may have taken Layla and Amy with him." Lily's face paled. "I need to get down there to investigate the situation. If I am to help your bess-tee, I need to know that you will remain safe."

Lily seemed to understand, yet a current of defiance zinged through the echo of her spirit. "Please be careful and let me know as soon as you learn anything new."

"I vow to do everything I can to help find Amy and Layla." I cupped her worried face in my hands and placed a soft kiss on her lips.

I'd planned on waking up my spirit mate with my cock surging inside her body, a leisurely stroke until she spilled her juices. Then we'd share a meal and lounge in the safety of my skypod, passing the suns-rise away exploring each other's bodies.

Instead, I left Lily behind as I descended the rope from my skypod. Even with my mouth twisted into a scowl, I could still taste her sweetness on my lips.

The settlement was in a complete uproar as my boots hit the ground. Males were running in every direction, trying to steer the unruly rynoses back out the hole they made in the wall without destroying anything else in their wake.

I felt the touch of Lily's gaze and looked up to find her standing at the lone window of my skypod. I flashed her my silver palm. She returned the gesture, and my heart swelled with pride. She was mine, and I was hers. I couldn't wait to rejoin her in our mated bed.

I tore away from her lovely face, my spirit screaming from the injustice, as I sprinted to the penitentrium. I found Nekko crouched down over obvious tracks left by Rayyar.

"The second set of footprints are female," Nekko traced his finger around the outline of the small print. "She ran alongside him. There's no sign of a struggle."

"Layla," Vallon muttered, looking stunned. "I saw her at the door to Rayyar's cell when the rynose pod attacked. I thought she was hiding because of the beasts ramming the wall. As I ran toward her, she sprang the lock and opened the door for him. Why would she do that?"

Vallon pinned me with haunted eyes. I suspected he'd formed an emotional attachment to her throughout our journey back to the settlement. He watched over her in the cave, fretted when she refused to eat and was never far from her side.

I clapped the young warrior on the shoulder. He needed a distraction. "We need to take accountability of all the females. Will you do that for me?"

"Yes, Sia."

"Go to Aggar's skypod and report the names of the females back to me. Make sure they remain inside until we secure the settlement. I'm appointing you as their personal guard."

Vallon's spine snapped straight, and his chest swelled with purpose. Charged with a mission, the warrior left me at a dead run. "What do you think?" I turned to Nekko.

"The tracks don't lie," Nekko swore. "Could Layla have somehow been under the Gretolic's mind control?"

"No," I said, walking the length of the penitentrium. All the barred doors faced forward so anyone passing by could see the prisoners locked inside their cells of the long, single-story structure, making guarding easy. "Their mind control doesn't work on the human females."

"Why is that?" Draggar asked, approaching.

"Nullar isn't sure yet. Amy volunteered for a body scan so he could study the differences between our species," I answered, following Rayyar and Layla's footprints around the penitentrium. "Yet another mystery to be solved. This brings up the question as to why Amy wasn't locked inside the medic bay at the time of the rynose attack."

"Nullar reported that Amy unlatched and opened the door when the commotion began," Nekko said. "She called to someone and ran out. Nullar went after her, but a rynose charged the medic bay and damaged the door, trapping Nullar inside. Sazzar and Wexxor are fixing the door as we speak."

"Fucking Helios!" I spat. "This suns-rise is off to a great start. Fan out. We'll search this area first."

I followed Rayyar and Layla's tracks while Draggar took a path behind the structure and Nekko toward the medic bay. The tracks stopped, then paralleled the settlement wall. My heart sank. Nekko was correct; there were no drag marks or shuffling of feet. Layla went with Rayyar willingly.

"Look at this." Nekko waved us over. "The tracks split here." Nekko pointed to the end of the tracks I'd been following. "Looks like Rayyar waited here then took off in the direction of the back gate while Layla went around the corner of the peni-tentrium. There's another set of prints that joined hers. They're small like Layla's. Another female."

I scanned the settlement. We were in perfect line of sight of the medic bay. Sazzar and Wexxor were just prying open the damaged door in the distance. Nullar raced out and towards us as soon as he could squeeze his body free. Sure enough, the petite prints had originated from there and were placed wide apart as if the person had run the distance.

"Amy," Nekko stated the obvious. "Looks like the two of them ran together—"

"Meeting up with Rayyar over here," Draggar finished Nekko's sentence from a distance away. "There are signs of a struggle. Only two sets of prints continued. One of the females was carried."

I crouched, swiping my finger across a bright fluid that sprayed the ground. I rubbed it between my fingers, contemplating the viscous texture. I knew exactly what it was. I'd seen the same fluid leaking from Lily's wounds when we first found the females on the crashed vessel. Human blood. And it sickened me to think that Rayyar had harmed Amy to subdue her.

"Amy did not go willingly," I said, holding up my blood-stained fingers. Rayyar had better pray to the Spirits that Amy and the other female still lived.

Nekko answered his comm's ping. "Is Sia Jakkar with you?"

"Here, Vallon," I spoke loudly so that my voice reached the comm.

"Marie," Vallon began gravely. "She's the only other female missing."

A low growl prickled over my scales. Swords were drawn, I swung around expecting to find a patooga ready to attack; instead, I met Draggar's ashen face, paled with his ferocity. The warrior looked prepared to engage and tear, limb from limb, anything in his path.

I'd seen him like this only one time before. When his spirit mate had accidentally wandered too close to a floratrap. A phosphorescent blue, the carnivorous plant was as deadly as it was beautiful. Once entangled in its tentacles, there was not much hope of escaping its digesting petals.

I knew better than to touch him, so I used words to try and calm him, "We will find Marie. First, we need to retrace her steps if we can."

My logic tempered Draggar's rage. "I will begin at Aggar's skypod. That's where I dropped off the females after they walked around the settlement."

Draggar took off for Aggar's skypod without another word from anyone. I tensed when he reached Vallon. I was proud of the younger warrior standing his ground against the seething male—a little worried for his safety but proud. Vallon was taking his guard duties seriously, proving himself a valuable warrior.

Words were exchanged in a civil tone, and Draggar began to track the small footprints that belonged to the women. With all the disturbance to the ground, it was a wonder he could pick out a single trail, yet he veered off and followed a path that swung a wide arc around the outer perimeter.

Nekko and I followed Draggar. He was locked on to something, taking slow, careful steps following Rayyar's trail. It continued in the back gate's direction and away from where the rynoses had punched through the wall. When the trail came to an end, my stomach dropped.

There, along the wall, we discovered a loose board marked with a scrap of white material all the females' dresses wore.

Draggar held the scrap to his nose, releasing a string of vile curses. "It's Marie's. I swear to the Spirits, I will kill Rayyar with my bare hands."

I didn't ask how he knew the female's scent. With the way he was acting, it was as if she were his spirit mate already. That was impossible, given he'd already bonded with another. She was waiting for him in the Realm of the Spirits. It was unheard of that a male could bond twice in a lifetime, but Marie was human and not Valosian. Anything was possible.

Draggar pulled back the loose board, creating an opening just large enough for a male to squeeze through. Draggar went first, then me and Nekko.

The jungle loomed before us—an endless stretch of thick vegetation with hidden dangers lurking everywhere. Despite the suns-rise, the jungle's canopy diffused the light leaving the ground in a wealth of shadows.

A squad of seasoned warriors could make the journey to Huren. One rogue warrior with three females on foot? They were as good as dead.

We searched the area closest to the wall until Nekko locked onto their trail. We followed, the jungle swallowing us within a few fates from the perimeter. After half a milose, I called off the search. It was apparent he was taking the females in the direction of Huren, and we were placing ourselves in danger, wandering this far away from help.

It took some convincing to turn Draggar around and back to the settlement, but common sense won out. He knew tracking them on foot would take too long, and by the time he reached the gates of Huren, Rayyar would have already made it inside.

We returned in the direction of the main gate, not surprised to come across a path of broken branches and bent leaves carved out by the thunderous hooves of the rynose pod. What got our attention was the area trampled in a circular pattern.

"I've never known rynose to run in circles while chasing a female ready to mate." Nekko studied the ground. "They normally travel in straight lines. Not even when startled do they circle back."

"We can attest to that," Draggar scoffed at me with a nod. "That stampede ran right off the damn cliff without a single thought."

Rynose were stupid, lumbering beasts. When a female was ready to mate, what little intelligence they had turned into a one-track mind. They'd give chase, not stopping no matter what was in their path, including the settlement wall.

"Definitely uncharacteristic..." My voice trailed off when I caught sight of something even more peculiar. "These aren't our footprints."

Draggar and Nekko looked to where I was pointing around the perimeter of the trampled-out circle.

"Those belong to full-grown males," Draggar uttered.

"And these do not belong to anything native to Valose," Nekko hissed, pointing down to two sets of tiny, three-toed prints off to one side of the circle.

"Gretolic," Draggar growled. "Those pricks compelled Sakkar's men to herd the rynose pod into our wall!"

I stepped into the circle, turning with the radius until the path to our damaged wall was revealed. Stretched out before me was a direct route to the solitarium, now laid waste under the weight of the stampeding rynoses. The broken body of the Gretolic prisoner lay on the ground in a mangled heap. "And they knew just where to hit us."

"Do you think it was a botched attempt to free their comrade?" Nekko came to stand with me, as did Draggar.

I considered the possibility but ultimately concluded. "Then why didn't they hit us at the back gate? With the rynose leading the way, they could have followed and freed their comrade before we had time to react. No. The Gretolics would rather sacrifice one of their own than allow it to remain a prisoner, which makes me wonder what information we could have extracted from its bulbous head."

The motives of this new enemy were endless. The Gretolics had made it known the strength of the foothold they had inside the city of Huren, and my brother was their primary prey. How much of the planet had they already infiltrated?

My gut twisted in a tight knot. The weight of uncertainty settled around me in a thick cloak. "When I was first exiled, I wore the burden of misfortune and was incensed when it spread to the few of you who followed me. Now, with this new enemy, it would seem we are the fortunate ones to be spared the mind control of the Gretolics."

The males grunted their agreement.

"They've proven they cannot only manipulate us with words but get into our minds and extract whatever knowledge they want." I deduced. "The settlement is no longer a safe place for anyone. The Gretolic have inside knowledge of our defenses. They have the numbers. We would easily be overrun if they were to bring a large enough army. As much as I dislike technology, under the protection of a dome is the safest place for all of us."

"Yes, given there aren't any Gretolic inside. If we are to take back Huren and save Sia Sakkar, we will need more warriors." Nekko looked in the direction of the majestic Jurigon mountains with their jagged caps thrusting above the wispy clouds. "We could elicit the help of Clan Jurigon and the forest clan, Trisess."

"That may be our only option." My gaze settled on my spirit mate's silhouette framed inside the lone window of my skypod floating high above the ruins of the settlement in the distance. "We must leave now. Find someplace safe where no one would think to look for us. We will have to lay low, scout for reinforcements if we are to defeat the Gretolics. And we must keep the females safe until we can secure a craft and a pilot to send them home."

I was at once contrite and joyful Lily would remain behind with me. Her spirit was too entangled with mine to sever the bond we created during the dark hurs. She was the only bright spot amidst all this chaos.

"The Gretolics think they can come here and take this world for themselves." I stood taller with resolution pounding through my veins. "We are warriors of Valose and fight for what is ours. This is not just about the city of Huren but for the whole of this planet. Even the Nuttaki—love them or hate them—this is their world too. Whoever decides to join us in this fight." I turned to face Draggar and Nekko. "It will be up to us to save Valose."

Not the End!

This is only the beginning.

Turn the page for a preview as the saga continues.

Sneak Peek!

Silver Seducer: Warriors of Valose Saga 2

Draggar

I had lost one spirit mate, and I refused to lose another. She didn't know it yet, but one way or another, I was going to make her mine. She was stolen from me and, I would gladly risk my own life to get her back. With a new enemy ruling in the city of Huren, there was no safe place. What we stumbled upon was worse than any of us could have imagined. Reunited with my female, the only way to safety was perilous. In the end, I would have to kill her in order to save her.

Marie

What happened on Valose stayed on Valose. I was not above some serious fooling around, but I had to resist going all the way. Why? Because sex equaled an unbreakable mated bond here, and I wanted off this freak show of a planet. Now that I was back in serious trouble guess who came to my rescue? The bristly, surly, otherworldly gorgeous male who I could hardly resist. How could I evade his heady seduction when he had a secondary heart that beat only for me?

Turn the page for a sneak peek of Silver Seducer: Warriors of Valose Saga 2 featuring the scarred warrior, Draggar, and the sass-talking, Marie.

Chapter 1

DRAGGAR

Sia Jakkar eyed me suspiciously as if he could hear the beat of my ancillary heart. It thrummed hard inside my ears; a rabid pulse needing to be answered.

The one that awakened me was out there in the thick of the deadly jungle with my enemy. If the torn and bloody scrap of her dress fisted in my hand were any indication, she'd put up one serious fight. That was no surprise. My spirit mate was a warrior, like me.

My feet were planted firmly on the ground, but I was twitchy, waiting for Sia Jakkar's answer. My scales flashed blue and silver with my need to get out there and look for Marie as the last of the rynose pod was pushed out of the same hole in the settlement's wall they crashed.

"We can't leave the settlement open to the jungle, even though we are leaving it behind," Sia Jakkar stated.

"I want a repair crew on this wall now," Sia Jakkar's second in command, Nekko, barked out orders.

Males raced to do his bidding, not out of fear, but out of respect. We were preparing to evacuate. Now that the Gretolic had shown what they were capable of, the settlement was no longer safe. And safety was paramount now that we had females under our protection.

"You know I can't let you go alone, Draggar," Sia Jakkar stated flatly. "We need to call Aggar and Tekkon back from their current mission, now that we are relocating."

My eyes dropped to his shawra. I hoped to appeal to his recent awakening. The mark of his bonding still glowed softly from a recent joining of the spirits. His spirit mate, Lily, looked down on us, shifting nervously in the window high above in the safety of Sia Jakkar's skypod.

I prayed to the Spirits he would soften to my request to go after Marie and the other two females stolen from the settlement by Rayyar.

"You know in which direction they head, Sia," I implored. "Rayyar will use the females to gain entrance through the gates of Huren."

"Rayyar has a lead on you. You won't be able to catch him before he reaches the gates. Then how will you gain entrance? You're an exile, the same as me—the same as all of us." Sia Jakkar gestured to the males rushing around the settlement.

"Which means the longer I stand here, the more ground he puts between us." I placed my hand over the welt of my first bonding. "The recon mission has already been planned. Let me carry out that mission while I'm there."

None would have been more surprised than me when the sight of Marie had breathed new life into a heart that once beat for another. What I thought was dead was resurrected by the slight human female. She had proven to be as steadfast as any Valose warrior. I couldn't have asked for a better match.

We hadn't mated to initiate the bonding, so I lacked the echo of her spirit. I couldn't read her emotions. It terrified me not knowing if she was afraid or hurt.

My first spirit mate awaited me in the next realm, yet I knew in my bones that Marie was mine. I'd never heard of a male having two spirit mates in a lifetime, yet the proof thudded behind my breastbone.

"I would prefer to ask for your permission rather than beg for your forgiveness." I squared my shoulders and straightened my spine. "I will go after her either way. And we need to know the status of Huren. Send me as recon, and I can place the scanner on the dome while I'm there."

"You are determined, aren't you."

Not a question. Sia Jakkar knew me all too well. "I have no choice but to act. She beats within me."

Sia Jakkar's eyes widened before he dropped his head with a curse. "Choose another to accompany you. Know that we are relocating to the Caverns of the Ancients. Take a rover. It will be impossible to catch up to Rayyar on foot."

"Thank you, Sia."

"I don't need to tell you to be careful." Sia Jakkar's gaze burned through me. "Valose cannot afford to lose you."

He didn't say the settlement or the human females we were protecting, but the whole of the planet. After recent events, didn't that just put things in perspective?

"I will see you at the caverns." To show respect, I presented my forearm for him to clasp. "I'll be taking Trisso as my second."

"Do not leave here without a comm."

"I won't." My words still hung in the air as my feet flew across the broken road to find our resident technology guru, Zikkar.

On the way, I found the companion I sought. Trisso, a craftsman who was also a budding warrior, I knew he would jump at the chance to exercise the fighting skills I taught him.

After a quick lesson from Zikkar on how to activate the scanner—armed with a comm and swords—Trisso and I rode together on our shared rover through the open gate as the rays of the twin suns rose higher above the horizon.

No longer our home, I didn't look back at the settlement. Everything had changed when the Gretolics showed their hand. We were gearing up for the battle of our lives, but first, I had to save Marie.

Chapter 2

MARIE

My head had never hurt this bad, not even when we crash-landed in the spaceship that had abducted us from Earth. I bounced on a wide shoulder, my body as limp as a wet noodle. Something dripped in my eyes—the tinny scent of my blood, the culprit.

I knew who was carrying me like a sack of potatoes. Rayyar. The enemy of the Valose males that rescued us from our abductors.

I fell into his clutches after Layla had grown some lady balls and slid down the rope of the skypod where we were all supposed to be sleeping.

She had snuck out, thinking we were all asleep. I'd kept quiet in the dark of Aggar's borrowed skypod, waiting until she made it to the ground and followed her.

Tiptoeing through the settlement in her Gucci shoes and matching handbag, the stupid bitch had freed Rayyar from his prison in exchange for an escort to the city of Huren. I had no idea what it was she hoped to accomplish by going there.

Granted, it was beautiful—a gleaming city with tall buildings nestled under a shimmering dome.

If it was safety she was after, she was barking up the wrong tree. The Gretolics, those alien a-holes that abducted us to begin with, had taken over the city.

Maybe she was too good to stay inside the war-torn settlement. Or maybe, it was a combination of her blonde hair and the fact that we were all a little lightheaded from the oxygen-rich atmosphere that she'd pulled that dumbass move.

The fidiot was walking us right into the lion's den!

My stomach slammed down on solid muscle and bone as Rayyar leaped across something wide. Every particle of air left my lungs with the crunch. More blood dripped, and I swiped it away, managing to pry open my matted eyelids.

It was still dark out. The ground beneath me moved fast under Rayyar's booted feet. I glanced around to get a bead on where in the hell I was. I couldn't see much of anything from my upside-down predicament. I struggled to lift my body. That earned me a hard slap on the thigh.

Red hair flagged out beside me. I turned my head to find Amy in the same position on the opposite shoulder.

"Wake up, Amy!" I yelled and struggled against my captor.

"Stop moving, or I'll bash you in the head again," Rayyar cursed.

I understood every word he said, so my translator was still in place behind my ear.

Amy was Lily's fiery-headed bestie, the girl I befriended back on the spaceship. I envied Lily's resolve. She had been so courageous when I couldn't have been, venturing out on her own into God only knew what. She'd even chopped off some alien's hand that was, apparently, still alive.

Here, I found myself a captive once more. It was time to take a page from Lily's book and woman up.

I swatted at Amy's flailing arms with no response. She was either dead or out cold. I twisted my head around and caught a glimpse of the King Kong-sized wall around the settlement off in the distance.

This was good. I had a landmark.

Now to figure a way out of Rayyar's clutches. I wriggled more, craning my body up and around to get a better look at the jungle. There were tons of huge creatures with giant teeth that wanted to eat me living out here.

It was still dark, and in the short time I'd been on Valose, I learned most of the animals were nocturnal. I didn't see anything around except thick foliage.

Rayyar slapped me again. "Stop moving around, female, before I drop you."

A proverbial light bulb switched on over my head, a devious smile crept across my face, and a plan began to form. Rayyar had two girls slung over each shoulder. If I struggled hard enough, Rayyar would be knocked off balance. Once he lost his grip on me, I could take off into the jungle and run towards the settlement wall. I'd be instantly lost in the lush foliage.

This could work, or I could find freedom only to be swallowed whole by a giant jungle creature. Yet, if I did nothing, and Rayyar made it inside the dome covering the city of Huren, I'd be screwed, along with Amy.

Decision made; I forced my body to relax, giving the impression of compliance. I could use the element of surprise to free myself.

Like a ragdoll, I hung limply off his shoulder with my limbs flopping around. When I thought he was off his guard, I struggled in earnest.

Rayyar lurched to one side, stumbled, and dropped to one knee with a harsh curse. His grip on me loosened—only for a second—but enough for me to scramble free.

Rocks dug into my knees. I ignored the pain and crawled away until I found my footing. My legs wobbled, and my head pounded as I sprinted headlong into the jungle.

Before the foliage swallowed me up, I chanced a glance back. Rayyar was rising from the ground, repositioning a limp Amy over his shoulder. Layla stood open-mouthed, glaring at me as I ran away.

Fuck Layla. She could get what she deserved, but Amy needed help, and the only way I could do that was to make it back to the settlement and round up some warriors.

An image of Draggar's scarred face popped into my mind as I fought through the thick vegetation.

I swiped away more blood trickling into my eyes as my legs pumped beneath me and looked back to make sure Rayyar wasn't following.

The pull Lily felt for Jakkar—the one she'd tried to explain to Amy—was real. I didn't completely understand it, but I felt it pulsating directly behind my breastbone.

It hadn't been for Aggar, though, who I was instantly attracted to, but for the most boorish, surly Valosian warrior on the planet.

Draggar.

Always a loner, I wasn't ready to admit that I needed him. As I battled through leaves as big as me and twisted tree branches acting as nets, I was not only fighting to get help for Amy but fighting to get back to Draggar. I didn't understand why I needed to see his face once more, but I did.

Suddenly, I broke through a small clearing. I stopped and took a step back into the edge of the jungle. I knew better than to expose myself to anything flying overhead.

Valose had winged monsters called wetlocks that looked like dragons. I'd seen one swoop down and pluck a thousand-pound rynose from the ground as if it weighed nothing. I wanted no part of that shit.

I stood quietly and listened intently to the sounds around me. Something big snorted off in the distance, probably a rynose. They were plant-eaters, but dangerous if provoked to stampede.

A roar belonging to the Valose version of a T-Rex, a rexose, was followed by a sharp screech from across the clearing. Something just became an early morning snack.

"Glad that wasn't me," I mumbled.

I looked up at the brightening sky. The twin suns were rising, and the jungle would soon sleep. A strong breeze pushed at the canopy, rustling leaves and parting branches. The settlement's wall revealed itself off in the distance. It was only a glimpse of the top edge, but it was enough to point me in the right direction.

With all the nocturnal creatures headed to bed, I had a better chance of reaching the settlement in one piece than I did under cover of darkness. If I ran my ass off and stopped for nothing, I could make it.

I flew across the clearing, my arms and legs churning out the distance. There was so much more than just my life riding on me reaching the settlement. It was Amy's, too.

Blood from my head wound dripped into my eyes. My lungs burned from the exertion. Having someone else counting on me gave me the courage to keep running. I'd never been responsible for anyone else before. I was determined to prove that I could be as brave and selfless as Lily.

The ground started to grow spongy, and the blue earth grabbed at my bare feet. My progress slowed. I trudged onward, having nearly reached the end of the clearing.

What was solid became hollow, and my legs punched through the ground until I was buried to my waist.

I clawed at the crumbling ground, yet the more I struggled, the faster I sank. My mouth and nose clogged with dirt as I fought for breath. Just as soon as I thought I was going to be buried alive, my flailing hands hit something hard, and I grabbed hold.

It felt like a root of some kind. I used every ounce of strength I could muster to pull myself out, but the thing was slick and studded with thorns. I kept sliding, my hands not finding purchase, despite the thorns biting into my palms.

I struggled for breath, sucking back small pockets of air as my face was, ultimately, covered by dirt. This was it. After everything I went through, I was going to die having been buried alive.

My legs kicked free. I scissored them back and forth in the open space. The ground covering me from the waist up began to loosen until it broke free, and I was in a freefall.

I landed hard on my back with a thud that robbed my lungs of air. I fought to suck back the musty air and stared up at the hole my body made in the ground above.

I'd fallen into a weird tunnel. The earth was dug out in a perfect tube. I recalled hearing the males talking about a mineral called nutrillium, a power source that had to be mined. It looked like I fell into one of the shafts.

I wondered, as my vision wavered and dimmed, if I'd ever see the scarred face of my warrior again.

Map of Valose

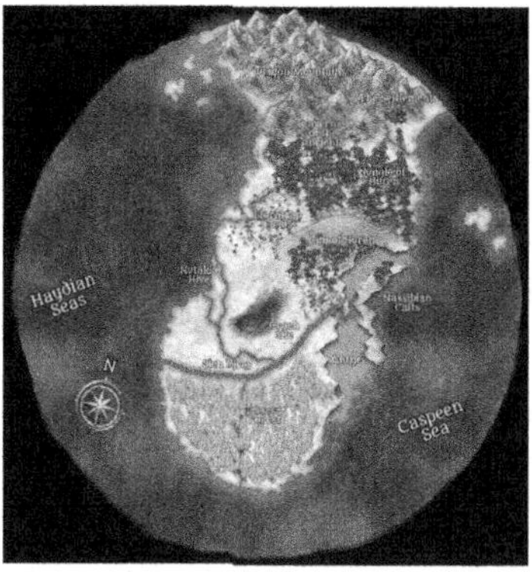

Also by Iona Strom

Nomadican Mates Series

Nomadican Mates Series Mega Box Set (books 1-7): Sci-Fi Alien Abduction Romance

Read Zaku and Ivy's Story!

Zaku: Sci-Fi Alien Romance

Warriors of Valose Saga

Silver Savage: Warriors of Valose Saga 1

Silver Seducer: Warriors of Valose Saga 2

Silver Savior: Warriors of Valose Saga 3

Silver Solace: Warriors of Valose Saga 4

Silver Scout: Warriors of Valose Saga 5

Silver Silence: Warriors of Valose Saga 6

Silver Spice: Warriors of Valose Saga 7

Silver Storm: Warriors of Valose Saga 8

Silver Steel: Warriors of Valose Saga 9

Silver Stealth: Warrior of Valose Saga 10

About The Author

Iona Strom writes for readers who love hot, erotic romance featuring exotic alien males who believe human females are a delicacy to be devoured—over and over again.

Don't miss out on Sales and New Releases when you join Iona's Readers Group.

Treat yourself to exclusive Sneak Peeks of upcoming books by signing up for Iona's Newsletter!

Follow Iona's Amazon Author Page and get the latest news about her books directly from Amazon!

Follow Iona on BookBub!

Printed in Great Britain
by Amazon

23619922R00169